Praise for *Night Falls Darkly*

"A new and fascinating mythos is being created before our eyes. . . . This spin on immortality has some hints of things that have been done in the past, but is also quite original. Readers are in for a mental treat, with no tricks."

—Huntress Book Reviews

"*Night Falls Darkly* is so compelling, it grabs the reader and keeps them entertained and on the edge of their seat until the dramatic conclusion. . . . Kim Lenox sketches extraordinary characters and visualizations that engage the reader. Her style of writing hooks the reader and keeps them interested to the last page. For those looking for romance, passion, suspense, and believable characters, this impressive read has it all."

—Coffee Time Romance

ALSO BY KIM LENOX

Night Falls Darkly

So Still the Night

A NOVEL OF
THE SHADOW GUARD

KIM LENOX

A SIGNET ECLIPSE BOOK

SIGNET ECLIPSE
Published by New American Library, a division of
Penguin Group (USA) Inc., 375 Hudson Street,
New York, New York 10014, USA
Penguin Group (Canada), 90 Eglinton Avenue East, Suite 700, Toronto,
Ontario M4P 2Y3, Canada (a division of Pearson Penguin Canada Inc.)
Penguin Books Ltd., 80 Strand, London WC2R 0RL, England
Penguin Ireland, 25 St. Stephen's Green, Dublin 2,
Ireland (a division of Penguin Books Ltd.)
Penguin Group (Australia), 250 Camberwell Road, Camberwell, Victoria 3124,
Australia (a division of Pearson Australia Group Pty. Ltd.)
Penguin Books India Pvt. Ltd., 11 Community Centre, Panchsheel Park,
New Delhi - 110 017, India
Penguin Group (NZ), 67 Apollo Drive, Rosedale, North Shore 0632,
New Zealand (a division of Pearson New Zealand Ltd.)
Penguin Books (South Africa) (Pty.) Ltd., 24 Sturdee Avenue,
Rosebank, Johannesburg 2196, South Africa

Penguin Books Ltd., Registered Offices:
80 Strand, London WC2R 0RL, England

First published by Signet Eclipse, an imprint of New American Library,
a division of Penguin Group (USA) Inc.

First Printing, May 2009
10 9 8 7 6 5 4 3 2 1

With love,
for Mom and Dad

ACKNOWLEDGMENTS

It takes a very special kind of person to put up with a writer. My sincerest thanks to the following individuals for their continued love, support, and patience:

Eric, who has my wholehearted love and devotion for believing in me and my writing from the start.

Cindy Miles, my cohort in daily mischief and mayhem—and NYC exploration. *Taxi!*

Kim Frost, for all the Empire Café and Java Dave's writing dates.

Kelley Thomas, for the talks, fun, and friendship.

Kim Lionetti, my agent, for being such a steadfast believer in my work and my abilities.

Laura Cifelli, my editor, for nailing me on the weak spots and pushing me toward bigger and better stories.

Gene, Victor, and Shirley, for creating such beautiful Shadow Guard covers.

Prologue

"They've found us." Professor Limpett burst into the tent. Ice crystals glistened on his gray beard. Snow dusted the slopes and crevices of his woolen toque, and the shoulders of his heavy coat.

Mina looked up from the ledger, where, by the light of an oil-fed lantern, she'd just recorded the coordinates of their encampment as provided to her by Lieutenant Maskelyne, their British guide. The gloves she wore made it difficult to hold the pen, and while the small stove beside her radiated a pleasant amount of heat, she remained so heavily bound and buttoned into layers of wool garments that she could barely bend an elbow. Wind battered the tent from all sides. The canvas walls snapped and the ropes creaked.

"We have visitors?" she inquired. Perhaps one of the local chiefs approached the encampment. Such a thing had been a common enough occurrence as their expedition traveled up through India and into Tibet toward the Himalayas. "Should I prepare tea?"

A few leaves of tea and half a tin of frozen biscuits were all they had left to offer by way of hospitality.

Two nights before—the same night they'd departed the mountainside temple that had been their sole destination—one of their hired Sherpas had disappeared from the camp, only to be discovered the next morning, bloodied, broken and dead at the bottom of a crevasse. The event had sent the camp into turmoil. Claims of whispering fog and moving shadows had rippled through the ranks of the Bengali pack carriers.

But the worst had come this morning when the English travelers awakened to the reality of a mutiny. More than half of the Bengalis had disappeared during the night, along with most of the camp's provisions and pack animals. Lieutenant Maskelyne had immediately sent for replacement supplies from Yangpoong. Because they could not continue the return journey to Kolkata until the necessary stocks arrived, the expedition could do nothing but wait, reduced in number and undeniably unnerved by the previous days' events. Though Mina had not spoken the suspicion aloud, it was almost as if a curse had befallen the expedition after its members had taken possession of the four ancient ivory scroll rods from the Tibetan monks. The sound of the temple's gongs still reverberated inside Mina's head.

Rather than answer her question, her father seized the hanging curtain that separated their quarters and shoved it aside. He leaned over his blanketed wooden cot to rummage beneath the pillow. "I have put you in such terrible danger by allowing you to come on this journey with me."

Mina slowly set the ledger aside and forced a light tone to her voice.

"No, you haven't, Father. These things happen. Remember the time in Gangtok when our horses were stolen, and we were left stranded for nearly a week?" She rubbed her gloved hands together. "Our supplies will arrive tomorrow or perhaps the day after, and we'll continue our descent as planned."

"I'm not talking about supplies." When he turned, he held a pistol. "I mean *they have found us*."

Her gaze fixed on the weapon. A chill that had nothing to do with temperature scraped down her spine. "Tell me who, Father. Who has found us?"

The professor had been behaving strangely for months, ever since being accused by the British Museum of "inappropriately borrowing" museum artifacts. His superiors had forced him to resign his position as a language scholar, and she wondered once again if the strain of those events had pushed him over an emotional ledge, because since that time his words and his actions had become tainted by paranoia. Swearing her into his confidence, he'd told her of a secret society of men who, like him, wished to discover the secrets of immortality—but for dark and wicked purposes. He'd warned her that the men would do anything to seize control of the two ancient Akkadian scrolls—the scrolls he presently kept in a locked case under his cot, and which had only days before been reunited with their original scroll rods.

Sadly, Mina did not know whether the dangerous men were real or whether the "secret society" was a creation of an aging and deteriorating mind.

The professor rushed toward her, extending the firearm with its barrel pointed to the carpeted floor. "Promise me you will carry this on your person at all times."

"*Father.*" She stood up from the chair and held her hands behind her back, refusing to accept the weapon.

"Take it."

"No."

"Do as I say." A frantic edge sharpened his voice.

"Tell me what has happened," she demanded. "Have you seen them? Are they here in the camp? Can you tell me who they are?"

Lips pressed firmly together and nostrils flared, he hooked his fingers into her belt and wedged the weapon inside the wide leather strap. In the next breath, he seized her face between his frigid bare hands and pressed a fervent kiss to her cheek.

Drawing back, he whispered, "You must return to Kolkata."

Her alarm grew. "Where are you going?"

He squeezed her shoulders, but avoided meeting her eyes. "We must separate. It's the only way."

She shook her head. "No."

He turned from her. "You will return to England. To London. Your uncle will not turn you away. You must tell them all that I am dead."

"Dead?" Shock numbed her lips.

"Yes, that I died here on the mountain in Nepal."

His words echoed in her ears, and yet still, she could hardly believe he'd actually spoken them.

"You're talking nonsense, Father," she whispered. "Madness."

He claimed a knapsack from the foot of the cot and spoke over his shoulder. "That poor Sherpa, dear . . . his death wasn't an accident. His injuries were so horrible, they couldn't have come only from the fall. They killed him as a warning to me. I won't have the same violence befall you." He exhaled raggedly. "Bury me, Willomina, next to your dear mother. Be sure everyone knows." He withdrew a crumpled slip of paper from his waist pocket. "This is the name of a man in Kolkata who will help you with the necessary papers and . . . everything else."

She stared at the paper as if it were a large, dangerous spider. He reached past her and placed it on the table.

"This must be our good-bye."

Was he telling her the truth? Had the Sherpa been murdered by these never-before-seen men or had her father lost his mind? In the end, it didn't really matter.

"I won't do it," she whispered. "I won't leave you, and

you're not going to leave me. We're staying together, no matter what."

Her father stilled.

"Father," she pleaded. "Look at me."

Shoulders rigid, he took up his folded woolens and stuffed them into the knapsack. Kneeling, he grasped the narrow box containing the scrolls. That, too, he shoved inside.

"That's it, then?" Tears stung her eyes. "You'll tell me nothing more?" She backed toward the tent's flap. "Then you've left me with no other choice. I've got to involve Lieutenant Maskelyne."

Her father reached for a leather-bound journal and a circular tin of tooth powder.

Mina claimed her parka from the wooden drying rack and pushed through the canvas flap. Frigid air frosted her lungs. A cluster of solemn-faced Bengalis looked up from where they crouched around a blazing fire pit, warming their hands. Above the camp, the mountain range stabbed upward through the purpling twilight, into a dense blanket of clouds. Mina thrust her arms into the coat sleeves, and tied the belt at her waist. Her boots sloshed in the mud as she maneuvered through falling snowflakes and the maze of canvas tents. A stalwart chest appeared in front of her. Large hands closed on her arms. From beneath a cap of dark fur, Lieutenant Maskelyne's square-jawed face peered down.

"Mina, you look distraught." His breath formed a small, vaporous cloud. "What has happened?"

"Please, you've got to talk to him." She swallowed down her tears and gestured over her shoulder. Wind tore at her hair, plastering a thick strand across her cheek. "I think he's lost his mind. He's claiming all sorts of wild things."

"Wild things?" he repeated, frowning. "Like what?"

"That we're being followed, that the Sherpa's death wasn't an accident."

He squeezed her shoulders, and tilted his head. "Perhaps it's a simple matter of elevation. Sometimes altitude does strange things to a person's mind. I'll go to him now."

She nodded, pressing past him and making a path toward the edge of camp.

"Where are you going?" he called after her.

"For a walk." She needed to be alone, needed time to think.

"Don't go far," he warned.

Her gaze settled on a small outcrop of stones. "I won't."

Chapter One

"I'll give you a damn good poke, that's what I'll do."

Mark perceived the words through a weighty shroud of slumber, but didn't consider the threat to be aimed at him. After all, he was invisible. Invincible.

A shadow.

". . . damn tired of waiting for you . . ."

The voice, male and teasingly familiar, hovered behind a curtain of darkness, along with other distant sounds. A pleasant, redundant creaking. Water slapping against wood.

The River.

Mark succumbed to the velvet embrace. Oblivion tugged him downward, into the dreamlike images he'd momentarily left behind. Shapely, floating limbs, arms and legs, all stained a warm and seductive shade of scarlet.

Something jabbed at his ribs. *Hard.*

Rage rippled through him. Like a provoked serpent Mark heaved up . . . only to strike a blazing wall of sunshine and sound. Horns and clanking. Distant voices. His linen shirt and woolen trousers lay wet and plastered against his skin. Every bone in his body, every muscle and every inch of skin seethed in dismay, as if his body awakened from a thousand years of sleep. As if he awakened from the dead.

His brain pulsed, threatening to explode inside his skull. With a dull splash he collapsed backward into the bilge water gathered against the center of the narrow hull. His teeth rattled as the skiff bobbed on high, choppy waves.

Mark curled onto his side, groaning, and ground his fists into his eye sockets, too weak to care that the brown river water lapped against his cheek.

"*Hell*," he rasped. Even his vocal chords stung, deep in his chest.

"No, Lord Alexander," the voice corrected cheerfully. "Not hell. *London*."

Through slitted eyelids, Mark confronted the soon-to-be *very unfortunate* individual who had forced him into this excruciating state of awareness. A gray-haired, mustachioed gentleman in trousers, crisp white shirt and green and black–striped vest grinned from his perch at the prow of the wooden skiff. A narrow black strap crossed his forehead, holding a black patch in place over one eye. The man chuckled, lifting a pole hook, and pointed the tip at Mark.

"You jounce me with that thing again, Leeson, and I'll kill you," he growled.

The immortal barked out a laugh and settled the pole across his knees. "My apologies, your lordship. Thought you were drifting off again. I've waited a good long while for you to awaken. Since Tilbury, no less."

Mark forced himself up onto one elbow. Planting the heels of his boots against the center of the hull, he shoved himself a few inches back until he could prop his shoulders against the wooden cross-bench behind him. God, he *ached*. Through grit-filled eyes he took in a familiar scene:

the quay and warehouses of the London Docks, swarm-
ing with laborers and watermen, and to the west, the
jagged, jaw-toothed spires of the clock tower and Parliament. A massive cargo barge lumbered past. Its wake set
the rowboat to rocking again. He curled his fingers over
the wooden rail.

How in the hell did I end up here?

"I can't say I know the answer to that, sir," Leeson
replied. "Last I knew, you were off to the far side of the
earth in search of that professor and his scrolls."

Immortals couldn't read one another's thoughts, but
they were capable of silent communication. Mark reminded himself not to speak in such a manner in Leeson's
company, unless he wished to be overheard. In the privacy of his newly shuttered mind, he attempted to recon-
struct some framework of memories. Last he could recall,
he'd been anchored in the Bay of Bengal, preparing to go
ashore in pursuit of Professor Limpett's inland expedition, when a dense fog had rolled in from the sea.

But London? London was the last place he wished to
find himself, if he wanted to stay alive. He fumbled at
his shirt pocket and brought out dark spectacles, their ear
wires hopelessly bent. With unsteady hands he angled
them onto his face. Blessedly, they dimmed the obscene
glare of daylight. God, it was warm. His clothing, the air,
smothered him.

"Blasted weather for February," he gritted out.

"Ah, for February it would be, sir," Leeson agreed
softly. "But it is May. The twenty-ninth of May, 1889."

Shock shot through Mark, numbing his lips and tingling
along his scalp. Everything around him—the temperature
of the air, the sunlight and activity—proved Leeson's statement to be true. *Three months of missing time.* Though he
kept the revelation—his internal thoughts—to himself, his
features must have slackened or even paled, for the jovial
smile faded from Leeson's gray-whiskered lips.

Mark whispered, "The *Thais* . . ."

Leeson tipped his head and redirected his one-eyed gaze just above Mark. "It's over there."

Mark shifted, flinching as heat tore along his muscles, and turned to look. A generous length of rope snaked over the water to ascend to the prow of his nine-hundred-ton steam yacht, which drifted, disturbingly unmanned. Mustering his strength, Mark hoisted himself onto the wood bench and fished the line from the water.

Leeson scrambled forth, ever nimble. "Allow me to do that, your lordship."

Mark ignored him, pulling the rope, closing the distance between the skiff and the yacht. His muscles roared to life, awakened by use and tension. Three months. Three damn months. The implications were astounding. He maneuvered beneath the dangling rope ladder. Grasping the sides, he hooked his sodden boot into the lowest rung.

"Did Black send you?" he demanded.

Behind him, the boat bobbed as Leeson lowered himself to the bench.

He answered quietly, "I remain in his service."

"But he's not yet returned to this side?"

"No, sir . . ." Leeson's voice drifted away. He looked off into the distance. "But soon, I think."

Swinging against the hull, Mark climbed until he came to the polished wood rail. Unlatching the hinged half door, he gritted his teeth and climbed onto the deck. Below, Leeson balanced and reached for the ladder.

Mark peered down. "Don't bother, old man."

As far as practicalities went, he didn't require Leeson's or anyone else's assistance to sail the vessel, though he preferred to keep the *Thais* fully manned for appearance's sake. Leeson further disqualified himself on the basis of trustworthiness. His loyalty belonged to Archer, Lord Black, Mark's former mentor within the immortal Shadow Guard. Black was also the Reclaimer most likely to be dispatched by the ruling Primordial Council as Mark's assassin.

He drew up the ladder, hand over fist. "Just tell him I'll be ready for him."

Dropping the weighty mass of rope to the deck, Mark turned on his heel and peeled his shirt from his shoulders and arms. He seethed with displeasure. God only knew where the professor was now. He could return directly to the open sea and begin the hunt anew, but he needed to regain his bearings and resupply. Closing his eyes, he envisioned the vessel's rudder. The boat responded, slowly altering its course along a westerly line.

He paused, his fingertips poised over the buttons of his trousers. Through two glass portals he viewed the interior cabin. Framed artwork hung on the walls at odd angles. Elegant curtains sagged, torn to ribbons. Trunks were upended and open, their contents strewn everywhere. Anything not nailed down had been thrown into disarray, as if the yacht had sailed through a typhoon. Yet a cautious relief trickled through him. There were no bodies, no blood, no sign of his mortal crewmen. He prayed they were alive somewhere, and that their murders by his hand or otherwise were not hidden in the dark vault of his mind.

He might be losing his sanity bit by fragmented bit, but he wasn't an idiot. Not yet, anyway. Clearly he'd been dragged to London over ocean and time for a specific purpose. But by whom? Until recently, because he was a member of the elite Shadow Guard, Mark's every move had been governed by the Primordial Council.

From their stronghold inside the protected Inner Realm, which existed on a parallel plane to that of Earth's mortal population, the three Ancients—Aitha, Hydros and Khaos—dispatched Guards to all corners of the globe for the purpose of protecting the interests of the Amaranthine race. The foremost of the Guards' responsibilities was the

hunting, or "Reclamation," of mankind's most dangerous
souls, souls so morally corrupt that they achieved a powerful, supernatural state known as Transcension. Such exceedingly depraved souls were capable of crossing into
the Inner Realm and wreaking destruction and death on
immortals. Jack the Ripper had been such a soul.

It was during the hunt for Jack—who had not only
Transcended, but had also quickly become a matchless
force of evil known as a *brotoi* after being recruited by the
Dark Ancient, Tantalus—that Mark's immortal destiny
had taken a dangerous turn, albeit by his own decision.

Mark, the immortal son of Cleopatra and her Roman
triumvirate lover, Marcus Antonius, had fought for centuries to break free from his parents' tragic legacy of passion
and death. Determined to define himself by *his* history—
by *his* victories—he'd undertaken a daring act of heroism
and crossed over into the state of Transcension. His sacrifice had leveled the Shadow Guard's playing field against
Jack and had guaranteed Archer's Reclamation of the
rampant, vicious *brotoi*, whom Tantalus had chosen as his
Messenger on Earth—one who would awaken a sleeping
brotoi army, and assist in freeing Tantalus from his underworld prison.

No, he wasn't the first Shadow Guard to offer himself
to Transcension to ensure the defeat of a powerful oppo-
nent, but he would not follow the same path as the others
who had gone before him: namely, banishment from the
Guard, eventual madness and ultimately death by capture and execution. The Primordials, after all, could not
allow such a dangerous threat to the Inner Realm to go
unchecked, valiant sacrifice or no.

Mark had only a brief window of time to save his immortal existence and regain his place amongst the Guard,
a feat that would ensure his unparalleled legend in the
history of the immortals. That window grew smaller with
each heartbeat and each passing breath. Sometimes voices

whispered, inviting him to succumb, but thus far he had remained strong and had kept them behind a thick, muting wall inside his head.

Ah, but blast his cursed luck. He had now lost three months of precious time. Had the insidious madness within him been delayed—or had it grown more powerful? More powerful than his strength to contain it? The coming days would tell.

They are here in London, you know.

Leeson's voice echoed inside his head.

The ones you seek.

An object was hurtled over the railing to land beside his boot. A newspaper, wound into a tight cylinder. He bent, taking the bundle in hand. Tugging off the string, he unrolled the paper, which had been folded to display the obituaries page. One announcement had been circled in black ink.

> William Demerest Limpett, Professor of Ancient
>   Languages and History
> Born: Egremont, Cheshire
> Died: February 12, 1889, Kolkata
> Interment at Highgate Cemetery; Thursday,
>   May 30, 6:00 p.m.

Mark returned to the rail and looked over. In the shadow of the yacht, the empty rowboat bobbed on the waves.

"Aren't you going to thank me?" said a voice beside him.

Mark ground his teeth. "Why are you doing this? In case you've forgotten, I'm an outcast. Banished. I'm slowly losing my mind. Who knows when I will turn slavering fiend and rip your head off."

Leeson chuckled. "I'd recover. I have before." He shrugged. "You made your decision for noble reasons. To

save the others. To save Archer and Miss Elena. I am in-
debted to you for that."

Mark winced at the rosy, inaccurate picture he painted.
"Let's be clear with each other, Leeson, or you leave now
and don't return. What instructions have you received
from the Primordials—or from Archer—with regard to
me?

An extended pause ruled the space between them.

Finally Leeson said, "I have received no instructions
from the Inner Realm. Not in regard to you or anything
else."

Mark's eyes narrowed at that. The very purpose of
Leeson's existence, as secretary to Lord Black, was communication. He was the man with the answers, the one
who relayed pertinent information from the Inner Realm.
"Why the hell not?"

Leeson's response tumbled out. "Because the portals
are closed."

"What do you mean, they are closed? All of them?"

Leeson nodded slowly.

"For how long?" Mark demanded.

The little man hesitated.

Mark spat, "As I said, either you tell me everything or
you go."

Leeson blurted, "Since shortly after his lordship carried Miss Elena through. We received word she'd survived the passage and then . . . nothing."

Never in the history of the earth had the portals closed
for more than a few days' time. Perhaps they had while
a particularly nasty Transcended soul was on the loose,
in order to protect the Inner Realm, but once the deteriorated soul was successfully Reclaimed and dispatched to
the eternal prison of Tantalus, the portals were reopened.

"Why have they been sealed for so long?"

His companion stared at him levelly. "From the reports
I've heard on this side, there has been a proliferation of

deteriorated souls bearing the particular symptoms of *bro-toism*. They appear to be organizing. Our Shadow Guards, at all locations about the world, have their hands full."

"But the Guard *has* been able to contain them?"

Leeson nodded. "But I assume the portals will remain sealed until they determine what's going on down below—whether just rumblings or a full-scale rebellion. Nasty bastard, that Tantalus. I hope they smite him and remind him who's in charge." He clenched his fists, but his attention quickly returned to Mark. "Needless to say, sir, without specific orders, I'm rather adrift."

Mark suggested darkly, "Why don't you join up with my sister? She's always looking for someone to order about."

Leeson sniffed. "She does not inform me of her assignments or activities, and I do not inform her of mine." His cheeks puffed out. "Do you know that after you left us in October, she ate my entire collection of penny novelettes?"

Mark could not help but grin. "She *didn't*."

His sister had an uncommon fetish for devouring the written word—literally. And though she had exceedingly good taste in eating material, when she was angry or frustrated, she'd rip into anything within reach.

Leeson continued. "Not only was she distraught over your decision to Transcend, but she's furious over her failure thus far to Reclaim her Thames killer."

Mark's gaze skimmed over the metropolis. Months before, when they'd all been embroiled in the hunt for the Ripper, Selene had mentioned that her present assignment—finding a killer who dismembered his female victims and deposited their body parts around London—was proving difficult.

Selene was here then, still in the city.

"She's on her own as far as I'm concerned." Leeson shrugged. "That girl's always been a bit high-strung for

my liking—with no offense intended toward you and
your illustrious forebears, sir."

"None taken. But why have you chosen to assist me?
I wouldn't be surprised if the Primordials punished you
for it."

"I've always been a bit of a gambler, your lordship. And
regardless of what you say, I believe you chose this path
for the right reasons—to save the others. My money's on
you, that you'll beat this. I'm proud to stand by you . . .
until . . . until . . . " He propped a fist against his waist and
added earnestly, "You understand, if his lordship returns
with the assignment to assassinate you, I've got to assist
him in carrying out that order."

"Certainly," Mark answered flatly.

Mina missed her father dreadfully, but despite her best
efforts, she could summon no tears for his funeral. Rather,
the urge to sneeze teased the insides of her nostrils with
maddening intensity, a result of the pungent incense that
clouded the small Anglican chapel, and the large sprays
of fragrant white flowers. She brought a handkerchief to
her nose.

"There, there," the Countess of Trafford consoled.

Her aunt Lucinda, fair as sunshine, was only a year
or two older than she, and was the second wife of Mina's widower uncle, the distinguished Lord Trafford. The
beautiful young woman wrapped a slender arm around
Mina's shoulders. "You're safe here with us now. No need
to be afraid, ever again."

Lucinda's deeply floral perfume enveloped her. Mina
nodded, feeling nauseated. The Gothic chapel. The smells.
The coffin. Her ridiculously tight corset. Really, it was all
just a bit too much. She was suffocating in black silk.

"Trafford," the countess said, urging her husband,
"fetch a chair. I do believe Miss Limpett might faint."

Fabric rustled. Voices murmured, low with pity. Although the actual service had concluded moments before, Mina allowed herself to be eased into an armchair. She'd never fainted in her life—never even come close—but it wasn't so terrible a feeling to be fussed over. Reluctantly her gaze returned to the long rosewood coffin, displayed on a velvet-skirted bier. Light from the floor candelabrum glinted off the silver handles. The lid was closed, of course, as the necessary documents placed her father's death in Kolkata as taking place some three months before.

It would have galled the professor to know that none of his associates from the British Museum or the university had come to pay their final respects, but in truth they had abandoned him long ago, even before the allegations of improper borrowings.

An orderly queue of black-garbed guests passed before Mina, offering their sympathies, all acquaintances of Lord and Lady Trafford and strangers to her. No doubt they would have been strangers to her father as well. After another few moments, her uncle peered down his narrow, hooked nose, and offered his arm. "Are you well enough, dear?"

Mina nodded and rose, accepting his escort. He led her past Lucinda and his two daughters. Astrid, blond and resplendent even in her detested mourning costume, stood arm in arm with her blander sister, Evangeline, who, dreadfully nearsighted, had a tendency to squint. The two young women, separated in age by less than a year, wore identical bored expressions. She knew they held her father's death against her, and she could not really fault them. He was a man they had never met, and his funeral proceedings had interrupted the festivities of their debut Season. She hoped the three of them might grow closer in subsequent days.

Crossing the threshold, Mina inhaled deeply of the late-spring air. Highgate Cemetery sprawled in lush splendor against the side of the steep hill. In the distance, stone angels prayed. Crosses, some draped in ivy, towered over flat stone slabs. A sudden grate of metal sounded from behind, startling her. Lucinda gasped, turning to look over her shoulder. Mina did the same and observed her father's coffin being lowered bit by jerky bit into a gaping hole in the ground. She closed her eyes, nearly overcome by . . .

Relief.

The coffin, once lowered to the level below, would be transported by cemetery workers to the catacombs, where finally, the casket would be placed behind a locked, iron door.

Forever.

When she opened her eyes again, she found the countess glaring up at her husband. "Could they not have waited a few more moments?"

"It's late." Her uncle touched the brim of his top hat and glanced to the sky. "I'm sure they'd prefer to . . . ah, *inter* dear William before sunset."

Dear William.

Mina smothered a smile. If only her father could have overheard the polite endearment. He had not enjoyed the best of relationships with his wife's elder brother. Lord Trafford had believed, as had the rest of society, the academic scholar to be far below his sister's status. But thankfully, Lord and Lady Trafford had been nothing but kind and accepting of her. Without them, she would have nowhere else to go. Her father's pursuit of all things related to immortality, and their extensive travels, had left Mina nothing short of penniless. Lord and Lady Trafford had already expressed their intent to present her next Season, once she'd emerged from mourning. At the present moment, Mina could think of nothing finer than immersing herself in parties, romance, piles of dresses and all the other female frivolities and anchors of permanence she'd thus far been denied in life.

She assured them, "It's all very well. Please don't be appalled on my behalf."

The Nonconformists' chapel lay just across the way. There as well, another funeral appeared to be ending. Guests spilled out the door, a sudden black surge.

Astrid gave a low purr. "Who is *that*?"

Mina's gaze snagged on one gentleman in particular. He hadn't come out with the other mourners. He'd been standing in the shadows beside one of the small oriel windows as if waiting for someone. Tall and broad of shoulders, he closed and folded a newspaper he'd apparently been reading. He wore a high top hat. Blue-lensed spectacles hid his eyes, but did nothing to conceal the sensual purse of his lips or the taut set of his jaw.

"Where?" Evangeline demanded, squinting. "Who?"

Folding the newspaper once more, he tucked the narrow parcel beneath his arm. Even at this distance, Mina could feel the intensity of his gaze. His unsmiling attention appeared to be focused intently . . . stunningly . . . on *her*.

"Is that not Lord Alexander?" her uncle mused.

"I'm sure I wouldn't know," Lucinda responded in a hushed voice.

The countess's cheeks filled with a deep, rich stain. Of course, Mina realized, the handsome gentleman had not been staring at her with such intensity, but at the beautiful Lucinda.

"He's not been seen in months," her uncle mused, chuckling. "Some of the chaps at the club even jested—"

His words broke off abruptly. His brows drew in, his smile faded and he appeared instantly contrite.

"*Suggested* what?" Lucinda demanded, her voice a strangled whisper.

"*Jested*, dear. They took to calling him Jack . . . Jack the Ripper, who . . . er, dropped off in his activities about the same time."

"*Trafford*. Such low humor, and on such an occasion as this. You must apologize at once to our niece—"

Suddenly a large flock of birds arose from the oaks, filling the air with the hiss of leaves and flapping wings. Bonnets and top hat brims turned in unison, as all who gathered watched the shadowy mass arise like a startled wraith and disappear over the treetops. In the aftermath, Mina vaguely registered that the handsome gentleman who had been standing beside the chapel was no longer there. Unexpected disappointment feathered through her.

Lucinda and the girls wandered off toward the carriages. Mina and her uncle followed a few steps behind until an elderly gentleman stepped into their path. After offering his condolences again, he politely asked to speak to Trafford on the matter of a horse. Excusing herself from the conversation, Mina wandered a few steps, knowing this would be her last bit of freedom before being overtaken once again by a thick, black sea. She had lived for so long at the edges of polite society, the remaining months of respectable mourning weighed heavy on her, a dense, smothering veil.

She stilled, listening.

Had someone spoken her name?

She tilted her face toward the voice.

He—the man her uncle had referred to as Lord Alexander—stood there, just off to her side, tall, elegant and intent. Her heart gave a little jump. The afternoon grew late and the shadows long, but how could she not have seen him approach? A dark thrill rippled through her, from the top of her crape-trimmed bonnet to the squared toes of her black leather shoes—a highly inappropriate response, given the event of the moment, but no one else needed to know.

Like her uncle, he wore a precisely cut suit of rich cloth, the sort only the wealthiest of gentlemen could command from the tailors of London's famed Savile Row. Somewhere along the way he had disposed of the newspaper.

"Miss Limpett?" he repeated, approaching in measured steps.

She had to consciously prevent herself from looking about to see if there were any other Misses Limpett in proximity. "Yes?"

"I hope you will forgive my breach of protocol in forgoing a proper introduction." His voice was rich and warm; his words elegantly spoken. He deftly removed his hat to reveal jaw-length blond hair, streaked an even paler shade of moonlight. "I am—"

"Lord Alexander," she whispered.

She flushed, mortified, not having intended to speak his name aloud.

His faint smile revealed a trace of vanity. "How did you know?"

"My uncle recognized you."

"Oh?" His brows went up good-naturedly. "That is good . . . or perhaps that is very bad." He chuckled, low in his throat, a masculine sound. "Time will tell, I suppose. But it is you I am here to see." His expression turned solemn again. "I saw the announcement in the paper and knew I must come to offer my condolences."

She warmed in surprise. "You knew my father?"

He reached up and removed his spectacles, a gesture that revealed startling, pale blue eyes. Slight hollows darkened the space just above his cheekbones, as if he hadn't had enough sleep of late. Their presence did not diminish his attractiveness.

"I dabble in languages. A personal interest, really. Nothing on the level of your father's expertise."

In that moment, his attractiveness took on a different dimension. "I see."

"I found myself in possession of something and wanted you to have it."

He had a way of speaking that felt very personal. Intimate, even. As if she were the only person in his world, at least for that moment. She remembered Lucinda's reaction and wondered if all women felt the same when fixed in his penetrating gaze.

"What is it?"

He produced a slender, rectangular object from his hip pocket, which he conveyed to her. Their gloved hands briefly touched, and a new rush of heat coursed high into her cheeks. Mina lowered her chin, purposefully retreating into the shadow of her bonnet, and at the same time considered the leather case. She slid her gloved thumb against the tiny gold slide-clasp, and inside found a photograph of two men crouched side by side, atop an immense slab of stone.

Her breath caught in her throat. For the first time since her father's coffin had been sealed in Nepal, tears rushed against her lashes. They blurred her vision of the picture—an image of her father as a young man, his hat cocked aside, and his face beaming with excitement. He had never lost that fervor, that zeal for adventure. Not even in the final moments when he had told her farewell.

He explained softly, "The photograph was taken at the ruins at—"

"Petra. Yes. I recognize the temple. Who is this man with him?" She pointed, lifting the frame for a closer look. "His face is blurred."

"Unfortunately."

"You favor him though. He is your father, is he not?"

His lordship cocked his head.

"Thank you," Mina whispered. "We traveled so much, from place to place. By necessity, I collected few mementoes. I shall treasure this always."

"I am glad." He pressed his lips together, as if pondering the words he would speak next. "Miss Limpett . . ."

"Yes, Lord Alexander?"

"I hope I do not overstep the bounds of propriety in choosing this moment to broach a particular subject, when the pain of your loss must still be so fresh."

At this proximity, his golden attractiveness was almost smothering.

"Please speak freely."

He nodded. "I am aware from the papers he published just prior to his death that the professor possessed an extensive personal collection above and beyond the one he curated for the museum."

Unease dragged up Mina's spine. She stared into the photograph, into her father's eyes.

"I'm afraid I know very little about my father's collections." She shut the case. "I can give you the name of his solicitors. Please feel free to contact them and make your inquiries."

Lord Alexander continued as if he had not heard her. "In particular, he owned two very rare scrolls—ancient facsimiles of two even more ancient Akkadian cuneiform tablets, which are no longer in existence."

Mina pressed her lips together and closed her eyes. If only that combined effort could make her disappear.

He gently prodded, "Do you know the scrolls to which I refer?"

Her first instinct was to lie, to feign insipidness and pretend she knew nothing about the two damn scrolls. She'd never been good at telling tales.

"I . . . do."

"Perhaps now that your father has passed, you might be willing to part with them?"

"I'm afraid that's not possible."

"I'm prepared to pay handsomely for them."

She attempted a polite, easy smile, while her mind threw out options for quickly extricating herself from his company—a regretful, but necessary reversal, given his line of questioning. "The scrolls are not available for purchase."

"Perhaps you have already sold the collection to someone else? To the British Museum?"

"No."

His brows went up. "The Boolak?"

Mina shook her head. He edged closer—so close she could hardly breathe for the magnitude of his presence.

"The Louvre? There must be a number of interested parties."

The boning of Mina's tightly laced corset cut uncomfortably against her rib cage, just beneath her breasts. Her heart pounded thunderously.

His voice lowered, becoming almost hushed. "If you could simply provide a name, I would be more than happy to approach them myself."

His eyes . . . they were so penetrating, as if they saw straight inside her. There had, indeed, been offers. There had also been one very nasty threat—which was why a pistol presently weighted the tasseled, jet-beaded bag on her wrist.

"I can give you no such name."

Her thoughts twisted inside her head, no doubt an unfortunate result of her tortured conscience. He radiated such a peculiar magnetism. She suddenly imagined herself kissing him, hard on the mouth, with her hands tangled in his hair.

He smiled, almost as if he knew. "Where are the scrolls, Miss Limpett?"

She experienced an overwhelming desire to confess everything, to give him anything he wanted.

"They are with Father," she blurted.

The smile dropped from his lips. "What do you mean . . . *with Father*?"

Chapter Two

Mina looked pointedly toward the Street of the Dead, where the dirt path disappeared into a shadowed corridor of oaks. By now her father's coffin would have been transported by cemetery workers to the catacombs.

Even in the dimming light, Lord Alexander's face appeared to blanch a shade lighter.

"You can't be serious. The scrolls were . . . *interred* with your father?"

"In the end they were—" She cleared her throat, and forced herself to speak around what felt like a ball of snarled twine in her throat. "They were his most treasured possessions."

"Ancient papyri, never translated or transcribed, and you mean to tell me"—he laughed, a deep, incredulous sound—"that they are lost forever?"

She twisted her hand in the velvet cord of her bag. "It's been three long months, you see."

"Oh, now that's *stellar*."

She glanced out from beneath her bonnet brim. "I suppose you'd like to have your picture returned?"

He responded with a rueful chuckle. The smile he

wore—though a bit tight—appeared surprisingly genu-
ine, as if she amused him.

"No, Miss Limpett, I do not wish to *have my picture returned*." His speaking of the words imitated her cadence
and tone, a light flirtation that sent a pleasurable tremor
through her. "I am disappointed, of course, but who am I
to object to the last wishes of a dying man? I should have
anticipated the same." He gazed out over the cemetery,
tapping his hat against a well-muscled thigh. "William always was rather eccentric. Or so I've been told."

Mina nodded. Her father's eccentricity had been the
bane of her existence.

"I suppose I must take my leave of you now, Miss Limpett, and allow you to return to your family." He lifted
his hat.

"Thank you for coming," she said, feeling both relieved
and disappointed that their time together had come to
an end. "Your attendance would have meant so much to
Father."

The edge of his mouth quirked upward, and she
glimpsed mischief in his eyes. He returned his hat to his
head. "I'd like to think so."

Mina watched him stride toward the gatehouse, and
eventually disappear through the archway, toward the
main road, where rows of coaches crowded Swain's Lane,
waiting to convey guests from the cemetery.

Her uncle approached, holding his cane midstaff. "I'm
so sorry for abandoning you."

"I was enjoying the scenery."

He extended his hand and led her toward the two funeral carriages that had been specially rented for the day.
"That *was* Lord Alexander speaking to you, was it not?"

"Yes, it was."

"Whatever was he saying to you?"

Their shoes crunched over gray gravel. As they arrived

at the carriage, the Traffords' footman, liveried in black, opened the door and pulled down the steps.

"Apparently he knew Father."

"Did he?" His lordship puzzled. "Imagine that. I wonder if I could catch up to him."

"I'm certain you could." She lifted a hand. "He just passed through the gate."

"Do go on to the house with the ladies." The village of Highgate was located on a hillside north of the sprawling metropolis of London. Lord Trafford had rented not only the mourning coaches, but a fully staffed country house. For ease of convenience, the family had lodged there, near the cemetery, the previous night. "Please convey to her ladyship I'll follow shortly behind and we can all travel into town together."

Her uncle urged her toward the carriage and hurried off in pursuit of Lord Alexander. Mina peered into the vehicle. Three feminine faces, framed by fur and feathers, peered out from the shadowed interior.

Yet her conversation with Lord Alexander left her uneasy, reminding her there were others, more suspicious and dangerous, who would not be so easy to placate were they to discover the truth. A sudden breeze brushed against the nape of her neck and she shivered despite the warmth of the evening.

Somehow she couldn't bring herself to climb the steps to join the others. The cemetery called to her, a keeper of secrets.

Her secrets.

How could she eat? How could she sleep, until she was sure?

Across Swain's Lane, hidden within a small copse of trees, Mark closed his eyes with the first powerful, heated surge of *aoratos*. He growled, deep in his throat, willing his every bone, his every cell and sinew to fade . . . to become nothing. To become *unseen*.

Transformed into shadow, he emerged, coursing low across the roadway to twist between carriages, returning whence he had come. He allowed himself one illicit pleasure. He brushed against Miss Limpett, curling about her from behind. He inhaled her delicious, orange blossom scent, but deeper than that, her *trace*—the singular essence she exuded, distinguishing her as unique from all those around her. He smiled, pleased, when she lifted her gloved hand to touch the bare skin above her collar in an unconscious acknowledgment of his presence.

He'd seen her once before, even spoken to her, although she would not know it because at the time his features had been transformed into the face and stature of another. He'd found her sultry beauty captivating then. He found her even more alluring now. Lovely. Delightful. But he had no time for play.

Abandoning her for the chapel, he narrowed thin as a razor to slip beneath the already-locked door. He gloried in his invisibility, the mercurial speed at which he moved and his heightened precision of thought. He could scarce allow himself to hope that within moments, he might finally hold in his possession the knowledge necessary to reverse the deterioration of his mind and his soul. Into the yawning hole in the floor he spiraled through the hydraulic catafalque that had lowered the professor's coffin, and easily latched on to the lingering trail of two cemetery workers. He pursued them along the dim tunnel, not continuing under Swain's Lane toward the East Cemetery, but diverting into the wan light of outdoors, through the dense clutter of cemetery monuments.

He slowed only when he arrived at the dark terrace of catacombs cut into the cradle of earth beneath St. Michael's Church.

*   *   *

Mina stepped back from the carriage. "Please, your ladyship, do go on without me."

"Go on?" Lady Trafford's blue eyes widened. "Whatever do you mean, Miss Limpett?"

"I . . ." Mina swallowed. She'd never been good at dramatics. "I just need a bit more time with Father."

Lucinda's placid expression fractured, but she quickly masked her impatience with a sympathetic tilt of her head and a smile. "Of course. Astrid, Evangeline, do accompany your cousin—"

A chorus of petulant refusals sounded from within.

Mina raised her hand. "No, please. I wish to be alone. I can walk back to the house when I'm finished. It's not far."

"Don't be ridiculous. There are Gypsies camped in the field just across the way." Her ladyship peered into the sky, and touched a gloved hand against the satin cording at her throat. "And it's getting late. The cemetery closes at sunset."

"If we remain here another moment, it will be *I* who expires next," muttered Astrid in a dour tone.

"I concur," added Evangeline.

"Please." Mina lifted her handkerchief to her nose and sniffled, acting upon the lessons of persuasion she'd learned from her cousins over recent days. She whispered, "I'm simply not ready to part with him just yet."

"Oh, dear, don't cry," her aunt pled, clasping her gloved hands together. "Very well. We'll leave Trafford with the second coach to wait for you. Please don't linger overly long. Remember, we'll be returning to the Mayfair house tonight, and in our own vehicle, as these must be returned to the local stable tonight." She pulled a watch from her bag and sighed. "We've a number of appointments tomorrow. The caterer and the florist, for my garden party next week. We don't wish to be exhausted in the morning."

A moment later, the carriage trundled onto Swain's Lane. Mina ascended the tree-shadowed trail. She knew the way because she had walked the path the day before when her uncle had shown her where her father's coffin would be interred. Only then, the sun had hung high in the sky and the cemetery had been alive with visitors. Now, evening shadows seeped up from the earth, along with low, curling wisps of yellow haze.

Only the sound of her shoes on the dirt path, and the furtive scratching of birds and other unseen creatures in the trees and underbrush, broke the silence. A mournful stone angel appeared to ward her away with open palms. Her pulse bounded, but she tamped down what were most certainly irrational fears—fears that would be set to rest once she confirmed her father's casket had been safely secured.

At the open iron gates of the Egyptian Avenue, Mina wavered. Massive twin columns and obelisks braced either side of the arched entrance, like a portal to an ancient temple. A dense veil of ivy tumbled down from above, and beyond . . . only shadows.

Her first instinct was to retreat, as fast as her feet would carry her, to the carriage, and all the trappings of safety, normalcy and sanity. Inhaling deeply, she swept beneath, onto the crypt-lined path. Quickly enough, she emerged into Lebanon Circle, where two rows of mausolea wreathed a towering cedar.

Although the Traffords owned a centerpiece crypt for the interment of their titled members, her father's casket was to be placed beside her mother's in the less exclusive terraced catacomb above. Mina grasped her skirts and ascended the wide stone steps.

A strong breeze lifted the boughs of the trees all around, filling the circle with a chorus of unintelligible whispers. She whirled, scanning the circle, certain she heard voices amongst the rustle of the trees. The whispers quieted. In their aftermath came the repetitive chink of metal striking against metal.

Chink. Chink. Chink.

Suspicion and fear twisted in her throat, and deeper, into her chest, but she swallowed it away. The sounds she heard were likely created by the cemetery workers doing their final bit of work for the day.

Chink. Chink.

Her lip throbbed where she bit into her flesh. What task could possibly require such repetitive and insistent blows? Warily, she approached the catacomb where her father's coffin was to have been deposited. The metal door featured a small, square opening, scored with iron bars.

Shuffling sounds came from within.

Chink.

Fear that her secret would be discovered surpassed any fear of what might be inside making the noise. She launched herself onto the tips of her toes and grasped the edge of the window. In the darkness, she perceived the dim outline of numerous coffins, stacked on shelves and blanketed in dust. The flowers she'd arranged yesterday atop her mother's coffin lay discarded on the floor.

A shadow moved.

"You there," she called.

The shadow merged with the darkness, making her question whether she'd seen anything at all.

She dropped from the window and grasped the thick metal handle. She tugged, to no avail. The door was locked.

She *had* seen something. And she'd heard something too.

Wood splintered.

She whirled, racing to the edge of the circle, searching for any worker, any guest, to whom she could shout out her accusations of desecration. She saw no one. Wind twisted her skirts. The whispers returned, filling her ears. Again she returned to the door, pressing her fingertips against her mouth, suppressing the urge to scream. Having no other recourse, she twisted the ball clasp on her bag and snatched out her pistol.

"I'm warning you. Come out of there!" she challenged, her voice reverberating in the silence.

Wood *crashed*.

She thrust her arm between the metal bars, gun in hand. She would fire a warning shot, and flush the person out—at least then she would know with whom she dealt.

A large stone hurtled from the darkness to slam against the door beside her head.

Mina stared. A shadow grew distinct. Became larger. Bronze eyes blinked . . . *glowed*.

She screamed. The creature roared, hurtling toward her. She fired.

Mark crouched in the darkness, silent in his rage.

He closed his eyes, and breathed deeply through his nostrils. He focused on the wound, working to disintegrate the bullet and repair his shattered shoulder blade. The intensity of the pain ebbed, but did not cease.

A clatter of footsteps approached, and an inquiry of voices. He opened his eyes. A key turned in the lock, its metallic rotation echoing through the narrow vault. The door groaned inward. An aged groundsman in rolled shirtsleeves, sagging vest and dirt-caked trousers lifted a lantern to illuminate the interior. His searching gaze passed directly through Mark.

"Ain't no one 'ere, miss."

"That can't be." Miss Limpett appeared in the doorway, her face luminous against the backdrop of shadows.

Fear and excitement shone bright in her eyes. Was it possible she'd grown lovelier since he'd last seen her? His eyes narrowed. Perhaps it was simply the fact that she'd shot him. He'd always admired women who handled their weaponry confidently, and well.

Her uncle appeared beside her. In his hand he clasped her pistol, barrel pointed to the floor. He too peered inward, his high silk top hat reflecting the lantern's orange glow.

"Are you *certain* you saw someone?" he prodded gently.

Miss Limpett's hard, glassy stare settled on the sturdy wooden shelf where her father's casket had been placed. Fortunately for her, Mark had released the lid so the weighty panel fell into its original alignment.

Her secret was kept.

The caretaker ventured inward, crouching low. The toe of his muddied work boot struck several of the rivets Mark had pried loose. The *ping ping ping* of metal as they struck the stone wall echoed through the crypt.

"What was that?" his lordship inquired, angling for a better look, but not going so far as to enter.

The caretaker lowered the lantern and examined the floor. Seeing the rivets, the old man's eyes widened. He swung the light toward the coffins in their niches. Fear slackened his features, and his Adam's apple bobbed. "Nothing, your lordship. Nothing at all."

He retreated backward, as if afraid to turn his back to the darkness. Despite his pain, Mark grinned in predatorial delight.

"We best be on our way now," he whispered. "They'll be lockin' the gates soon."

"He's right, Willomina." His lordship attempted to gently draw her away, but her gloved hands gripped the stone edge of the doorway.

"Dear girl, you're overwrought," he surmised. "Your grief plays tricks on you, making you see phantoms where there are none."

She nodded, still staring inside. "You're right, of course, I am . . . overwrought."

"Let us go on to the house," her uncle urged. "You can rest a bit there, and soon we'll be away from here."

"One moment . . ." She pushed inward and bent to retrieve a length of greenery twisted with white flowers. Grasping the lengthy mass with both hands, she draped it over two coffins, her father's and the one beside it, which he assumed to be her mother's.

Turning on her heel, she froze.

Mark followed her line of vision to the floor where her gaze fixed upon the stone he'd hurled at her at the height of his fury.

He couldn't resist the temptation. He reached out and, after allowing himself one illicit brush of his fingertips against the lace hem of her petticoat, gave her silk outer skirt a stiff pull. Miss Limpett yelped.

Mark heaved up—

Male voices exclaimed from the door.

She whirled about to stare at nothing.

To stare directly at *him*. Nose to nose, breath to breath.

Oh, yes . . . she was pretty.

Miss Limpett was a picture of lustrous skin, rosy lips and gleaming chestnut hair, perfectly twisted into a simple coil at her nape. Even in the midst of his anger over finding nothing but rocks and stale air in the casket, he was what he was. He'd always enjoyed the ladies, especially adventuresome ones with secrets.

The heels of her narrow black shoes tapped against the floor as she backed away.

"What is it?" her uncle demanded.

"Nothing," she whispered. "Just my nerves."

The door slammed. A subsequent roll of metal signaled the turn of the lock. Through the tiny window, the lantern light ebbed to nothing. Their footsteps faded. He stood, surrounded by dust and darkness, and the scent of moldering wood, flesh and bones. His mood quickly returned to foul.

Damn rock-filled coffin. Mina Limpett had deceived him, and everyone else. Odd how he hadn't sensed her lies. Was she so good at telling them? He rubbed his shoulder. The pain had dulled to almost nothing. The only outward evidence of the gunshot was the lingering scent of discharged gunpowder, and the destroyed sleeve of his garments beneath, which his mind, even now, worked to repair. How he despised sewing.

They are with Father.

Realization swept through him. He hadn't sensed her lies, because she hadn't lied to him. Not really. She'd spoken the truth, and with a few frantic miscues, allowed him to make his own assumptions. The scrolls *were* with her father.

The professor wasn't dead, though clearly, he and his daughter had undertaken some elaborate scheme to make everyone believe he was. Three months before, Mark had been so close. He'd tracked them across the earth and across the ocean with all stealth, certain they had no knowledge of his pursuit.

His blood pounded in his head like a clock ticking off time. He had no time for intrigues. The very fact that he'd resisted the deterioration of Transcension this long was a testament to his strength as an immortal warrior, and the centuries of stringent mental training as a Guard. How much longer would he last?

Worse yet, the manner in which Miss Limpett had wielded the gun revealed she had anticipated danger, raising the question in his mind. . . .

Who else wanted the scrolls? Apparently he had competition, which was no surprise, given mortal society's interest in metaphysical subjects, life beyond the grave and immortality. There were all sorts of silly cults and secret societies with shadowy rules, funny robes and ceremonies, all striving to discover the *truth* about life and life beyond. Some of them were not so nice, and intended

darker purposes. Perhaps one of those organizations
sought possession of the scrolls.

One thing for certain, he wasn't finished with the
prickly Miss Limpett. Six months ago, while working
toward the Reclamation of Jack the Ripper, he'd stood
in the small, shabby drawing room of her father's Manchester house, his features transformed into those of Mr.
Matthews, assistant director of the British Museum. He
had interrogated her on the whereabouts of her father
and an ancient cuneiform tablet that had gone missing
from the secret underground archives. The tablet recorded the dark history and even darker prophesies of
the Tantalytes—an ancient chthonic cult that worshiped
the wicked, immortal Tantalus, the Dark Ancient, forever
entombed by the Shadow Guards in the underground
realm of Tartarus.

Without the tablet, Mark, Lord Black and his twin
sister, Selene, had been forced to make do with a poor
duplicate—a badly fragmented scroll. Mark, an expert in
ancient languages, had been tasked with the translation
of the relic.

The scroll preserved the history and prophesies of this
chthonic cult. The papyrus had also contained a series of
numerical coordinates, which when translated, coincided
with all manner of horrific events throughout time, and
leading into the present. Murders. Blights. Plagues. Natural disasters. Most recently, the violent eruption of the In-
donesian volcano, Krakatoa, in 1883. It was through these
occurrences that Tantalus conveyed, via currents of invisible energy, communications from his eternal underworld
prison in an effort to rouse his sleeping army of *brotoi* followers. Through observation, the Guards had determined
that *brotoi* were nearly identical to the evil, deteriorated
souls they were already tasked with Reclaiming.

Yet unlike Transcending souls who sought solitude for
their wicked deeds, *brotoi* displayed an unfortunate incli-

nation to join forces and organize toward the ultimate demise of civilization—not only mortal civilization, but also that of the Amaranthines and their protected paradise, the Inner Realm.

But most important to Mark now was that in its closing, the scroll had mentioned the existence of two sister scrolls that would contain details about the location and use of a powerful conduit of immortality. The unidentified conduit was his only hope of reversing the dark state of Transcension presently at work inside his mind.

The sooner he persuaded Miss Limpett to divulge the whereabouts of her father and the scrolls, the sooner he could reclaim his derailed destiny and his place of honor amongst the Amaranthine Shadow Guards. Remembering her eyes and her lips, and the enthralling fit of her austere mourning garments, he regretted there was no time for a gentle seduction.

A warm breeze swept through the open window of the carriage, sending the curtains fluttering rearward like the wings of a great night moth. The dark, sumptuous interior, combined with the vibration of the wheels on the roadway, and months of exhaustion . . .

Evangeline's head lolled onto Mina's shoulder. A faint snore staggered from her lips.

Mina wished she could do the same. She was so tired. The funeral was supposed to put an end to the running, the hiding and the fear. She had hoped that at last, tonight, she could find peace in sleep.

Astrid sat on the other side of Evangeline. Across from her, Lady Trafford frowned, appearing tangled in her own thoughts. On the far end of the bench from his wife, Trafford stared out the solitary open window. Mina had been so appreciative when he'd thrust the shuttered panel out, dispersing the dizzying miasma of perfume that had accumulated inside.

She, for her part, sat rigid in her seat, trying to rational-
ize everything she'd seen and heard at the crypt. It was, of
course, as Trafford suggested. She had been overwrought
and imagining things.

The glowing eyes had most certainly belonged to a
monstrously large cemetery rat. The stone that struck the
door—obviously it was a chunk fallen from the ceiling of
an aging and shifting crypt, dislodged by her yanking on
the handle. The *chinking* and *splintering* and *roaring* were
all likely due to the activities of the aforementioned sep-
ulchre rat and an unexplained anomaly of wind and echo.
She blinked into the darkness . . . almost believing herself.

Lord Alexander. She recalled his blue eyes, so uncommon, and the way they'd focused so intently on her. Was
he one of them? The men she'd come to fear? Her imagi-
nation twisted sharply, transforming his striking blue
eyes into impenetrable bronze. Men didn't have glowing
bronze eyes, but her mind balked at any notion of the supernatural. Her father might believe in all that nonsense,
but her feet and her suspicions remained firmly grounded
in reality.

Everyone who was anyone in the world of archaic
languages knew her father possessed the two Akkadian
scrolls. The scrolls themselves weren't Akkadian, of course,
but ancient still, and exact copies of Akkadian cuneiform
tablets, which had long ago been destroyed or had dissolved to dust. She, herself, had been present at the time
of their purchase in a nomad's dark desert tent, eighteen
months before. They had been missing their scroll rods,
but were otherwise remarkably well preserved.

At the close of the expedition, she had done as had become customary. She'd organized her father's notes and
penned an academic account that only as a brief aside
made mention of the acquisition. At the time, they hadn't
even been certain of the artifacts' authenticity. She'd sub-

mitted the paper under her father's name to the Royal Geographical Society.

Yet with the publication of that paper, their world had gone mad.

Across from her, Lord Trafford went rigid in his seat. He twisted, his vision fixed on something on the side of the road. Hoisting his cane out the open window, he rapped against the carriage roof. The driver shouted out and amidst a jangling of harnesses, the carriage jerked and slowed.

Lucinda blinked. "What is it, Trafford?"

Evangeline jerked upright. She muttered sleepily, "Why are we stopping?"

Crouching, Trafford opened the door. Without waiting for the footman or the stairs, he clambered down onto the grass, cane in hand.

"I *thought* that was you," he chuckled, speaking genially into the darkness. "Having a bit of horse trouble?"

The carriage side lamps illuminated a broad circle of gravel and grass, littered with miscellaneous rubbish. Carriages and wagons clattered past, the road into London just as busy at this hour as during daylight.

A figure emerged from the shadows, the upper half of his face obscured by the brim of his top hat. A long black overcoat descended to midcalf and rippled in the wind. He held a pair of reins, and a dark, gleaming horse lumbered along behind. The unidentified gentleman's lips pressed together in a grim smile.

Mina's eyes widened, and her heartbeat thundered in her ears. She recognized those lips. She recognized everything from the masculine outline of his shoulders to his towering height and confident stance.

Lord Alexander removed his hat and tapped it brusquely against his thigh, sending out a faint cloud of road dust.

Lucinda shoved back into her seat, her shoulders very straight, her face a pale moon in the darkness. The girls edged toward the windows, straining past Mina for a better look.

"Indeed." His lordship lifted a horseshoe. "I rummaged in the grass until I found it. Might you have a farrier's kit I could borrow?"

"Even better." Trafford pointed his cane in the direction of the road. "We've a farrier."

A brief moment later, the servant—one of two who had followed on horseback—came round on foot. He extended his gloved hand for the shoe.

Her uncle said, "Why don't you ride to the house with the family? Mr. McAlister will bring your animal along once the repair has been made."

Lord Alexander lifted a gloved hand. "Thank you, Trafford, but I suspect your family, and in particular your niece, must be exhausted and desire their privacy."

Through the shadows, his gaze captured Mina's. She dropped the curtain and shrank into the shadows.

Lord Trafford countered, "My dear niece tells me you knew her father. I can't imagine she would want a family friend stranded on a dark night street. Isn't that right, Miss Limpett?"

She heard the crunch of her uncle's shoes on the gravel, just outside the window. Evangeline jabbed an elbow into her side.

Every muscle in her body shrank by at least an inch. Mina called out from behind the curtain, "Do, please . . . ride along with the family, Lord Alexander."

Chapter Three

A moment later, and he was settled amongst them.

Elegant and long of limb, he occupied the corner opposite Mina, his top hat on his lap. The carriage lurched, then rolled onto the road, and soon they coursed along at their previous speed. Gas lamps flashed intermittent light across his features. The wind coaxed a lock of his hair over one eye, an eye that, like its brilliant match, rested on her far too often for peace of mind.

Trafford sat beside his lordship. "I saw you at the cemetery, but didn't get over to speak to you in time. Earlier, I had commented to her ladyship how long it's been since I've seen you at the club."

Lord Alexander adjusted his legs, sliding his booted foot alongside Mina's smaller one. Not touching, but almost. "I've been abroad for the past several months, and only returned to London yesterday."

"Where did you go?" Lucinda whispered.

"Pardon?" Alexander leaned forward a few inches to peer at the countess around Trafford.

"When you left London." Her voice grew stronger, but

held a thready edge. "Did you go somewhere far away? Somewhere more . . . *exciting* and *exotic*?"

Mina listened in silence. Was she the only one who realized Lord Alexander and Lucinda shared some sort of past?

In her corner of the carriage, Astrid stretched like a pampered cat and interjected herself into the conversation. "I *love* to travel."

Lord Alexander smiled easily. "I spent time in Rangoon, before proceeding to Mandalay."

Mina licked her lower lip. Two locations not so far away from Bengal and Tibet.

Astrid gushed breathily, "I *adore* India."

Evangeline hissed, "*Burma.*"

"*Buhhr*-ma," Astrid purred, smiling coquettishly at Lord Alexander. "Isn't that what I said?"

Jaded amusement lit their visitor's eyes. He seemed the sort of gentleman who was used to being fawned over. With a slight tilt of his square-jawed face, he met Mina's observant gaze. Like a shot of morphine, the feeling of intimacy they'd shared in the cemetery returned to dizzy her, to warm her through and through. She felt attractive. Mysterious.

Seduced.

If only Trafford had returned her weapon, she would just pull it out and shoot him now. She could not help but sense he was a danger to her, in more ways than one.

Lord Trafford rotated his cane against the carriage floor. Its faceted glass pommel glimmered in the dark. "Have you taken residence somewhere?"

"I'm actually still on the river, moored at Cheyne Walk."

"I've heard talk of your *Thais*." Trafford smiled. "Envious talk."

"Someone you were very fond of?" Lucinda prodded.

"Who?" asked Lord Alexander.

"Thais," the countess repeated.

He responded, "Thais was . . . a paramour of Alexander the Great."

The girls giggled behind their gloved hands, looking only half scandalized.

His lordship pointedly returned his attention to Trafford.

"I'll take you out some afternoon."

"A spectacular idea," Trafford agreed.

Astrid effused, "I *love* to sail."

"As do I," Evangeline echoed faintly.

Lord Alexander glanced between them. "You are certainly welcome to come along." To Mina, he said, "You are . . . *all* . . . welcome to come along."

Trafford twisted in his seat and crossed one leg over the other. "Now that I know your accommodations, I must insist you accept an invitation to pass the night with us."

Mark shook his head. "I couldn't impose."

"Nonsense," Trafford declared. "It's late, and we've empty rooms begging for guests."

Evangeline and Astrid nodded in concert. Lady Lucinda mustered a blithe smile. Mina prayed his lordship would decline.

"I'm afraid I just can't. I've a full morning of appointments, and all the documents I require are on the boat."

Astrid and Evangeline let out little sighs of disappointment. Lord Alexander grinned, and a boyish, heart-melting dimple appeared on his left cheek. Mina wondered how many women he'd seduced wielding that weapon.

Just then, the carriage rolled into Mayfair.

"Open all the windows so we can see out," exclaimed Astrid, her face bright with excitement. She pushed her shutters open.

Mina did the same, cowardly focusing her attention on the passing scenery, rather than returning the interest of the man in front of her.

Gone was the sweet air of the countryside. Here, every-thing smelled of dust and horses. Well-appointed vehicles crowded the roadways. Gas lamps illuminated the night, reflecting off the façades of the great houses, most of which were lit up like glittering bonfires. Flashes of color could be seen through the windows—silk gowns and flowers—along with glowing faces and sparkling crystal. Even from the street, laughter and strains of music could be heard.

After a half hour of slowing and lurching in traffic, the carriage rolled to a halt in front of the Trafford house. Though just as impressive as her neighbors, the win-dows were solemn and dark. Footmen rushed to assist the ladies down from the vehicle, guiding them between two towering post lamps, toward black lacquered doors. Moments later everyone gathered in the entry hall, an impressive structure of gleaming wood and plaster or-namentation. To the side of the central staircase, several large busts of notable historical figures perched atop Corinthian display columns. A solitary chandelier illu-minated the vaulted ceiling, leaving the periphery of the room in shadows.

"Alexander, I've recently acquired a box of Havanas. Care for a smoke until your mount arrives?"

"Certainly." Lord Alexander's face came around. "Good evening . . ."

Mina looked away before their eyes could meet.

"Ladies." His voice carried a distinct lilt of amusement.

He and Trafford disappeared through an arched doorway.

Lucinda was already halfway up the staircase. "Come, girls. It's been a tiring afternoon, and we've a full day of appointments tomorrow." Her skirts rustled as she ascended the stairs. Evangeline and Astrid cast longing looks in the direction of their father's study, and with dual sighs, slowly followed their stepmother up.

On the first-floor landing, Lucinda paused. "Miss Limpett, are you coming?"

Mina responded, "I'm not sure I'll be able to sleep just yet. I believe I'll step into the library and find something to read."

Lucinda pressed a hand against her temple, and after an extended moment of silence, descended the stairs to stand before her. "I've been unforgivably withdrawn this evening. I've allowed my preoccupation with the planning of Thursday's silly little garden party to distract me when today should have been all about you and the terrible tragedy of your father's passing." She grasped Mina's hands and looked earnestly into her eyes. To Mina's surprise, she saw the gleam of tears against the young woman's lashes. "Please forgive me."

Mina suspected Lucinda's emotion had nothing to do with her silly little garden party or her father's funeral, a perfect example of why she should avoid Lord Alexander. "There's nothing to forgive."

"You are a darling girl, and we're so glad you've come to be part of our family." Her ladyship embraced Mina, fiercely, yet fleetingly, before returning up the stairs and disappearing with the girls around the balustrade.

Mina glanced to the closest of the plaster busts. Lord Nelson stared at her, steely eyed and resolute.

"I've had such an interesting day."

He did not ask for details.

Moving in the direction opposite to that which the gentlemen had taken, Mina traveled a dim hallway dappled on either side by framed oils. Eventually she passed through two behemoth wooden doors into a warmly lit room. In the week that she'd resided with the family, the library had become her haven in the massive, always-busy town house. Two enormous plaster medallions, painted a glacial white, spread above her on the ceiling. Busts of all the great literary masters peered down over their learned noses from identical nooks around the decorative upper border of the room. She walked the full length of shelves, filled to the ceiling with books. She had already paged through and made a few selections when her eye fell upon *Debrett's Peerage*. A sudden curiosity sprang to mind. She claimed the weighty volume and made her way to the far side of the room, taking her seat at a desk situated within a large and deeply bowed and curtained window. A small lamp provided all the light she would require. She paused only a moment to open her bag and retrieve the small photograph case. This she propped open and upright beside her. Glancing at her father and the blurred gentleman who accompanied him, she took up *Debrett's*.

A for Alexander.

She skimmed the aristocratic titles and found the place where . . .

A frown turned her lips. After A-L-E-X- there was nothing but an illegible smudge, an entire half page blurred to nothingness. She fanned through the rest of the pages and found them all in perfect form. Just her luck that the one page she wished to read had suffered some sort of publishing mishap.

Mina shut the book and banished it to the far corner of the desk, more disappointed than she ought to be.

"I believe I owe you something along the order of forty-four pounds from our last card match." Trafford sat in a thronelike armchair behind a mahogany desk. Smoke arose in gray tendrils from the cigar he held pinched between his fingers. He opened a drawer. "Let's see what I've got here."

"No, don't." Mark waved him off, savoring the sweet, woodsy essence of the cigar. "You've allowed me to intrude on your family and gifted me with this excellent cigar. Consider us square."

Trafford grinned. "It's not really gambling if someone doesn't lose. I fully intend to fleece you next time around."

"I don't want your money, Trafford."

"How about a daughter, then?" The earl pointed the ash end of the cigar at Mark. "I've got two, if you hadn't noticed, both in their debut Season. So if you're of a mind to wed . . ."

Mark's throat closed on the smoke, and he coughed. "They are both *lovely* girls. I'm sure they are drawing potential suitors like flies."

Trafford chuckled. "I believe their list of favorites went out the window when they caught sight of you."

"I'm . . . ah . . . flattered. But at present, no, marriage is not a priority."

"The bachelor life. I remember it fondly."

Mark sensed no spite in the man that might indicate knowledge of the minor dalliance he and Lucinda had shared during her debut Season, just one year ago. They'd flirted, and they'd kissed. His hands might have wandered a bit—all at her encouragement—but that was all. In retrospect, he regretted things had gone as far as they had. It made his presence in the Trafford household damn awkward.

Mark nodded, leaning forward in his chair. He extended his hand over the broad expanse of the desk. "That's right. You've celebrated your own recent nuptials. I must offer my congratulations."

They shook hands, a firm exchange.

Trafford puffed around a smile. "Lucinda and I married in December, at my family's chapel in Lancashire."

"You're a lucky man."

"I am, indeed. She's done wonderfully with the girls."

Out of nowhere, a twinge of pain radiated through Mark's temples. He pressed his fingertips against them, and the discomfort faded. His mood grew solemn. Sometimes a similar sensation warned of an oncoming spell of what he'd privately come to refer to as his Inconvenient Madness, which so far revealed itself in black moods of irrational temper and impulse, thus far within his ability to contain. He did not know how the missing three months of time, and his return to London—the place of his original Transcension—might affect their frequency, or intensity. It was for that reason he'd already declined his lordship's invitation to stay the night. Despite his desire to court Miss Limpett's immediate favor, he'd thought it best to exercise caution, at least until he was certain of his mental bearings.

"Unfortunately, Trafford," he said, "it's time that I go."

As if on cue, the gilt-work clock on the mantelpiece chimed eleven. Trafford squinted at the dials.

"I concur—it's been a dreadfully long day." His lordship stood up from the chair. Lifting a silver salver, he ground his cigar onto the gleaming surface and offered the tray to Mark so he could do the same. Cornering the desk, he lifted a guiding hand toward the door. "Let us see about your horse."

The butler met them at the base of the stairs and bowed deferentially to both men.

Trafford rested his hand on the balustrade. "Has Lord Alexander's mount been delivered?"

The butler responded, "The groom took him to be watered. I'll ask that he be brought around."

"Very well."

"And your lordship?" The butler edged forward, his hands behind his back. "Might it be possible to have a word with you on a household matter before you retire?"

"Of course, Mr. George." Trafford lifted a hand. "Just let me see his lordship to his horse."

Mark waved him off. "No, you go on. I'm sure he's being brought around, thank you. I'll just wait here."

Trafford added, "Lucinda's planning a garden party for Thursday. We'll send round an invitation."

The perfect opportunity to return and seduce—yes, why wait?—Miss Limpett.

"I wouldn't miss it."

Left to his own company, Mark drifted to the door, his hat clasped behind his coattail. He peered out the window into the dark but crowded street. Thank God he was on horseback, else it would take him an hour to get out of this jam. His blood quickened in awareness of *her*. A smile turned his lips. Behind him, light footsteps sounded against the marble. He turned.

Miss Limpett emerged from a hallway, her path of intent clearly toward the stairs. Her bonnet hung from her elbow, suspended by its ribbon. She also carried her purse and several books. When she realized his presence, she froze, midstep. Her cheeks pinked, but she didn't smile. She straightened her shoulders, as if to steel herself against him, but in the process, provided him with a tempting display of high, full breasts and an hourglass figure.

His mental net filtered the space around her. *Suspicion*. He loved seduction twined with intrigue, but realized, in this matter, he could not move too fast or she would fly. "Miss Limpett."

"Lord Alexander," she responded with all cordiality, but the emotional buffer she installed between them arose as stalwart as a twelve-foot wall of stone. She would resist being undone. Despite the urgency of time that he could not spare, the challenge thrilled. "I see you're returning to the river after all."

"I am." Hat in hand, he sauntered forward. "I was hoping to see you again before I left. Might we have a word?"

"Yes, of course." Her glance fell upon his tie. His chin. Everything but his eyes.

"I wanted to ask you . . . well"—he smiled his most dashing smile—"if you might grant me permission to call upon you some afternoon, here at the house?"

Wide, dark-lashed eyes fixed directly into his. "Call on me?"

"I'd like to see you again," he clarified softly.

"I see." She shifted her little stack of books from one arm to the other, holding them over her breast—her heart—like a shield against him. "As I told you at the cemetery, I don't know the details of my father's collection."

"My request to call on you has nothing to do with your father, or his collection."

Her dark brows went up, in elegant question. "No?"

"No. I'd like to see you. Spend time with you." He waved his hat in the direction of the rest of the house. "Not even all of them. Just . . . you."

A flush crept into her cheeks. She moistened her lips. "I see."

"Do you understand?" He smiled again, but only slightly, not wishing to appear overly confident—for in this endeavor, strangely he was not. Though an undeniable frisson of tension existed between them, he sensed there would be no guarantees when it came to Miss Limpett and her favors.

"I think I do."

The door swooshed inward, and the footman appeared, bringing with him the sounds of hooves clattering on pavement. "Your horse, your lordship."

"I shall inquire, then?" Mark pressed her gently, lifting his hat in adieu.

Her gaze went dark. "I'm flattered by your request, but . . . I don't believe I'm ready for callers. And I don't believe I shall be at any time in the near future."

Surprise and displeasure clouded his mind, but he easily held his smile.

"I must respect your wishes, of course." Slowly, he lowered his hat to his head. "Good night, then, Miss Limpett."

He exited the door held by the footman. On the street

he accepted the reins of his horse. Hoisting himself into the saddle, he glanced through the polished front windows to see her still there on the stairs, an alluring silhouette, watching him as he watched her. His blood warmed a degree hotter, and every muscle in his body drew excruciatingly, deliciously taut. He touched the brim of his hat, and turned his horse in a wide circle, departing in the direction of the Thames.

An hour later, he descended the creaking steps of the public stable and set off on foot, east down King's Road. Two- and three-storied shop fronts and houses lined his way. Steam hovered in the warm, stagnant air, forming hazy haloes around the large gas lamps lining the avenue. Here in Chelsea, the green, decayed scent of the river permeated everything.

His thoughts lingered on Miss Limpett—*Mina*—an intriguing enigma. A delightful turn of tables, when it was he who always played that part. Even now, the delicious agony of their parting lingered. Delicious it was, because her reluctance to trust him—to allow him to draw closer as quickly and easily as he wished—only heightened his interest, an interest that had nothing to do with her father or the scrolls, and everything to do with the first sensual strokes of a growing flame.

A sudden fluctuation deep inside his bones, within his very immortal marrow, alerted him that he was not alone on the street.

The occasional hansom clattered past and small groups of men and women clustered on deeply shadowed stoops. But there was something else. He passed an alleyway, and from the corner of his eye glimpsed a shadow moving against shadow.

He did not alter his pace, but mentally dispatched a penetrating wave of energy, one that revealed, like an explosion of white light, everything around him in luminous relief regardless of brick walls, wood or stucco: A fishmonger pushed his cart down the back alley. Three rats, tails snapping, feasted on a heap of fresh rubbish. A swarm of cockroaches scurried in the basement of the butcher shop two streets away. And someone—or something—tracked him, just along the edge of his awareness, too fast and too erratic of movement to positively identify. His assassin or some other foe? An anticipatory smile pulled Mark's lips at the impending combat. His palms itched to wield an Amaranthine silver sword or dagger, but, denied that privilege since his Transcension, he would make do with his hands.

A public house occupied the distant side of the road. A lively tune, being hammered out on a piano, jangled through the door of the Queen's Elm. Perhaps a drink before confrontation. He enjoyed his vices, tobacco and liquor, and because of his immortal constitution, fortunately suffered no ill effects from their consumption. He entered and made his way through a jumble of mismatched chairs and tables, toward the bar, where he stood, rather than taking one of the stools. The sour-sweet scent of wood cured by spilled ale tainted the air. Two boy-faced sailors hunkered over the piano, joined arm over arm. They sang a slurred tune, swinging their pint tankards in time with the music.

> Six little whores, glad to be alive,
> One sidles up to Jack, then there are five.
> Four and whore rhyme aright,
> So do three and me,
> I'll set the town alight.

Jack the Ripper. Bastard didn't deserve a song. Peculiar how mortals glorified those things they feared the most. More men in military dress sat at the tables, likely on pass from the Chelsea Barracks, only a few streets away.

"Good evenin', gov'na." The bare-pated publican

moved close, wiping down the polished wood bar with a green checkered rag. "I'd offer y' the snug"—he gigged his thumb over his shoulder—"but someone's already there."

Mark glanced to the window, cut into the wall at a raised level so as to offer its occupant anonymity and privacy—but a full view of the room.

"I won't be staying long." He pointed out a bottle of Irish whiskey.

The man hoisted the bottle. "Looks like we're almost out. Don't want to give y' the dregs. I'll go back t' get another."

Mark nodded. Eventually, the publican returned, bottle in hand. With a knife, he wedged out the cork and poured a stream of amber liquid into a battered and chipped glass. Mark slid his hand into his pocket for the necessary payment, but the man tapped the bar.

"No need, it's paid for."

Mark stilled. "By whom?"

"The gentleman up there." The barkeeper jerked his head in the direction of the darkened window.

A gloved hand lifted a mug in salute.

Slowly . . . Mark did the same.

Lowering the glass to wood, he smiled. His pulse surged. God, despite the danger, it was *good* to be back in London. Rounding the bar, he ducked up the narrow cut of steps and shoved the door open. The small room was empty, save for a wooden bench.

Sensing her, he whirled.

A figure lunged, a blur of wide-brimmed hat and cloak, planting a knee-high boot at the center of his chest. The impact sent him crashing inside. His back slammed down, and skidded across the bench. He'd already identified his tracker, and by way of greeting, good-naturedly allowed the violence. Her full weight landed on his chest, crushing the laughter from his lungs. God, a knee to his ribs. Hands wrenched his head up by the collar.

Selene glared down at him, her eyes entirely black.

He grinned. "I've missed you."

"I should kill you now, Brother."

"Mirror, mirror on the wall." With a stiff flex of his muscles, he flung his twin against the wall. *Crash.* Plaster rained down about them both. She fell, a tangle of long, trouser-clad legs and cape, to the floor. "You're your mother after all."

"Don't talk about her," she hissed, springing onto her feet and lunging close. "You've no right. She'd despise you for what you did as much as I do. You threw it away, Mark. You threw it all away, for a moment of vainglory. And let there be no doubt, I've sent missive upon missive to the Primordial Council, begging them to let me be the one."

"*Selene* . . . ," he warned.

"Your *assassin*," his twin seethed, adjusting the brim of her hat. A fat, purple feather quivered against the band. "I'm just waiting for the order."

Before his eyes, she twisted, her features collapsing into nothingness. Into shadow.

With that, she was gone.

Mark knew the violence of their exchange had brought on a shift in the color of his own eyes and quickly thrust on his spectacles to conceal the bronze glow—just as the publican rushed up the stairs.

"Wot the 'ell?" he shouted.

"It's a private family matter," Mark growled.

"Where'd 'e go?"

Mark brushed past. At least now he knew who had been tracking him along the street. Straightening his necktie and returning his hat to his head, he ducked again and clambered down the stairs. He didn't expect to find Selene in the public room below, and she wasn't there, not even in shadow.

The other patrons gave him a wide berth, though goddamit, if someone hadn't made off with his drink. He caught the eye of the barkeeper.

"Another," he growled.

Mark seated himself on a stool and glared into the large mirror spanning the wall behind the bar, and sipped his whiskey. His spectacles glinted in the hazy darkness. The thin layer of silver beneath the glass had deteriorated, leaving his reflection mottled and incomplete—a far more accurate portrayal of himself than he would have liked to admit.

Selene was clearly just as furious at his decision to submit himself to Transcension as she had been six months ago. He understood the underlying source of her anger—her fear of being left alone. For centuries, they'd had no one but each other in the world, no one else who truly understood the emotion and history behind their mercenary and solitary ways. That she would wish to be his assassin . . . well, he would not expect anything less from her.

At the same time, her lack of confidence stung. She shared his ambition, and the burning desire to make a name for herself. Surely she understood that if he returned from Transcension, he'd be an unparalleled legend amongst the Guard—and amongst the entire Amaranthine race. Once he found the scrolls, and the reparative conduit they promised, she could be certain he would present himself and demand her apology.

Someone slid onto the stool beside him. The mirror showed her to be dark haired, dark eyed and slender, and one of several prostitutes who trolled the pub for customers. Her unbuttoned bodice displayed a profusion of shabby lace and bosom. She leaned, positioning her breast so that it crushed against his arm.

"Want t' work off some o' that frustration on Annie?" An audacious smile curved her lips.

He'd never had a taste for street prostitutes. The reality

of their lives put him off. They were dirty, desperate and diseased. Still, if he crossed his eyes, this particular girl might look something like . . . Miss Limpett.

Take her.

Use her.

Devour her.

Pain shot through Mark's temple. He pressed his fingertips against the throbbing pulse. The command echoed inside his head. Staring at the mirror, into his own flat eyes, he reminded himself the voice didn't belong to him. It wasn't the first time he'd heard it, the whispers and sly instruction. Sometimes the voice belonged to a man. Sometimes there were several. Tonight . . . the voice was distinctly female. Velvety soft, she not only offered dark suggestions, but painted lurid pictures and urged him to do exceedingly wicked things.

He strongly suspected his brief indulgence in violence moments before had awakened the predator inside him, though only a mere fraction of the monster he could become. With that slight turning, he must have opened his mind to the madness within, so best he return to the boat, and quickly.

Just then another woman drew his attention, perhaps because of the way the light glinted off her bright, red-gold hair. Young, and certainly beyond her twentieth year, she stood in the open doorway, eyeing the crowd. Fatigue painted itself in dark streaks beneath her eyes. An ulster coat hung from her shoulders, much too large for her frame. A brown linsey skirt peeked from beneath, bits of grass clinging as if she'd spent the day, and perhaps the previous night, living in the rough on the banks of the Thames.

"What do you say," whispered the woman, just beside his ear. Her hot breath bathed his neck. A heavy pulse stirred his groin. *Devour. Devour. Devour.* "Want to give Annie a try? You won't be sorry."

The girl, the bright-haired one, circled the room, a forced smile turning her colorless lips. She sidled up to the nearest of the two sailors and rested her hand on his arm.

Annie's hand, however, slid beneath the cover of the bar to press against his upper thigh. His vision blurred, and he imagined he was somewhere else, with someone else. The idea of losing himself in his false Mina Limpett, and forgetting his present troubles, if even for a quarter hour, held a sordid appeal.

"I said no," a man's voice shouted. All conversation in the room ceased. The seaman glared down at the girl. "Ain't interested. Somethin' you don't understand about that?"

Mark focused on the girl. Her cheeks went apple red and her eyes glazed over with tears. Slowly, she retreated to the door and disappeared into the night.

The intensity of her desperation soured Mark's arousal. He gripped Annie's wrist and thrust her away. Whom was he trying to fool? The woman beside him would require a pillow over her face to even remotely resemble Miss Limpett. He dropped several coins to the bar and stood. The prostitute cursed him.

The room flashed orange—as if illuminated by an invisible fireball.

His hand shielded his eyes. Heat, greater than a desert sun, scorched his skin and heated his clothes.

Skeletons. Everyone in the bar . . . a skeleton.

Mark stared, trying to make sense of the moment. They weren't *really* skeletons. Instead, the peculiar orange light rendered their skin and muscle transparent. All around him, in a surreal caricature of normalcy, the bones talked and laughed. They wagered with hats perched on their heads, and uniforms or dresses or whatever garments hanging from their matchstick frames.

He felt a tug on his jacket sleeve. The prostitute stood

behind him. Her clawed hands rested on the butterfly-wing bones of her pelvis. Hollow eyes peered up at him, and her yellow teeth clacked. "Change your mind, luv?"

The bartender threw back his white skull and cackled.

Mark hurtled out the door into the night. He bent at the waist, his palms on his knees, and gasped for air. Confusion crowded his thoughts, as if a thousand pincer-headed worms ate into his skull and multiplied a thousandfold. He looked through the window, into the pub, and saw everyone there . . . as they had been before.

No skeletons. No maniacal laughter.

His skin went clammy . . . cold and hot at the same time. Two doors away, a pair of shoeless old men in rags, probable residents of the local workhouse, eyed him from a darkened stoop. Likely they'd missed the evening locking of the door and would be forced to spend the night on the street. Like them, it appeared he'd run out of time. He reached out to touch the brick wall as vertigo threatened to send him sprawling. Rigidly, he continued south at as rapid a pace as the lingering dizziness in his head would allow.

Beyond the Embankment rail, the Thames shimmered like a black serpent, covered by a vaporous blanket of haze. Grand terrace houses overlooked the river. Distant lights bobbed on the water, lanterns on unseen ships and barges. Once returned to the *Thais*, he would release the yacht from its moorings and take it out into open water, where he'd anchor for the night. By secluding himself in such a way, he would be aware of anyone who approached, and isolate himself until his mind returned to course.

In the distance, Albert Bridge illuminated the night with its blazing pagoda lamps and lattice of suspension cords. Cadogan Pier waited just beyond. He felt cautious relief.

A dense wave of despair struck him, from the direction of the bridge. At the railing stood the girl from the Queen's Elm. She leaned over—too far for safety—precariously peering into the black water below.

Chapter Four

Mark's heart should have beat more quickly when he realized what she intended, but years of jaded existence merely fixed him to the spot.

The girl whispered to herself and climbed onto the rail, her leg swinging up to bunch in her skirts. Shadow Guards, by strict rule, were forbidden to interfere in the life and death matters of common mortals. But now, banished from the Guard, he supposed he lived by his own rules.

As if to challenge that assertion, the voice inside his head commanded:

Take her.

Claim her.

Devour her.

An echo of its previous demand. His mental fortitude faltered, and for a shattering moment . . . wrong became twisted into right. He staved his fingers into his hair, wishing he could tear the voice from his brain. In defiance of the voice, and all the things it commanded him to do, he advanced toward the girl. Oblivious of his presence, she pushed off, her arms and coat spread like the wings of a bird.

He evanesced . . . and twisted, veering deep.

A scant moment later he lowered her to the bridge.

The voice raged louder in his head, insisting that he—

He hissed in defiance. With a touch of his hand to her cheek, he dazed her, muddying her memory of her rescue. At the same time he drew from her recent memories and most vivid thoughts. She stared at him, her eyes wide and incredulous. Her lips parted, but no words issued forth.

"You're having a very bad night," he said.

Through white lips, she wheezed, obviously perplexed by the chunk of missing time and the sudden presence of the stranger beside her.

"He misled you. And now he's left you. You're without any means of support. You've had no choice but to turn to the streets."

She blinked and whispered, "Yes."

"And you've no family to go to for help."

She shook her head, and a tear spilled over her cheek. "My mum, she's in the workhouse. My da' . . . 'e won't never forgive me for all I've done."

Mark slipped his hand into the breast pocket of his coat. "Things will be better now." He pressed a slim leather wallet into her hand. "It's enough to see you well kept in a respectable lodging house for a month, until you get back on your feet."

Suspicion furrowed her brow. "What do you want from me?"

The voice supplied an array of wicked suggestions.

"I want you to go," he gritted.

Oblivious to his torment, she peeked inside the wallet. "Oh, sir." Another tear fell. "Yer me bloomin' angel, aren't you? Sent down from 'eaven?"

The voice cackled, clearly amused. She taunted him— told him there was still time to snatch the girl. That no one would see.

"Go . . . *now*." Even to his own ears, his voice sounded strange. Hollow.

She seemed to sense the danger in him. Backing away, she clutched the case against her breast and hurried off the bridge. Just before she disappeared into the shadows, she turned to look back. She lifted her hand in good-bye. With that she was gone.

He followed the path she had taken off the bridge, but proceeded west toward the moorings, just yards away now. He could not help but claim a dark satisfaction. In saving the girl's life, he had defied the voice and proven that *he* remained in command, that some kernel of humanity still existed. He was not yet completely consumed by Transcension.

From off the Thames a cold gust of wind struck, causing a dramatic change in temperature.

Pain ripped through his temples.

He staggered—

Mina awakened to darkness. Paralyzed, she blindly stared at nothing, too fearful to move. Too fearful to make a sound. Then she saw it, a sliver of lamplight from one of the tents. She scrambled toward the glow, clawing frantically through the fog.

No, thank God. . . .

She almost sobbed with relief.

Not fog. Bed curtains, striped in green and gold. She twisted her fingers into the cool brocade and raked them aside, exhaling her fear and inhaling the comforting scents of lemon oil and orange blossom soap. She had survived another night. Three nights since the mysterious event at the cemetery. Three months since her father had left her to make her way alone. She collapsed back onto smooth sheets, buttery and delicious against her skin.

A moment later she padded across the floor. Starting at one window, she pulled the heavy curtains and did not stop until she'd pulled them all wide, exposing every inch of the elegant room to light. She stood behind one panel, her dishabille hidden from any gardener or passerby, and took comfort in the sight of Hyde Park, which spread in the distance just beyond the courtyard. She must have slept late, because riders already obscured the Row and hunger gnawed at her stomach. Through the speaking tube she called down to the kitchen for breakfast.

Last night she'd lain in bed until her lamp flickered out for lack of oil. She'd lain there some more, listening to every creak and shift of the house, waiting for a pair of bronze eyes to appear. At some point, she must have fallen asleep. One glance at the sunshine out the window, and at the white, yellow and purple crocuses cheerily dotting the flower beds, and she felt assured she would soon forget her fears and be able to fully embrace this new life.

Even now, her pulse trilled with the melodramatic symphony of a theater orchestra each time she remembered the far-too-handsome-for-words Lord Alexander's request to call on her. Two days had passed, with no sight of him. She prayed, in defiance of her feminine heart, that he'd forgotten her. His attention had unnerved her. He was too much—too golden, too audacious and, she strongly suspected, too wicked. And he understood the importance of the scrolls. He was exactly the sort of man she could never allow herself to trust.

There came a soft knock at the door. At her answer, a maid entered with a silver, dome-lidded tray and a few calling cards. The only one she recognized was that of Mr. Matthews, from the British Museum. Mr. Matthews had once been a close friend of her father's, but six months ago it had been he who accused the professor of theft. She wasn't ready to receive him just yet.

Over the next half hour, the girl helped Mina into her petticoats and corset, and finally, one of her three dull, black dresses. She also brushed and pinned Mina's hair before pouring her a cup of tea and leaving her alone again. The assistance of a maid was something Mina had never before had the opportunity to enjoy. The experience had taken getting used to. Because she had traveled so much with her father—and because such a luxury could never have been afforded—she'd always tended to her own needs. Since coming to stay with the family, she could not help but feel spoiled. To her surprise, she rather liked it.

She unlatched the nearest window and pushed it open. Outside, birds sang in the trees, and carriages trundled past. As she turned back for her teacup, her glance settled on the leather satchel in the corner, filled with her father's notebooks and papers. The smile faded from her lips. She'd carried them with her all the way from Nepal, never allowing them out of her sight. She'd even slept with them on the ocean voyage over. One day soon she'd open them and begin organizing and transcribing his notes. Eventually, as she'd always done for him after her mother died, she'd submit a paper to the Royal Geographical Society— under her father's name, posthumously of course—but she wasn't ready to face them yet.

Instead, she enjoyed a point of toast with marmalade and a second cup of tea before washing up. Wrapping a few uneaten sausages in a napkin, she let herself into the hallway and proceeded downstairs. The house was quiet, with only the servants moving about. Likely Lucinda and the girls had gone for their daily constitutional in the park.

Two days ago, while reading in the conservatory, she'd glimpsed three pairs of green eyes peering out at her from the shrubberies along the back wall of the garden. A few moments later, Mina crouched, gathering her skirt against her legs so the noise of her petticoats wouldn't frighten the skittish felines away.

"Come on, darlings." She unfolded the napkin and

laid it on the flagstones. "That's right. I've brought you breakfast, but shh, don't tell. I don't think the cook would approve."

Soon, green eyes blinked from the shadows. Eventually, one small, glossy black feline emerged from the shrubs. With queenly grace, she turned her back to Mina and sat, pointedly ignoring the sausages.

Another emerged to circle her skirts, while a third swatted and sniffed at the sausages, finally attacking, and sinking his teeth into one. Mina hugged her arms around her knees. She didn't attempt to pet the animals. They were feral and still learning to trust.

She'd always loved animals—even the slobbering yak she'd ridden in the mountains those final days of the expedition with her father. But their constant travel made it impossible to ever have a pet. Pets required constancy. Permanency. Something that—after her mother's death, the succession of shabby boarding schools and endless travels—she'd always craved.

A shadow darkened the stones. "Don't let Lucinda catch you doing that."

The cats darted off into the shrubs. Mina turned to find Astrid on the stairs behind her. She stood as her cousin came down.

"To my dear stepmother's way of thinking, cats and dogs are no better than rodents."

Mina retrieved the empty napkin and folded it in her hand.

"You look lovely today, Lady Astrid."

The young woman smiled, a picture of fashion and grace. Her upswept blond hair had been curled and pinned to perfection, and she wore an elegant plum-colored day dress, trimmed in purple. Unlike Mina, the family had observed only one week of mourning, that being the week of the funeral. Three months had passed, and by all accepted rules of etiquette, there was no expectation that they should continue the practice further for a relation they'd not spoken to in two decades.

"Lucinda wants to know if you'd like to go to Hurlingham this morning. We've a musicale to attend at the club."

Mina agreed. "That would be lovely. I'll just get my things."

Perhaps . . . perhaps, by chance, Lord Alexander would be there.

Upstairs in her room, she tied on her bonnet and gathered up her gloves and purse. From her bedside table, she retrieved the book she'd started the night before and turned toward the door. Her gaze fell upon the leather satchel containing her father's writings.

Odd. She could have sworn that earlier this morning, when she'd been eating her breakfast, the flap side—the one bearing the small brass lock—had been facing the room, rather than the wall.

She approached the satchel. Kneeling—a move that left her breathless due to the constriction of her corset—she tipped the case. The lock hung there. She gave the brass a tug and found it secure. Certainly she had remembered wrong. Though she'd made the bed herself, the breakfast tray remained on her desk, so the maid hadn't even come round to tidy up.

No one had been in her room.

"Your lordship."

Mark awoke, the voice and its seductive song of unintelligible words still an echo in his mind. Pale blue light streamed through a portal to bathe his skin. Dawn, or twilight? He did not know. He sprawled shirtless, in trousers, his limbs tangled in dark blue sheets. A hazy figure moved closer, into focus. He distinguished a face and a black patch.

"This is getting to be an unfortunate habit," he growled, rubbing his eyes.

"And good morning to you." Leeson carried a plain white teapot and matching mug—an improvement over his prior choice of a sharp, pointed article of torture. He poured and set the steaming cup on the chest beside the bed.

Mark pushed up and peered out the portal.

The Chelsea Embankment. Terrace houses. Trees. All painted in the same blue light . . . and all in the distance. He sensed the movement of the yacht, drifting in the direction of the moorings under Leeson's command. He exhaled sharply, relieved to find himself, at least, in the familiar waters of the Thames and not off the coast of San Francisco or Samoa.

The girl on the bridge. He must have done as intended, and anchored the yacht away from shore. But why couldn't he recall?

Remembering Leeson, he scowled. "Don't tell me it's January."

"Oh, dear. No, sir. It's early Tuesday morning." The elder immortal's lips pressed together. "You vanished for three days."

Frustration shattered his calm. More missing time. What did it mean?

"I wasn't here, on the *Thais* all that time?"

"I cannot say." Leeson shrugged. "I spied the vessel adrift only this morning. I had a carpenter come out on Saturday to finish up the repairs to the galley. It will be damn difficult to get him back again, in any timely fashion."

The idea he'd been sleepwalking around London for three days with no memory of his activities did not sit well. Mark remembered the voice and all it had encouraged him to do.

No . . . he didn't like the idea at all.

Only then did Leeson's words register. Mark took notice of the change in his surroundings. The curtains, the furniture . . . everything had been returned to its previous order. Leeson retreated to the desk where a short stack of papers lay.

"I've got another newspaper for you. Several, actually."

Leeson's interest in all things mortal was a known trait. Lord Black's secretary ravenously read newspapers, books and periodicals—anything to forward his study of mankind. He maintained a meticulous collection.

"Of course you do." Mark shoved his fingers into his hair, resting his forehead against his hands. "I don't want to see it. Just tell me what's happened."

Leeson turned round, his expression grim.

"Well then . . ." He glanced to the paper in his hand. "I regret to share that three days ago a horrible event took place in America. Pennsylvania, to be more specific. The event began with torrential rains and flooding, and in a matter of days, the excess of water led to a cataclysmic dam failure."

Mark nodded, looking to the floor. "Go on."

"The deluge swept whole villages away. Even a city. Thousands are lost—men, women and children."

"Tragic news." Mark nodded solemnly. "What does that have to do with me?"

Natural disasters happened from time to time. As immortals, they'd witnessed hundreds of them through the centuries, and from a necessary distance, observed the misery left behind in their aftermath. There was nothing he or any other Amaranthine could do to stop them.

Leeson's gaze held unspoken meaning. "I just thought you should be kept aware."

Mark sat silent and rigid at the side of the mattress, not wanting to acknowledge his mind also raced along the same dangerous path. Mark stood, his unbelted trousers slipping to his hips. He growled, "Where're the rest of my clothes?"

"Bundled to go to the laundress, sir. There's a selection of clean garments in the cabinet."

Mark dropped the trousers he'd slept in. Wearing only his smalls, he unlatched the cabinet. Leeson swept forward and claimed the discarded garment from the floor. The secretary retreated to the far side of the room and busied himself at the desk, clearly offering Mark privacy to wash and dress. Mark poured water into the basin, and within moments, donned a clean pair of linen trousers.

Leeson prodded quietly, "Now that Jack the Ripper is gone . . . there's no danger, eh? The Tantalyte Messenger is silenced. I'm sure it's just a . . . nasty coincidence that you suffered one of your spells at the same time this collapse of the dam occurred."

"Miss Limpett, I hope you don't mind if we attend to a few errands along the way," said Lucinda, looking out the window.

"Not at all," Mina responded.

The carriage coursed along Bond Street. Smart shops with polished windows tempted from all sides. The curbs were crowded with carriages, the sidewalks with splendidly outfitted ladies and their accompanying footmen. Mina could not help but feel a bit invisible in comparison in her plain, dark clothing.

"First, I've got to stop at the stationer." The countess adjusted the seam of her glove and addressed Mina's cousins. "Evangeline and Astrid, Miss Gerard is just two shops over, so you may go inside and inquire about your riding habits. They ought to be finished by now."

Smiling to Mina, she said, "Young ladies must go to Paris for their trousseau and their couture, but remember the very finest riding habits are to be found in London. Don't let anyone ever try to convince you otherwise."

Mina nodded. She didn't own a riding habit or anything that might be remotely considered couture. As for a trousseau, she didn't believe she'd have a need for one in the near future.

"We've arrived," Lucinda announced.

The carriage ended its travel in front of a pristine row of shops, all with gold lettering painted on their windows, identifying the wares they offered for purchase. The footman opened the door and the girls climbed down. Mina followed, and last came Lucinda. They gathered on the sidewalk, the footman hovering close by to offer any assistance that might be requested.

"Miss Limpett, why don't you accompany me? I realize you've not had an opportunity to order your mourning stationery."

Mina agreed.

Lucinda waved the sisters on their way. "Girls, we'll join you as soon as we're finished. Ask if the new style plates have come in from Paris."

Astrid and Evangeline drifted off in the direction of a well-kept shop, some two doors down the sidewalk. Lucinda watched them until they disappeared inside. "I like to be sure they get to their assigned destination. Astrid can be a bit mischievous."

Together they turned back toward the stationer's shop. To Mina's surprise, a man waited there, holding a large Kodak. Lucinda paused, and turned her head to the side and slightly downward, as if to display the profile of her straw hat, the crown of which boasted an artful display of faux flowers, gilt berries and organza ribbon. She smiled demurely.

Mina quickly stepped away, so as not to spoil the picture. *Click.*

The photographer nodded to them both, then set off down the sidewalk.

As if nothing had happened, Lucinda continued on to the shop. Mina followed her inside.

The shopkeeper stood up from behind a small, partitioned desk.

"Lady Trafford," he greeted.

"Good morning, Mr. Abbott. My niece, Miss Limpett, would like to view your samples of mourning stationery."

"Right away, my lady, and I'll bring out your order as well."

Once he returned, it took only a few moments for Mina to make a selection, because there was no true *selection* to speak of. There were white cards with thick black borders, white cards with thin black borders, and all thicknesses of borders in between. She chose something in the middle.

Mr. Abbott filled out the appropriate form. "Let me just go see if we've got this particular card in stock, or if I'll have to bring it from the warehouse." He disappeared into the back of the shop.

At the counter beside her, Lucinda pulled the lid from a small box. She extracted a calling card and scanned the wording. A heavy sigh escaped her lips.

"I'm afraid these are all wrong, and this is the second time." She frowned, looking exasperated. "It appears we won't be leaving anytime soon."

A tall, fashionably dressed woman entered the shop. She and Lucinda greeted each other brightly.

Mina took advantage of the pause in their conversation. "Your ladyship, I think I'll join Astrid and Evangeline."

She knew very little about current fashion, and wanted to look at the plates from Paris as well.

"Very well, dear. Have the footman follow you," Lucinda instructed. "I'll be there as soon as I can."

Mina gathered her purse from the counter, then stepped onto the sidewalk. The Trafford carriage no longer waited immediately outside the door, having apparently pulled forward a few spaces to make room for others. She made no effort to gain the attention of the footman, who was presently engaged in conversation with the driver. It was the same distance to the carriage as it would be in the opposite direction to the modiste's shop, and Mina would feel like a ninny requesting an escort for such a brief walk.

She'd managed marketplaces, tent cities and curious lo-
cals in far more exotic settings—why not Bond Street?
Really, some of the rules by which she now had to abide
were silly.

She passed a narrow alley on the way. The next window displayed a charming collection of porcelain music
boxes. She paused. There were scores of them, the retti-
est ones shaped like flowers. Her gaze moved from one
to the next, and she marveled at the detail and workman-
ship. Eventually she turned to continue on—

And froze.

A person in a white theatrical mask lurched toward her,
costumed in a black tentlike cloak that descended to his
knees. His legs were clad in white stockings and ended in
black buckled shoes. At least she assumed the street actor
to be a man. The costume made it difficult to tell.

A governess and her young male charge passed by,
traveling in the same direction as Mina. The actor spun
in a circle, and from nowhere produced a rose formed of
red and white–striped petals. He bowed gallantly and
presented it to the child. The boy laughed and accepted
the gift. He and his governess kept walking. Mina, too,
proceeded toward the modiste's. She smiled politely.

He leapt in front of her and posed his arms wildly. Perhaps his antics were all intended in fun, but she found it
unnerving. Unable to see his eyes for the shape and depth
of the mask, she found the effect almost ghoulish.

She laughed, a tad edgily. "Yes, I can see you are . . .
very nimble."

She sidestepped him, and again he veered in front
of her—then feinted dramatically to the side and high
marched past her with the stiffly posed arms of a soldier.

Relieved, and a bit flustered, she moved forward, only
to feel a hard tap against her shoulder.

Chapter Five

Exasperated, she said, "Sir—"

A gloved hand shot from inside the cloak, grabbing her forearm. The world spun. He flung her into the alley. A shout came from the direction of the carriages.

He yanked at her hair. Pain tore at her temple.

"Ouch!" she shouted.

Metal flashed. A blade. Footsteps sounded on the sidewalk.

Something struck her at the center of the chest, and fell to the ground. The assailant fled into the alley.

Mina gasped for breath. At her feet lay a rose, like the one he'd given the boy.

The Trafford footman clambered around the corner, his expression fierce. "Are you all right, miss?"

"Yes." She pressed a hand to the center of her chest, trying to calm the rampant beat of her heart.

The coach driver raced past them into the alley. A few moments later he returned, wheezing and red-faced. "I'm so sorry, miss. He's gotten away. I can't even tell which direction he's gone."

A number of onlookers clustered around, drawn by

the excitement. A Metropolitan police constable tweeted a whistle and elbowed through. After a moment's inquiry, he escorted Mina to the stationer's shop. There, amidst exclamations of feminine horror from Lucinda and her acquaintance, Mrs. Avermarle, Mina found herself ensconced on a velvet-covered stool. The girls, apparently having heard of the incident at the modiste's shop, rushed through the door.

A strand of hair dangled against Mina's cheek, severed bluntly midway down. She supposed she ought to be thankful her assailant hadn't taken more.

Evangeline pulled a pin from her own brown hair and quickly tucked the abbreviated lock into place.

"There, you can't even tell now," she assured her.

Astrid touched Mina's shoulder, looking more traumatized than Mina felt. "Are you sure you're all right, Miss Limpett?"

Mina nodded, unable to shake the memory of the mask. "I'm fine. Just startled. Her ladyship was correct, I suppose. I should have asked for an escort. I just didn't think it necessary."

"What is the city coming to?" Lucinda whispered, squeezing Mina's shoulders. "Clearly we need more police making the rounds."

A constable scratched out details into a small notebook. "We try our best, my lady, to keep the mountebanks off the finer streets, but sometimes they get through. Usually they're only a nuisance. I suspect, however, that this fellow was a common criminal in the guise of a street actor. The boldness of his crime is shocking, but it's not the first hair thief we've seen."

Lucinda peered down at Mina. "Let's get you home."

The girls' faces fell with disappointment. Mina could not help but sympathize. They'd given up a week of their debut Season to mourning her father, a stranger, and then spent several days confined to the house while preparations for the garden party were finalized. And truly, all Mina wanted was to forget about the incident.

Mina assured Lucinda, "I'd prefer it if we went on to Hurlingham as planned."

Leeson turned to the table. "Speaking of danger, your box at the mooring contained a number of correspondences, which by their scent, are from various *ladies*. There are a number of calling cards and invitations as well." He sifted through a stack.

Mina. At just the memory of her, something inside him grew less sharp, less angry. It was one thing to allow Leeson into his service, but perhaps . . . gads. Skeletons? Burning orange light? Perhaps things grew too dangerous. Perhaps *he* grew too dangerous. Despite her own deceptions, was he wrong to involve her? Bemused, he approached the table.

When had he ever worried about anyone but himself? He refused to start now.

Leeson spread out three cards, all in a row. Mark frowned. He recognized the writing on one, and left it for last. As he tore open another, the scent of lavender spilled out. Inside he found a brief note, written with dramatic flair.

Hurlingham.
Tuesday, midday. The Clubhouse.
—A.

The second note smelled of violets and contained identical information. The authoress had simply signed "E." The third, of course, was from "L." and thankfully contained no scent; yet the words "Please come" had been added—and underlined.

"There's one from all the women in that house but the Limpett girl."

"I see that."

"How is she? What information were you able to glean from her at the funeral?"

Mark paused. Leeson wouldn't know about the professor's falsified death. Under normal circumstances such a thing would be easily verifiable by the immortal secretary, but if the portals had closed, he was effectively cut off from the informational resources they had all previously enjoyed.

He considered whether he should share any of his hard-won knowledge with the enthusiastic little man, but in the end, decided he had no choice but to trust him—at least in this.

"The professor isn't dead."

"What?" His eye patch moved up on his face with the raising of his eyebrows.

"He and his daughter falsified his death. I'm certain to throw someone off their trail."

"'Someone' as in *not you*?" Leeson frowned quizzically.

Mark nodded. "There's someone else out there who wants the scrolls. Whether it's an individual or some sort of cult of immortality, I don't know yet. I just know I've got competition."

Leeson drifted closer. His temples creased in thought. "I realize they are valuable artifacts, but do you think their true value is known?"

"Hell, I can't even claim to know their true value. All I know is that the first scroll provided a glimpse of the information contained in the second and third scrolls; specifically, that they would provide details of a conduit of renewal and immortality—one that could repair an immortal stricken with Transcension," Mark answered. "I've got to believe the professor is still in possession of the scrolls—or at least knows where they are."

"So what is your plan to seduce the girl?"

Mark flinched. Were his methods so predictable? So clichéd?

The old man prodded. "Come on now. We're not two rascals telling tales. This is strategy. Have you managed to bed her yet?"

"*Leeson.*"

"Don't be shy, boy. Have you danced the horizontal polka or no?"

"Good God," Mark exclaimed. "We only met three days ago and I've been . . . I don't know where since then, but I think I'm safe assuming not with her, so no. We've only talked."

"Talked." Leeson chewed his thumbnail in thought. "I'm not sure that method will be quite as effective or expedient as what you require. Lucky for you, a mortal woman turns to veritable putty in the masterful hand of an immortal lover. You and I both know that." He winked. "Get her in bed and she'll tell you anything you want to know."

Mark said firmly, "I haven't made any decisions yet on how, exactly, I will proceed with Miss Limpett."

"Your only other alternative, as I see it, is to cut off her fingers one by one until she talks." He made scissor motions.

Mark clenched his teeth. "That's not an option."

"I'm inclined to agree." Leeson nodded. "I saw her myself. She's got lovely fingers, and so seduction is the desired plan of action. All you've got to do is work your Marcus Antonius magic on her and she'll spill the details of the professor's whereabouts."

Mark shared his deepest doubt. One he'd refused to address, even with himself. "Bloody hell. What if she doesn't know where her father is? What if I'm wasting my time?"

"Oh, I vow he knows where *she* is. If you had a daughter like her, would you just give her up to the nasty old world, and forget her? No. He may be off on an adventure, but he's got his paternal eye on her somehow. He's got to have trusted connections here in London, who would relay any cause for alarm to him. And if any man is cause for alarm—it's you."

"I'll take that as a compliment."

"As you should. But in this case, I think you need to go above and beyond as far as the girl is concerned. You've got to come out big, right out of the chute. No time for dillydallying."

"What might you suggest?" Mark asked sardonically. Clearly the man did not understand sarcasm.

Leeson crossed his arms in thought, his eye focused on the ceiling. "We're experiencing the oddest summer, either roasting or chilled, but no rain in sight. So that excludes a carefully orchestrated, trapped-in-the-gardener's-hut-during-a-downpour seduction." He grinned. "Always my favorite scenario. Everyone's clothes all wet and clingy."

Mark shook his head. "I'm not doing this. I'm not strategizing with you over a seduction of Miss Limpett. She's not a hackneyed cutout like . . ."

"Like all the others?" Leeson grinned. "Then we've got to think of something big. Something truly spectacular."

Mark poured himself a glass of water from the carafe on the table. "If you didn't understand what I just said, allow me to translate: Stay out of my business where Miss Limpett is concerned." He consumed the tepid liquid in one gulp.

Leeson shrugged, but his eyes still twinkled with too much mischief. "Have it your way. I am, after all, at your service."

He turned to peer out the portal. "We're nearing the wharf. Before we arrive, there is one more thing you need to see. Something I've . . . ah, purposefully delayed in showing you because . . . I don't think you'll be very pleased."

"What is it now?" Mark responded suspiciously, and set down the glass.

"I think you'd better go outside and have a look." Something in Leeson's face—the drop of his lips, the hardening of his jaw—told Mark to not ask questions, to simply do as he asked. He slid the lacquered wood door into its casement and stepped out into the cool morning air.

White rose petals carpeted the threshold. Slowly, he followed them all the way to the prow of the yacht.

Rose petals. Unpleasant memories surfaced in his head. Jack had preferred red roses. These were white.

Well, mostly.

Some of the petals had become stained by the bloody footprints underneath.

Leeson joined him, mop and bucket in hand. "Go get yourself together, sir. I'll clean up this mess. Go on to Hurlingham and see if you can get your name, along with Miss Limpett's, into the gossip rags."

Hurlingham, located at the private end of Ranelagh Gardens, was not far from Cheyne Walk. Indeed, the grounds of the private club were so close, Mark chose to walk the distance. He'd used the time alone to think, and think he had.

He'd thought about scalding orange light.

Skeletons.

The damn voice in his head.

And now, on top of everything else, white rose petals stained with blood. At least, clearly, the footprints hadn't belonged to him. They'd been smaller and narrower. Whether they'd belonged to a woman or a man of smaller stature, he had been unable to discern.

His mind kept returning to the same thought. As Leeson had suggested, why should he be surprised that he, a Transcending immortal, might also be susceptible to the same message-bearing waves intended for deteriorated souls, such as Jack the Ripper and the rest of the fiend-ish *brotoi* attempting to populate the earth? The admission was not a happy one. It served only to emphasize how little time he had left in which to save himself.

Mark paused in the shadow of the Hurlingham club-house. The structure's massive colonial columns offered a grand salute to the ships sailing down the Thames. Visible from where he stood, the river coursed along the southern border of the property. With his current spate of luck, he'd likely encounter Lucinda, Astrid, Evangeline, or—God, please no—all three at once and be informed Mina had remained behind at home. He prayed a weekday walk on the grounds would be a desirable excursion for a young woman in mourning. If only he could get her alone.

His own dear mother had written the book on strategic seduction, and he supposed the apple had not fallen far from the tree.

Mark proceeded in front of the clubhouse, and down the slope. He dispatched a thousand mental feelers, in all directions, in an effort to pick up her trace. The dramatic crescendo of a string quartet drifted out from the open windows, adding an almost comical score to his quest. Just last year, he had thundered atop prime horseflesh on the distant polo field, to the applause of the crowded grandstand. The club also hosted lawn tennis, cricket matches and male-member-only pigeon shoots. Likely Miss Limpett would not be undertaking any of those sports. He rounded a thick copse of trees, which led to a smaller clearing. Ah, there. *Close . . . yes, she was close.*

However, his gaze narrowed on a man in a straw hat and dressed in white duck—a familiar man who had no business being at Hurlingham. Mark had often wondered if Leeson were part sprite, for his ability to move about so quickly.

A large square of white canvas blanketed the clearing.

At its center, a large wicker basket lay on its side and beyond that, a half-inflated gas balloon. Mark pinpointed the source of a faint hissing sound—a cylindrical metal dispenser of compressed gas, inflating the balloon via a large filling tube. Mr. Leeson shouted orders to four harried club groundsmen, who staked lines and assisted in spreading the plumping silk.

Mark approached him from behind, and growled, "What are you doing here?"

Leeson cast him a sideways glance. "I think that's obvious, sir. I'm airing up my balloon. My *big . . . spectacular* balloon. Don't worry. I shan't interfere with your plans. I realize you don't need me or my silly-old-man ideas. So I'll just be here enjoying myself with my own thrilling diversion. Perhaps I can persuade some pretty, *adventurous* lady to go up with me. By the by, yours is just around that bend of trees."

Mark narrowed his eyes in warning and backed away.

Mina stared down into her book, but saw only the mask. She blinked the image away, and looked out over the lawn. Married couples walked arm in arm. Children chased each other through the trees. Nannies pushed babies in gleaming perambulators. Everything around her appeared so normal. Everything *was* normal. That morning, outside the shop, she'd been the victim of a random crime. If her attacker had wished to harm her, he would have, but all he'd wanted was a strand of her hair. According to the constable, the person suffered from a *hair fetish*, and they'd seen the crime before.

So why did her mind insist on painting the world in shades of danger and impending doom? And on making hazy connections where there ought to be none?

Trafford had unexpectedly met them at the club. Unfortunately, he'd forgotten his ticket, so Mina had insisted on surrendering hers. Understandably he'd been mortified at the news of her attack, and though he had voiced nothing but concern, she could not help but feel as if she were being branded a damsel in constant distress. First there had been her gun-wielding panic at the cemetery, and now this. For the express purpose of proving the event hadn't phased her, she'd calmly waved them off to the musicale, insisting she'd rather read her book out on the grounds.

Mina's breath stopped as she caught sight of a tall, dashing figure in gray trousers and a dark blue frock coat. Broad shouldered and confident, Lord Alexander strode in her direction. She bit her lip, half praying he did not see her—and half praying he did.

His cool, blue-eyed gaze surveyed the lawn, skimming over everyone, disinterested . . . until they settled on her. His pace slowed. A smile turned his lips. *That* smile. Endearingly boyish with a sharp glint of rogue. Pleasure curled up through her belly, to warm her throat and her face.

Her inner shrew—the one she imagined as a grumpy, dour-faced version of herself—counseled her to remain on guard. That he was too handsome and too tempting for even a strong, forward-thinking young woman like her, who wouldn't, under the right circumstances, shy away from romance. But how could she not be thrilled by the notice of such a remarkable man?

"Good morning, Miss Limpett," he called as he drew close. "Certainly you're not here alone, are you?"

"Not at all." She pulled the ribbon between the pages to mark her place, and closed the book. "The family received tickets to the musicale at the clubhouse, and rather than stay alone at the house, I came along."

"How fortunate for me." His shadow slanted across her.

She watched him beneath the brim of her hat, and inquired politely, "What brings you to Hurlingham?"

"An invitation from some friends," he answered vaguely.

Yes. He would have lots of friends. He had the sort of magnetism that would draw all kinds of personalities, admiration and favor. He was both attractive and likeable, but beneath all that, a bit mysterious as well.

He added, "They must have been delayed, but I am just as pleased to find you here. May I sit?"

Best she avoid such a tempting situation. Although he was a different kind of danger, she'd had quite enough imperilment for one day. She did not want to risk the chance he would try to resurrect the matter of the scrolls. She opened her purse and glanced at her watch without even making note of the time.

"Actually, I'm supposed to meet the family. Would you like to walk with me to the clubhouse?"

His smile faded the slightest noticeable bit. "Of course."

She slid her book into her purse and stood. After brushing a few bits of stray grass from her skirt, she joined him. They walked side by side along the path, with him towering above her. Furtively, she studied him from beneath the brim of her hat. Did she only imagine the thick air of tension between them, or did he feel it too? She curled the gloved fingers of both hands around the ebony handle of her purse.

"You've been well these past few days?" he inquired, his eyes riveted to her face.

No, she didn't imagine the tension. She reminded herself men like him had *tension* with whomever they chose, and wielded the talent like a weapon. He'd apparently experienced some sort of *tension* with her aunt, and perhaps still did. Her spirit of individuality rejected the idea of becoming one of a bevy of admirers, a competitor for his attention.

She nodded. "There's always something going on in

the house. The girls have been busy, of course, with their social activities, and Lady Lucinda has been thick in preparations for a garden party she will host on Thursday. She has marvelous taste. I'm sure the event will be the talk of the Season."

"But what of you?" he probed, forcing the intimacy she avoided.

She shrugged. "I read. I walk. I read and walk some more."

He chuckled, deep in his chest, good humor mixed with masculine power. She liked the sound—too much. In her mind, she almost dared him to ask about the scrolls so that she would have good reason to avoid him further, but he did not.

"You've other things to occupy your time, I'm sure," he said.

"I've some of my father's papers. His notes." She did dare him now, quite recklessly. "There's nothing of real importance in them, but I think they'll shape up nicely into several different academic papers. I'll submit them to the Royal Geographical Society, and we shall see if they publish them."

"Under your father's name?"

"Yes," she replied, then emphasized, "Posthumously, of course."

"You've always written your father's articles, haven't you?" he asked.

She shrugged. "More or less. My mother used to do it for him. He was always very good at making translations, observations and measurements, but for some reason, organizing his thoughts and getting them onto paper never came easy."

"I've read them all, you know." He inclined his head, casting the shadow of his top hat across her skirts. "They are exceptionally well done, and I'm certain that you, as an Englishwoman, have set a few records when it comes to territorial exploration and mountain ascensions. You ought to publish them under your name, at least jointly with his."

"Thank you." His admiration and encouragements were like a physical caress.

"Perhaps sometime you could"—he shrugged elegantly—"assist me in making sense of my own expeditionary papers."

"Perhaps."

His gaze fell to her lips. "I suspect we've many interests in common."

She felt almost certain his words carried hidden meaning, and perhaps even an invitation—one that had nothing to do with writing or papers or foreign expedition. To her dismay, she found herself craving an advancement of the intimacy between them. She wanted to ask him questions about his family, about his interests in languages and artifacts. Much as she wanted a home and family and permanency, she supposed a need for adventure also thrived in her blood.

They rounded a thick outcropping of trees. To Mina's surprise, in front of them floated a *charlière* balloon crafted of alternating vertical gores of scarlet and gold silk. A narrow basket hovered beneath, about a foot off the earth.

"How *exciting*. Someone's brought a balloon," she said.

He didn't even look at the aircraft. His eyes remained unnervingly on her. "Have you ever . . . been up in one?"

"No, but I've always wanted to go."

Flight had always intrigued her. She could not imagine how thrilling it would be to look down on the earth from a bird's-eye view.

She stiffened as Lord Alexander placed his hand on the center of her back and led her toward the balloon. "Shall we have a look, then?"

So firm. So confident. So nice. As they drew closer, his

wonderful hand dropped away, and he strode ahead to speak to the person who appeared to be in charge. The gentleman, a sprightly little fellow with distinguished gray hair, an eye patch, and a mustache curled at the tips, nodded enthusiastically.

Lord Alexander turned to her, his gaze darkly inviting, and beckoned with his hand. Mina moved to stand at his side.

The silver-headed fellow announced, "My honorarium is twenty pounds."

His lordship's eyes narrowed on the man. "Of course. There *would* be a fee, wouldn't there?"

His lordship withdrew his purse and selected the necessary pound notes.

Mina's heart leapt. "You're going to go up?"

"No, *you* and I are going up."

"Oh." Her lips pressed shut. "I don't know . . . I was supposed to meet the family at the clubhouse."

"It's a quarter to," he countered. "I'm sure the musicale will continue until eleven."

She looked about, perhaps for rescue. Her cheeks flushed. Two hands descended between her and his lordship—one presenting a long sheet of paper filled with printed words, and the other, a silver ink pen.

The diminutive balloonist interjected, "Before you board, I must request that the both of you please sign on the bottom line indicating you hold yourselves responsible for all damages you may do to your own life and limbs, to any third parties on the ground below and to the balloon and/or its accessories."

"Oh, dear," she laughed softly. *Anxiously.* It appeared she was going for her first flight in a balloon. Perhaps that was just what she needed, literally, to permanently lift her spirits above the events of the previous months.

Defying caution, Mina scrawled out her name. Lord Alexander did the same. The operator unlatched the door and with a dramatic bow, assisted her inside. The floorboard, which was stacked around the edges with narrow bags of sand, wobbled ever so slightly under her feet, and she grasped onto the rail edge of the wicker car for support.

A small crowd gathered. Lord Alexander climbed in beside her. The door closed.

"I thought the operator was coming."

"We don't need the extra ballast." Mischief glinted in his eyes.

The gray-haired gentleman backed away from the balloon, gesturing upward. He shouted to the groundsmen. "Slowly, slowly . . . Easy, gents."

Mina gasped, deep in her throat. Too late. *Too late to turn back.* She didn't know if she felt more frantic about going up in the balloon alone with Lord Alexander, or the fact that they'd be up there without the operator. Pushing her purse handle to the crook of her elbow, she gripped her gloved hands around the thick ropes on either side of her.

"My stomach is doing flips." She looked up into the cavernous center of the balloon. "I can't believe I'm doing this."

His lordship, tall and stalwart, mirrored her position, curling his long arms around the ropes. He grinned. "Hold on."

Suddenly, the balloon shot like a bullet, straight up into the sky. The people, the grass and the trees all disappeared in a blur. The downward crush of air flattened the brim of her bonnet against her cheek, and a wild, ticklish exhilaration speared through her, as if her stomach would swoop out through the bottoms of her feet. His lordship's hat flew off, spiraling into the blue. He laughed, a deep, wonderful sound. She let out a little shriek—but to her amazement, realized her lips were smiling.

Just as suddenly as the balloon had risen, it bobbed to a solid halt. The basket jerked, careening wildly.

Despite her hold, she stumbled into Lord Alexander. "Oh!"

With one hand on the rail, he seized the other around her waist, firmly bracing them in place. The floor leveled and ceased its erratic movement. Her heart crashed against her ribs at the realization they now hovered, suspended over the earth in a tiny basket, but even more so for the pleasurable sensation of his arm flexed so tightly around her waist. Under his expensive clothing, his chest seemed formed of stone, more akin to the physique of an ancient warrior than an erudite London gentleman. And he smelled good. *Divine*. Like spice and skin and man.

She shouldered free and stepped backward, two very small steps, for that was all the small area of the basket would allow. Her skirts crushed against the wicker.

"Was that supposed to happen?" she gasped.

She gripped the railing with both hands. Her gaze wavered from his handsome, amused face, to the view below. The shadow of the balloon drifted over the canvas, moving in the direction of the lawn. A guide rope dangled all the way down. The crowd waved and cheered. Mina pried her hand loose long enough to wave back.

"I thought we were supposed to stay tethered, and much lower to the ground."

"There must have been some . . . miscommunication." The emphasis on the final word, as well as his smile, revealed everything.

In realization, she blurted, "You wicked man. You knew the ascent would be like that, didn't you?"

The gentle wind feathered his hair against his cheek. He grinned, a mischievous rogue who'd just pulled off a well-planned trick. "I don't deny it."

She couldn't even be angry. The moment was perfect. He was perfect. She melted inside. Why did she have to like him so much?

There was scarcely a touch of wind. The balloon lumbered in the direction of the clubhouse. All around them she saw rooftops and steeples and roads and alleys. She marveled at the sight of the Thames undulating like a dark asp against the southern border of the club grounds, water vessels dotting its surface.

"How did you know I'd agree to come?" she asked.

"Because you're like me," he answered. "You're adventurous."

Music drifted up from the clubhouse.

Palms skimming over the rail, he stepped toward her. The car tilted, and Mina gasped, her shoulders slanting against the ropes. With the heel of his boot, his lordship deftly shoved a sandbag to the opposite end. The basket leveled.

"Here's an adventure for you." He offered his hand. "Have you ever danced in the clouds?"

Her pulse leapt in her throat. Mina stared at his hand. Elegant and steady, it was upturned, with long, square-tipped fingers. Something sparked deep in her chest: It was the adventuresome spirit he referred to, reawakening.

How could he know about the young woman she had been before life had left her scared? *Scared*. She hated the word, indeed, the whole idea. It was too close to "timid," and she'd never been that.

Her heart beating faster, she took his hand.

With a gentle tug he brought her closer, to the center of the basket. The music lilted, as light and airy as the sky around them. His arm came around her. His hand spread against the center of her back, drawing her closer—closer than proper—toward his chest, so close that only an inch of space separated them. Her body awakened—her mouth, her nipples, her thighs, aching to close the gap. Mina licked her lower lip.

Together they moved, ever so slightly, shifting weight and turning with the music.

A sudden gust of wind shifted the balloon. The basket

tilted just enough to sway her against his chest. The hand on her back spread, increasing in pressure to hold her there. In a split second, she made the decision to allow the familiarity. They stood, no longer dancing, but embracing and listening to the music.

"Miss Limpett . . ."

He bent. She closed her eyes, sensing his intent.

A gentle pressure lifted her chin.

"Lord Alexander . . . ," she warned softly.

"Mark. My name is Mark."

He pressed his mouth to hers.

With that kiss, Mark lost his senses. Or rather, he found them. The realization occurred, like the weight of a stone wall collapsing over him, that he wanted her more than he'd wanted anything in a very long while, for reasons that had nothing to do with strategy, or saving his own skin.

Innocent, perfect lips pressed up against his. Heat slowly diffused his groin.

"Mark . . ." She turned her face so that her cheek pressed against the hollow of his jaw.

"Yes?"

She pulled abruptly away.

"You shouldn't have done that." Her brown eyes, which had been bright and excited, instantly clouded.

He felt certain his did as well. "Why not?"

"I'm not *that* sort of adventurous."

She planted her hand at the center of his chest and exerted pressure until he had returned to his side of the car. What could he say? If he tried to persuade her otherwise, he'd come off sounding like an ass. From this distance, kept at arm's length, he could only admire—and curse himself for having apparently misjudged the level of attraction between them.

"I offended you." The impulse to kiss her had felt completely natural. "I meant no disrespect."

She frowned, then glanced over the grounds, and back to him again. "It's not that I didn't enjoy the kiss—it's that I'm afraid I shall like you too much. I hope you understand what I mean by that."

No illicit affair. Hands off. That's what she meant by that. Not waiting for a response from him, she turned back to the rail and fixed her gaze on the scenery below. "I'm assuming you know how to land this thing."

"I do."

"Then I think you'd better take us down before we leave the grounds. I don't know if you've ever tried to swim in petticoats, but it's not easy."

Mark knew she was right, but damn it, he'd hoped for a different outcome from their time together. He'd never made love in a gas balloon, and he'd be lying to say the idea hadn't crossed his mind. Short of that, he'd at least hoped to have formed a more solid connection between them.

His tug on the valve rope released a measured amount of gas. The balloon descended over the club where it appeared the musicale had just let out. Fingers pointed. Voices called out. Everyone's faces turned upward. He recognized Lucinda and Trafford on the steps, as well as the girls. Four jaws dropped in unison.

"Hello," Miss Limpett called, waving.

Mark pulled the valve rope again.

The ground rushed up a bit more quickly than he'd intended, a likely result of his distraction over Miss Limpett's unanticipated rebuff.

"We're dropping awfully fast," she squeaked. Her cheeks were pink, and she, radiant. She didn't appear frightened, only excited. "Are we going to crash?"

He chuckled and dropped a bag of sand over, and then another for good measure. The descent slowed a bit, and they skimmed horizontally across the grass, delving along an avenue of trees. Slower. Slower. The balloon tilted behind them, a rippling silken wake.

The lead corner of the basket caught against the turf and tipped.

The car bumped, pitching them in a tumble onto the grass.

Mark rolled, settling on his back, with Miss Limpett sprawled atop him.

Moving quickly, he twisted, pulling her beneath him. He stared down into her eyes.

"I already like you too much," he murmured.

Framing her face with his hands, he kissed her hard, with lips, tongue and teeth, so thoroughly, so pleasurably, that his *own* toes curled in his boots. Hearing the approach of footsteps on the grass, he quickly rolled off.

Miss Limpett sat up, her cheeks bright and pink, her hair loose and her bonnet askew.

Glancing in his direction, she whispered, "I withdraw my earlier decision, Lord Alexander. You may call upon me at will."

A smile spread across Mark's lips.

Chapter Six

Mark sat with Mina and Lucinda atop a red and white–striped blanket in the shade of a large tree, enjoying the last of a cold luncheon. A male servant had attended to them, serving from three large baskets. There were crusty rolls of bread, hard-boiled eggs, roast beef and chicken, cheese, fruit and even champagne.

Not to mention a score of secret, fleeting glances between him and Mina. Each one sent a stab of anticipation through him, for what would come. Scrolls. Mina. Mina. Scrolls. The morning had turned out better than he'd anticipated.

In the past he'd drawn criticism from fellow Amaranthines for his dalliances with mortals. Yet there was something about mortal women in the prime of their life that never failed to excite. They were like an exotic flower that bloomed only once. Miss Limpett was such a flower. Each time he saw her, it was as if a layer of invisibility were lifted away from her, revealing the incomparable jewel beneath.

Trafford had gone off to see if he could find the shooting master. Mark had avoided direct eye contact with Evangeline and Astrid long enough that they'd finally given up and agreed to a game of badminton with two well-dressed young men. A brightly feathered shuttlecock flew back and forth between the couples in a gentle rally.

Lucinda pressed a hand over Mina's. "Miss Limpett, are you certain you're recovered from your spill? You look a bit feverish."

The countess's gaze veered reproachfully to Mark.

"I'm just a bit warm." Mina lifted her white stoneware cup and sipped her lemonade. "Other than that, I'm very well. Not so much as a bruise. Lord Alexander is an excellent aeronaut. I'd recommend his piloting skills to anyone."

Astrid approached, twirling her racquet. "Miss Limpett, we've just lost Lord Kilmartin to an afternoon appointment and have a need for a fourth. Might you like to play?"

Mina's features warmed with obvious surprise. "Yes, of course."

Her gaze touched on Mark as she stood and joined her cousin on the grass. Together they walked the short distance to the net, which was strung between two bamboo poles. She bent at the knees to select a racquet from the grass. The servant collected the remainder of the dishes. Nesting them in the last open basket, he hoisted two and set off to return them to the carriage.

"Your lordship," said the countess.

"Lady Trafford."

"Mark."

"Lucinda."

The countess twirled her parasol in terse, jerky whorls. "We've grown exceedingly fond of our niece."

He'd known this discussion would come. He sighed. "I can see why. She's a remarkable young woman."

Her brows drew in, and her lips quirked down as if even with that mildest of compliments about another woman, he'd wounded her.

"I don't like this game."

"What game, Lucinda?" he asked quietly. "The only game I'm aware of is just over there on the grass."

Even now, in the midst of this ridiculous conversation, he couldn't seem to take his eyes from Mina. Not the lovely curve of her cheek, or her pretty neck. Not from the slender taper of her waist, or the alluring sway of her bustle. Their kiss had only enflamed his interest. His mind buzzed with it. Yes, he wanted her father for his scrolls. But he could not deny that he also wanted Mina Limpett. He'd have her too. For as long as he liked.

"It's very clear what you're trying to do," said Lucinda.

"What's that?"

"Make me jealous of my niece." Her parasol twirled faster. "The idea is ludicrous."

"Especially ludicrous when I'm not at all attempting to make you jealous."

"Then what was that? The balloon ride? Flying just over our heads, and then drifting off where we couldn't see you? An obvious taunt."

"I've no control over the forces of nature." A true statement, much to his consternation, though he had to admit to a manipulation of the basket.

She hissed, "You're a profligate."

He calmly answered, "I don't see anything wrong with trying to lift Miss Limpett's spirit. She's spent three very somber months surrounded with all the details of her father's death. I was acquainted with her father through his academic pursuits. What is the harm in my offering her a completely proper half hour of diversion?"

"Her hair was *disheveled* when we came upon you there on the lawn. She was smiling that secret little smile women do. Are you sure flying was the only diversion going on in that balloon?"

Her words unexpectedly angered him. They echoed upon those spoken by Leeson that morning. Lord Alexan-

der, the conscienceless *seducer*? Had he become such a caricature of a man? In that moment, he realized he had. Her
accusation, at its core, was true. It had been his intention to
seduce Miss Limpett, to whatever degree possible, in the
balloon. Even now, he plotted about how he could have
her. Keep her. For however long it pleased him to do so.

"I assure you my intentions toward Miss Limpett are
honorable and sincere."

He vowed that to be true, at least to the full extent of
his ability. He also vowed that however grievously he
manipulated Mina toward the end purpose of saving his
own mind and soul, he'd make it up to her tenfold, even if
it meant building a palace for her finer than the Queen's.
Thousands of women would give anything for such an
honor.

"But your intentions weren't sincere or honorable toward me, were they Mark?" she accused.

"I never misled you."

"No." She cast off the umbrella and sagged against the
trunk of the tree. "Clearly, I misled myself."

"It was a flirtation, Lucinda."

She stiffened. "Not just that."

"You and I *kissed*."

She looked away, shaking her head and smiling bit-
terly. "Thank God I saved myself for Trafford. He's the
grand passion of my life."

He saw the lie in her eyes, and for a moment, he pit-
ied her. She'd done as every young lady of her class
and social standing was trained to do. She'd charmed
a wealthy, titled gentleman and had her grand society
wedding. Now she found herself wed to a man she
didn't know all that well—an older man for whom she
held no particular attraction. But their marriage was
none of his concern.

"That's wonderful. I wish only the best for you,
Lucinda."

"You'll grow bored with her quickly," she muttered spitefully. "She's a little brown mouse, Mark, the complete opposite of the sort of woman you need."

There was something cruel in the set of her lips, and the brightness of her eyes, something he'd never perceived before. Jealousy could do terrible things to a person, or so he'd witnessed. He couldn't recall any firsthand experience with the emotion.

Trafford crossed the lawn from the direction of the shooting trap, which was located down the adjacent corridor of trees. He planted his walking stick with every other step. An uncomfortable silence hovered in the air while they waited for him to arrive.

"Lucinda." Trafford slowed at the edge of the blanket. Sunshine transformed the prism of his walking stick into a miniature rainbow of color. "The shooting master has agreed to let you shoot. Of course, I've agreed to pay for the plantings of the north gardens in the spring, but it appears you've got your wish. Just for today, though."

"Do you see, Lord Alexander, it's just as I was saying." Bright spots of color crested her cheeks. "My husband spoils me completely."

Trafford smiled, clearly pleased by her praise. He offered his hand and assisted her up from the blanket.

The earl inquired, "Lord Alexander, would you like to come along and watch? They're going to score Lucinda on a pigeon shoot."

"Thank you, Trafford, but I'll stay here," Mark responded politely. He'd always considered pigeon shooting a cowardly sport.

Lord and Lady Trafford disappeared between the same banks of trees from whence the earl had just come. He remained on the blanket, watching the match—watching Mina. Yet, feeling the distinct intensity of someone's attention upon *him*, he scanned the grounds. Across the expanse of lawn, a woman walked slowly behind the columns of the clubhouse, staring out from beneath the brim of a flamboyant scarlet hat. It was Selene, dressed in all her customary elegance.

The sound of gunfire echoed over the trees—a series of three shots, right in a row. Lucinda was shooting at fleeing pigeons released from a trap. The reverberations faded.

Mark felt rather like one of those pigeons, except fixed within his sister's sights. If Selene wished to be his assassin, so be it. But there was no reason for her to lurk about in the shadows, stalking him—and letting him see her stalk him.

He rose from the blanket. He'd just go talk to her. Certainly she hadn't come here to do battle with him on the cricket field.

Starting across the grass, he glanced once more to Mina. She waited for the next volley. The dim-sighted Evangeline swatted at a shuttlecock that had long since soared past.

His senses shouted a warning.

Something hurtled toward Mina through the trees at a dangerous speed. In the next second, the unmistakable crack of a shotgun tore all around. Forgetting Selene, he raced toward Mina, fear crashing in his chest.

She jerked, but remained standing, her racquet dangling from her hand. She didn't move. Instead, she stood as if paralyzed. A report echoed through the trees.

"Are you hit?" Mark seized her by the shoulders and lowered her to the grass. He touched the destroyed silk of her skirt and glanced at her face, which was completely blank of expression. If she was shot, she didn't realize it.

Lord and Lady Trafford rushed toward them. Lucinda, ashen faced, carried a double-barreled shotgun pointed toward the earth.

Mark lifted Mina's skirt, and the petticoats, just a few inches. Blood stained the stocking beneath.

She whispered dazedly, "I am rather tired of having interesting days."

Five minutes later, he carried her toward the drive where the Trafford carriage waited. "What do you mean, someone attacked Miss Limpett on the street this morning?"

He had to struggle to keep the full strength of his fury from his voice.

"I wasn't hurt," Mina insisted, her arms wrapped around his neck. "And I'm not hurt now. It's just a scratch from a tiny pellet of birdshot."

If she wasn't hurt, why was she so pale? Why did she tremble in his arms?

When they neared the open door, she wriggled down out of his grasp, her cheeks flushed. "Thank you, Lord Alexander."

He wasn't sure what the message in her eyes conveyed, but under the scrutiny of her family, she quickly climbed inside the vehicle. He hated to let her go.

Lucinda, her face lowered and hidden beneath the brim of her hat, climbed in afterward, followed by Evangeline and Astrid.

"Oh, darling girl. I'm so sorry!" the countess exclaimed, gathering Mina into her arms.

"It's not your fault," Mina assured her quietly.

On the badminton field Lucinda had tearfully proclaimed herself and Mina to be the victims of a misfire. She'd demanded to anyone who would listen that the rifle be examined for defect.

"Astrid, lift your cousin's legs onto the cushion."

Mina protested, "That's not necessary."

Trafford tipped his hat to Mark, shaking his head. He muttered gruffly, "Damn far too much excitement for one day."

He also climbed in.

Lucinda, her eyes flashing, announced in a hushed voice, "I'm sorry, Lord Alexander. There just isn't room for you."

The footman shut the door and went around back to climb on. The driver tapped his cane whip against the back of the horses, and the carriage rolled away.

Mark exhaled. Slowly, he walked back to the club. Selene was nowhere to be seen. He departed the private grounds, going south to the Embankment. Looking out over the water, he wondered what the hell had just happened. He couldn't believe Lucinda would shoot Mina on purpose, but something didn't sit right. He'd felt entirely unsettled, sending her off in that carriage.

He came alongside the Physic Garden, and slowed. A thick crowd gathered on the walkway at Cheyne Walk and beyond, past Albert Bridge. Pedestrians clustered the rails of the bridge. A powerful wave of emotion—morbid curiosity and horror—reverberated from the area. In retrospect he supposed he'd felt the sensation even upon leaving the grounds at Ranelagh, but tangled the negativity up with his alarm over Mina.

Police officers in blue uniforms and bobby hats dotted the Embankment, and newspapermen crouched behind tripod cameras. A Thames River Police galley coursed along the river's edge in close proximity to the bank. More officers waded in the water, wearing rubber hip trousers. They poked with poles and fished out pieces of rubbish with nets. Looking across the river, Mark magnified his vision and perceived the same degree of activity on the Battersea side.

Leeson emerged from the crowd and rushed toward him. "Your lordship!"

"What's going on here?" Mark asked.

"Horrible stuff." The immortal lowered his voice. "From what I have gleaned, a young man went down to the river midmorning—over on the Battersea side—and discovered something there under the bridge."

Mark closed his eyes. "Tell me."

Leeson nodded. "I've not seen the evidence myself,

but I've been listening very carefully, and heard several of the officers here refer to a *thigh*."

Mark blinked in disbelief. He looked into the sky to be sure the sun was not crashing into the earth, for that was the kind of day this had been. "As in part of a person's leg?"

Leeson nodded. "*A woman's* thigh. Dismembered."

The *Thais* floated just a short distance away. *Flower petals and blood*.

The same thing had to be on Leeson's mind.

"That's not all. They apparently found an arm around the same time this morning up by Horslydown."

"Horslydown. That's far down river."

Leeson's mustache glinted silver. "Both, they say, were carefully tied into cut sections of clothing."

Mark pondered the details. "Are the body parts from the same person?"

"That I don't know, sir, but of course, a huge search is ongoing along both sides of the river."

Mark looked out over the water. He nodded. "This might be the work of Selene's Thames torso killer."

Mina lay back on her pillows, feeling like a child who had been ordered into her nightgown for an early bedtime. It was not even seven o'clock, and daylight still lit the sky outside her windows.

"There," announced Lucinda. She sat at the foot of the bed, tucking the end of the bandage at Mina's ankle. "How does that feel? Too tight? Too loose?"

"The bandage is perfect, thank you," Mina answered calmly, despite her thready nerves. "But as I've continued to say all afternoon, the scratch is so minor, it couldn't possibly qualify as a wound."

"I know, I know." Lucinda positioned Mina's foot on a tasseled cushion. "Fussing over you makes me feel better. I feel as if I am completely at fault for what must have been a terrible day for you. I should have insisted you stay in the stationer's shop until I could accompany you down the street—and then this horrible thing with the gun misfire."

Mina smiled in sympathy. "Please don't trouble yourself any more on my account."

Lucinda arranged a lap blanket across her legs. "Mina, dear, despite all this . . . I hope you realize you can always trust me and speak to me in confidence about anything."

"Thank you for that offer, Lucinda."

Pressing her lips together, Lucinda appeared to ponder the words she would say next. Her expression was one of concern. "I must say . . . I was rather shocked to see you up in that gas balloon with Lord Alexander this afternoon. I know you must be accustomed to making your own decisions, and living more . . . well, *freely*, but . . . this is London."

Mina paused before answering. "Our ride was very brief. I admit though, when I agreed, I thought we would remain tethered in one spot. I apologize if I made a spectacle of myself."

Her aunt tilted her head. "Young ladies in mourning are held to an even higher standard than those who are not. You wouldn't want it to appear that you were . . . unmoved by your father's recent death."

Mina said nothing, but her cheeks burned at receiving such a lecture on propriety. Perhaps she *had* chosen poorly in going up in the balloon with Mark. Still, deep in her heart she could not regret the time she'd spent with him. Aside from the kiss, he'd reawakened a part of her she'd missed—and admired.

"If I could give you any advice, dear Mina, any advice at all, it would be to steer clear of gentlemen of Lord Alexander's ilk."

Mina swallowed, trying not to appear shocked. The discussion on mourning etiquette was one thing, but she hadn't expected any advice of this sort to come out of her ladyship's mouth. Whatever had happened between her aunt and Lord Alexander had clearly tainted her opinion of him. Or could it be that Lucinda spoke out of jealousy?

Lucinda gathered Mina's hands and held them between both of hers. "He's all flash and finery but very little substance. He's dashing, yes, but his motives where the feminine sex is concerned are rarely aboveboard."

Mina thought it best to respond conservatively. Now was probably not the right time to inform her aunt that she'd given his lordship permission to call upon her.

She said, "Lord Alexander is apparently quite interested in some of the more archaic languages my father specialized in, as well as the artifacts he collected. Perhaps his interest is nothing more than that."

The answer appeared to please Lucinda. The tightness around the edges of her mouth eased, and with a fleeting glance over Mina's face and hair, she concluded, "I'm sure you're right."

Mina wasn't sure how she should respond to that.

Lucinda touched her cheek. "You're very sweet. I'm sure you'll meet all sorts of wonderful gentlemen when the time is *appropriate*. No one can make sensible decisions when their mind is clouded with grief." She smiled suddenly. "Once Thursday's garden party is past, I should like to take you to my modiste. Perhaps you'd like to make a few selections to see you through your mourning into next year?"

A knock sounded, and Lucinda left Mina to open the door. Upon her return, she held a tray. "I thought you might be hungry. I've had supper brought up for you."

"That's very kind."

Lucinda lowered the tray to her lap. "How delicious it all smells. But we've the Nevils' dinner to attend at nine, and then Lady Winbourne's ball at eleven, so I couldn't possibly indulge. In fact, I'd better dress and see that the girls are doing the same."

Part of Mina wished she was putting on a colorful gown and going to a party as well. But of course she was in mourning for another nine months. Not only that, but her leg had been half blown off, at least by everyone's account but hers. Wistfully, she wondered if Mark would be at the Nevils' or Lady Winbourne's. When would she see him again?

"Have a wonderful night," Mina said, looking down at her plate.

There were boiled parsnips and . . . something she didn't recognize. A savory-scented mishmash of stuffing and shredded meat and vegetables. Several narrow stick-like *things* poked out of the culinary morass. She poked at one. A bone? She bit her lower lip.

"This does smell very . . . good." She swallowed hard and looked up. "Could you tell me what this is? Not the parsnips, the other."

Lucinda paused, her hand on the handle.

"One of my favorites. It's pigeon pie, of course."

With a smile, she drew the door closed behind her.

Mina unfolded her napkin and draped the cloth over the entire plate. Lifting the tray from her lap, she scooted to the edge of the mattress and abandoned the untouched tray to the hallway. Back inside, she considered a few of the books she'd brought up from the library, but her mind was too scattered to focus on any of them.

Her gaze fell on the satchel of her father's papers. She couldn't put them off forever. Now was as good a time as any to begin sorting them. The bandage loosened, and she paused to unwind it from her calf. She deposited the narrow length of cloth into her wastebasket and took up the satchel. She chose to sit on her bed rather than the desk. Climbing onto the cool sheets, she tugged the slender chain from her neck. Turning the little key in its lock, she lifted the flap. Her father's scent wafted out—one of paper, ink and tobacco.

She put the notebooks in one stack, and the little scraps of paper in another. There were diagrams and lists, as well as notes and hand-drawn maps.

A drop fell to warp a stroke of ink. Mina blotted it carefully with the edge of her gown, preserving the word in its entirety. She swiped at her eyes. No tears. No more tears. She'd given up crying over that man a long time ago.

Lifting the next page, she paused. Something lay between the two pieces of paper—something she didn't recognize. She lifted the rose by its stem. Flat and dry, it appeared as if it had been pressed between two heavy books for some time, like a memento. Though the color had faded, it was easy to see the petals were striped . . . red and white.

An alarm went off in her head, as loud and resounding as a temple gong. Three months ago she'd been the one to collect every bit of paper that went into the leather case—albeit frantically—from her father's tent on the side of a Tibetan mountain. She felt very certain there'd been no stray red and white–striped roses there.

She rolled over the pillows and opened her bedside drawer. She rummaged about until she found the little folded paper that had come in her tin of orange blossom soap, the one about the language of flowers.

She drew her finger down the paper to the place where roses were listed.

Red and white . . .

A love that could not be shared.

Chapter Seven

A full two days later, Mark maneuvered through the hallways of the Trafford house. All the notables of London society crowded the drawing rooms and galleries. There were beautiful women in Doucet and Worth gowns. Candlelight and the fractured sparkle of crystal lusters illuminated their faces. Gentlemen preened like peacocks in evening dress. Several older fellows boasted the vivid sashes and glinting medals of the various orders of the Empire. The cheerful notes of a blue Hungarian band carried over the voices of the animated throng.

Thick sprays of flowers spilled from massive, decorative urns and hung above the arched doorways. The event had already been under way for several hours, starting off as a late-afternoon garden party. The invitation had specified there would also be a formal dinner, and later, dancing on the terrace, continuing into the night. He perused the ballroom, but found no dancers—and no Mina. Instead, servants collected silverware and porcelain from long rows of tables, the remnants of a formal meal.

He had not called on Mina the day before, though he had dispatched Leeson to observe the Trafford house.

After the report of the "random" attack on her, and the shooting, he couldn't shake the feeling she was in danger. Yet he, by necessity, kept to the river, observing the continued search for body parts. Though he was no longer a Shadow Guard, old habits died hard. This morning, a woman's trunk had been discovered off Copington Wharf, bundled into a cut section of clothing and tied with string . . . again, just a stone's throw from the *Thais*. Although he had crossed paths with Selene a number of times, he could not shake the suspicion that the killer taunted *him*. Goaded him. Sought to draw him out for battle. Such intention would indicate the existence of a powerful *brotoi* in London, one whom he, as a cast-out Guard, had no authority to Reclaim.

Despite all that, it could not be assumed that the mutilated remains were the work of the torso killer who had made similar gruesome deposits about the city in the midst of the Ripper crimes six months before. A number of hospitals lay in proximity to the banks of the Thames. It was completely possible the body parts were illegally dumped medical refuse. It would not be the first time such discoveries had been made. Death and incidents of the macabre were an unfortunate but anticipated reality of the river. In one recent year alone, more than five hundred corpses had been discovered in the Thames.

At last he happened across Mina's trace and followed it until he found her in the yellow drawing room. In her simple black gown, she knelt in front of Evangeline. With needle and thread she mended some imperfection in the debutante's skirt. Astrid stood at the far wall, staring into a gilt-framed mirror and pinching her cheeks. Seeing his reflection, she spun around, a whirl of ivory organza.

"Lord Alexander," she exclaimed.

Evangeline yanked her yellow skirts free of Mina's hands. Mina looked up and her gaze locked on his. The muscles along Mark's abdomen tightened, evidence of his attraction, mingled with sensual intent. Much depended on this evening, and whether he would be able to successfully gain her trust. He'd reviewed his translation notes from the first scroll. The current waves of Tantalyte power—the ones likely triggering his spells—no longer coincided with the prophesies. It was as if Tantalus knew, with the Reclamation of his Messenger Jack the Ripper, that the game had changed. Mark had no way of knowing when the next wave would travel across London.

"We've been waiting hours for you to arrive." Astrid rushed toward him. She whispered, out of hearing of the other two, "You'll dance with me, won't you?"

"Of course," he agreed. Though it was a rather bold invitation on her part, he would be uncouth to decline. "Miss Limpett, how does this evening find you? Are you recovered from your injury?"

Mina nodded, as polite and aloof as before their kiss.

"Completely, your lordship." She only fleetingly met his gaze. "I thank you for your concern."

Astrid sighed impatiently.

Not wishing to lose sight of Mina in the crowded house, Mark extended an invitation. "Miss Limpett . . . Lady Evangeline, shall you accompany us into the garden?"

"Of course, your lordship." Evangeline, giddy, grasped her skirts and hurried toward him, obscuring his view of Mina. When he saw her again, she had turned her back to gather up her scissors and thread.

The message stung. Though he wished to grasp her arm, drag her off into some darkened corner of the house and remind her of the attraction between them, left with no other choice, he proceeded to the rear of the house. With one debutante on each arm, he played the part well—the flashing-eyed rogue—fully aware of the female admiration and male envy he collected upon the way. Only the knowledge rang hollow. Vanity no longer satisfied. Worst of all, the woman he'd come to see tonight, the one he'd imagined in his bed during the darkest hours of the night, had barely offered him a glance.

He and his two pretty albatrosses passed through a crowded gallery. All the windows hung open to the night. Outside, Oriental lamps dotted the trees. A servant presently worked to clean up the shards and splatter of a broken champagne glass.

The next hour passed in a miserable blur of dances and inane conversation, Mark purposefully forbidding himself to go off in search of Mina.

"Aren't you going to ask your hostess to dance?" Mark glanced down to find Lucinda beside him. She wore a rose-colored gown, cut to display her bust and narrow waist to their finest. A thick cluster of diamonds glittered at her throat. Hers was an undeniable beauty, but one that did not elicit the faintest reaction within him. Had he truly found her a temptation before?

Her icy façade melted before his eyes. "I'm so sorry about what happened at Hurlingham. I behaved like a fool." She grasped her closed fan in both hands.

He studied her carefully and saw a glimpse of the happy, vivacious girl he remembered.

She continued on, tears glazing her eyes. "It's just that marriage is nothing like I'd expected. Don't misunderstand me; Trafford is wonderful and indulges me my every desire." Her gloved hand touched the necklace at her throat. "Even so, I suppose I must confess to being very envious of the girls for the choices they still have ahead of them."

He offered her his arm, if for no other reason than to remain in her good graces—and continue his welcome in her household. "No apology is necessary."

Stepping into the waltz, he guided her into the midst of the other couples. Chairs circled the perimeter of the terrace and scattered the lawn. His gaze continually wandered, yet Mina did not appear. Yes, she was in mourning, but given the passage of time since her father's death—albeit an *untrue* death—it would not be out of place for her to sit under the stars to enjoy the music with a glass of tea or lemonade. When the waltz ended, he extracted himself from Lucinda, smoothly depositing her amongst a cluster of friends and rivals.

Over the past half hour, a dull, nagging headache had come upon him, but so far, no odd light or dancing skeletons. The dangling paper lamps offended his eyes, along with all the frenzied talk and movement of the guests. Their chatter, and their thoughts, clouded his mind. He followed a garden path that wended into the deeper shadows against the house.

He dropped to a bench and rubbed the bridge of his nose.

For the first time in nineteen centuries, he wondered secretly, in the private depths of his mind, how death might feel.

Mina sat in a chair, her elbows resting against the darkened windowsill. From her window she'd watched the party and admired the ladies and gentlemen in all their finery, dancing, romancing and politicking. She'd learned all the dances in boarding school, but she'd only ever tried them out with fellow students, in the presence of a dance master. Certainly it would be different to dance in the arms of a gentleman, especially one for whom you had feelings.

Mark had moved from one dazzling partner to the next. Tall, golden-haired and striking, he clearly held the attention of the ladies. A smile had broken across her lips when he'd taken an elderly matron for a slower turn about the floor. The silver-haired vixen continually lowered her fan, and her hand, to his bottom. Each time he removed her hand, it drifted down again. The battle went on until the song ended, and he chivalrously returned the smiling lady to her chair. His expression had revealed nothing but the faintest trace of amusement.

Then Lucinda had appeared. After a brief yet intense conversation, they'd danced. Could any couple be more perfectly matched? Golden and elegant, they had cut a graceful path across the floor. She could not help but notice the way Lucinda clutched at his arm, even more so at the end of the dance, as if she were loath to let him go.

Even if there had been no affair between them before Lucinda's marriage—and even if none continued now—Mina suddenly felt very sorry for Trafford.

At present, Mark sat in the dark, just below her window—as he had for the past five or so minutes. She warred with herself over whether to let him know of her presence. Here, out of the light of the lanterns, he seemed quiet, even pensive. He rubbed his nose, as if weary. Finally, she could resist no longer.

"Are you enjoying your evening?"

He looked up. "There you are. What are you doing up there?"

There you are. Spoken as if he'd been looking for her. Every inch of her skin warmed with cautious delight.

"Watching. I've a delightful perspective of all the evening's happenings."

"Tell me something interesting."

"Well, if you must know," she answered lightly, "the American faction is behaving rather badly."

"How so?"

"The Misses Bonynge have just arrived with their father, and as a result, their archenemy, Mrs. Mackay, has stormed out, taking her entourage with her. According to Astrid, they've a longstanding feud over some perceived slight or another."

"Now that *is* interesting."

Mina laughed. He didn't.

"Are you all right?" she asked. "You don't seem yourself."

"It's my neck. I'm breaking it to look up there at you. Why don't you come down here and sit with me."

His request sent a dangerous curl of excitement through Mina's stomach. She knew she shouldn't.... If Lucinda saw, there'd be another lecture on propriety, likely spurred by the countess's feelings for his lordship, but Mina did not wish to rub salt into any wounds.

Still, she'd been so isolated these past two days. Yes, she'd been constantly surrounded by people, assisting with the preparations for the party, but she'd largely been left alone to her nerve-wracking fears, and images of striped roses—between constant thoughts of Mark, of course.

"I'll be right down."

She pulled the windows closed, and fastened them securely—always securely. Taking the servants' stairs down, she passed through the bustling kitchen. From an unattended serving tray she claimed a glass of tea sprigged with mint, and exited the service door. Avoiding the lights of the party, she slipped along the garden path and found Mark sitting just where he had been moments before.

Mina appeared like a shadowy nymph from the trees, her face luminous above the dark collar of her gown. He immediately sensed the wall she put into place between them, one built of caution. He didn't throw her any smoldering looks or speak any clever words. He simply made space for her on the bench.

"I have something for you." He reached into his inside breast pocket and handed her the card.

"Another picture?" Her brows furrowed with confusion. "What's this?"

"It's you," he answered softly.

She examined the photo. "I remember this. I was outside the stationer's shop with Lucinda. I just assumed the man on the sidewalk took her picture. Where did you get this?"

Leeson had returned to the *Thais* from the Chelsea shops that afternoon with supplies and the photo. He collected such novelties for his collection of mortal paraphernalia.

"It's posted in half the shop windows in London, beside those of Jennie Churchill and Lilly Langtry."

She paled. "You can't be serious."

"I am. Each day your photo is being snatched up by ladies all over town. By next week, they'll all be wearing your bonnet."

She laughed. "But it's such an ugly bonnet."

"The bonnet has nothing to do with it."

She glanced away, as if both pleased and discomfited by the idea. "Have you got a headache? You keep rubbing your head as if you do."

No, not exactly a headache . . . but it wouldn't do to tell Miss Limpett that malevolent forces of evil presently worked to claim his mind and his soul for wicked and destructive purposes, and that even now one voice in particular filled his head with such a screeching cacophony of demands, he could barely form a sentence.

"Yes." He nodded. "A headache."

"Here."

She pressed the glass she'd been holding into his hand. It was cool and refreshingly damp against his palm.

"It's a bit of minted tea—I picked it up on the way down, and haven't so much as taken a sip. Perhaps you'll find it soothing. They say peppermint sometimes eases such pains."

He pressed the cool glass against his temple. If only a sprig of peppermint would solve his problems.

She looked up at the sky. "Perhaps your headache is

the result of all this peculiar weather we're experiencing. Can you believe how it can be hot one moment, and gusting cold the next? And there's been no rain. I don't recall anything like this ever before, not in England. The grass has started to turn crisp and brown."

"Very unpleasant," he answered, not really caring what she said, as long as she kept talking. Her voice soothed his head and seemed to mute the incessant demands.

She mused, "One has to wonder if the terrible weather in America is somehow connected. It's so tragic, what happened with the flood, and the dam breaking. I spent the morning reading through all the accounts. So many lives lost." She shook her head. "Aunt Lucinda insisted Trafford wire over a generous donation for the reconstruction efforts."

The events were connected. Would she believe him if he explained about exploding volcanoes and residual ripples of doom that, if uninterrupted, would eventually bring about the destruction of mankind?

He almost laughed at the preposterousness of it all. He wished his intuition were wrong, that the eruption of Krakatoa and the revelations of the previous months had never happened, and that all of it had no effect upon him. He'd never wished to be mortal, but the obliviousness of the race to the true happenings of the world had its attractions.

She tilted her head in sympathy. "If you felt so badly, why did you venture out tonight at all?"

"I wanted to see you."

"Oh. . . ." She blinked rapidly and looked into the shrubbery. Suddenly she stood. Damn, he'd frightened her off. But no . . . she walked around the bench to stand behind him.

"A Bhutanian temple monk once showed my father a remedy when he suffered an altitude headache. Would you like to try it?"

"I'll . . . try anything." He'd let her cut off a finger as long as she touched him to do it. Her fingertips lowered against the crown of his head . . . hesitantly at first, and then slid through his hair. They circled, scratching lightly with the nails. Her touch left a path of pleasure against his scalp, one that shot a heated bolt of pleasure directly into his groin.

He closed his eyes, gritting his teeth against a hiss.

She said quietly, "You've very nice hair."

Suddenly she grasped hold of his hair and pulled. *Hard.*

His mouth fell open. *"Ow."*

Not what he expected. But to his surprise, each solid, extended tug eased the pain.

"Better?" she asked.

"Yes."

Mark's hand circled her wrist. Mina stilled. Slowly, he pulled her hand over the high cut of his cheekbone, and lower . . . to press his lips against the center of her palm.

Her knees weakened. Everything inside her melted. She braced her other hand on his shoulder. That one he also claimed, drawing her down to sit beside him, her knees and legs opposite his on the bench. Her breasts just touched his chest. He drew the backs of his fingertips along her cheek, softly at first. All the old warnings echoed inside her head, but this time . . . this time, she closed a solid door against them. She ached at the touch and prayed he did not stop. He bracketed her chin and gently kissed her.

A peculiar sound came from the darkness . . . a breathy gasp.

Mark's lips stilled against hers.

Another sound . . . this time a masculine groan. A curse.

Mina felt his lips curve into a smile. He pulled away, his eyes gleaming in dark amusement. Mina's cheeks went hot. She would like to have claimed ignorance, but she'd spent many a night in shabby foreign inns and tent encampments. She knew the sounds of a man and woman being intimate. The sounds came from the thick cluster of trees between them and the terrace. She and Mark were effectively trapped.

She bit into her lower lip, mortified. Mark chuckled.

"Ah . . . we'd better just stay here until they are . . ."

"Finished."

"Yes."

They sat beside one another, rigid. Mark's hands pressed lightly against Mina's shoulders. The sounds became more fervent and frequent.

"Oh, my," Mina whispered, lifting a hand to her mouth to smother her nervous laughter, yet her nipples hardened against her chemise as she imagined Lord Alexander touching her in intimate ways. She clenched her thighs against a sudden profusion of damp heat.

Mark tipped his head closer, murmuring against her cheek. "I don't believe she's pulling his hair. Or . . . perhaps she is."

The warmth of his breath on her skin only intensified her discomfort. She turned her face aside for fear she would kiss him.

"Who do you think they are?"

Firm fingers caught her chin. Dark blue eyes stared at her mouth. "Who cares?"

He bent his head to hers. His mouth, his breath, teased her lips until she . . . *she* . . . in a mindless delirium of pleasure, swayed, and pressed her lips to his.

He groaned softly, deep in his throat. He tipped her head back onto the hard pillow of his arm. His tongue in her mouth, his hand slid down her neck. Warm fingertips brushed against the base of her bare throat, twisting one button. Two. He explored a bit lower. When his hand slipped between her bodice and corset, she arched against him.

The sky cracked loudly. A narrow streak split the darkness.

Another crash followed, and a brilliant shattering of light.

Alarmed voices arose from the direction of the terrace. Dazed, Mina opened her eyes to the sky. "Is that . . . lightning?"

Boom. Flash. Crack. The earth shook. The windows above them rattled.

Mark stood, pulling her up. He deftly buttoned her bodice. "We're not safe under the trees."

His face had gone pale, and he pressed his hand to his temple.

Crash.

"This way." Mina led him along the path, and to the service entrance she'd utilized just a short time earlier. They entered, their togetherness concealed by the crush of servants crowding the rear hallways. Yet turning, he pinned her against the wall, his hands against her shoulders.

"I've got to go," he said.

"In the storm? Why don't you wait—"

"I'll return tomorrow." He looked *tortured.*

"Mark—"

"Be careful, Mina."

Another boom sounded. The floor moved under Mina's shoes. Trays of silverware and crystal rattled.

Be careful, Mina. What did he mean by that? Mark released her, backed away and disappeared out the service door. From a narrow window, she watched him go. He cut through the garden gate, and between two waiting carriages. His elegant gait had gone abnormally straight and stiff. A spear of lightning cut across the sky. The muscular span of his shoulders stiffened. He stumbled.

Chapter Eight

The strike of Mark's boots against the cobblestones echoed against the storefronts and warehouses and up into the night. His coat snapped in the wind. The streets were abandoned, a result of the extreme atmospheric display above. Light flashed, brilliant and surreal, illuminating the avenue.

Crash.

He passed alongside a great heap of pavement, torn up from the street. A cast-iron pipe jutted out of the resultant hole. A long plume of flame rippled and hissed from the open end, a startling banner in the night. On the adjacent pavement a lantern wavered, evidence of an interrupted repair to the gas main below.

The voice attempted to turn him predator without his consent. He'd been forced to leave Mina for fear he would suddenly transform into a hulking fiend with glowing eyes and ethereal skin, and all the terrifying attributes that had made him a ruthless, vicious hunter. Removed from her, he surrendered to the beast within.

Mark sensed a peculiar pattern of movement in the darkness on either side of the street—one distinguished

not by the moral deterioration of a Transcending soul—
but by vacant emptiness.

Stellar, his conscience growled. He wasn't particularly
in the mood for new discoveries. He was, however, in the
mood to slay, and as this particular soul was neither Transcending nor *brotoi*, its life was fair game for a banished
Shadow Guard with an overwhelming need to hunt.
Shoulders forward and chin down, he passed the next
alley. Tilting his head, he glimpsed a figure leaping into
darker shadows. The mental echo he cast out filled in the
picture, revealing the wiry figure of the one who stalked
him. Two more beings scurried like rats along the high
roofs above. The dark power of his hunger sluiced like
fire through his veins.

Let them come. He bit into his lower lip, craving the
kill.

They circled closer. . . .

Mark transformed into shadow and veered up the
side of the warehouse. They clung like spindly legged
cockroaches, high against the alley wall. Skimming close
against the bricks, as with the vicious swipe of a chain, he
sent each one spiraling down from its perch.

The strike of his boots as he landed amongst them
echoed off the walls. On filthy cobblestones littered with
rubbish, the three men lay groaning and wheezing. Peculiarly, their eyes rolled in their sockets in a constant whirl
of agitation. They scrambled to crouch and lower their
heads into a perplexing pose of subservience.

"Get up," he hissed. "Face me as you die."

One whispered, "Your lordship."

"*Our* lordship," echoed another.

Dismay, dark and vicious, cut through his chest. "What
did you say?"

The nearest fiend dared to lift his face to Mark. A bes-
tial smile pulled his lips. "We're not here to issue a challenge. We've been sent to serve you."

Mark planted his boot against the fiend's shoulder and sent him toppling. *Serve him?* The words, the very idea, disturbed him.

The sound of wheels on cobblestones repeated off the walls. From the far end of the alley an enormous town coach appeared, led by a team of four. Wisps of white vapor curled off the wheels and surfaces of the cab, and even the backs of the horses. The vehicle was like something he would have seen on these streets a century before. The large side lamps were shattered. Orange flames licked through the jagged shards of glass, high and uncontained.

The driver, a twig-thin fellow with the same peculiar eye affliction, dug his heels into the footboard and pulled the reins.

The three fiends leapt up. Mark tensed, prepared to end their lives, but they only skittered midway up the brick walls, and gestured for him to follow.

Whoever they were, they certainly knew how to make an impression.

The driver dropped to the cobblestones. He wore a livery, one fashioned of black cloth. The same vapor curled from his shoulders. His suit appeared crushed and mottled and damp, as if snatched off a moldering corpse. A wide, black sash crossed him from shoulder to hip. Upon it, embroidered in red stitching, appeared the monogram "DB."

"Me mistress begs the pleasure of yer company." He lifted his stovepipe top hat and swept low.

"Your mistress . . . ," Mark repeated. "Who is your mistress?"

The fiends leapt closer, like frogs, and crouched low about his knees. Thunder crashed, and in an instant, they appeared as skeletons, bathed in orange light. When the lightning faded, so did the effect.

Their whispers sounded in chorus.

"She's waiting for you."

"*Waiting* for you."

"Waits to *join* with you."

Mark growled, "How flattering."

The driver, who had remained in his courtly bow all this time, now swung his arms and his hat in the direction of the coach. "Get in, if you please. We'll take you to 'er."

The door flew open, crashing back against the side of the cab. The stairs unfurled, only to promptly dislodge from the vehicle. They fell with a metallic crash to the cobblestones below. A handful of moths fluttered out from the dark interior and bobbed off into the night.

He narrowed his gaze on the driver. "Call me prudish, but I like to know more about a woman before I commit to a liaison. Why . . . I don't even know her name."

The driver's eyes widened, their pupils whirling faster. "She's the Dark Bride."

The fiends echoed, "The Dark Bride."

"You *know* her."

"You *do*."

In that moment, Mark realized he did. A frisson of dark anticipation scored through his chest.

He strode forward to grip the handle and climbed in. The driver followed. With a grunt he hurled the stairs inside. They skidded across the floorboard to strike against the far wall. The door slammed shut. The vehicle bounced as the driver returned to his perch, and the three fiends clambered onto the back.

The carriage left the alley. Beneath him, the seat bounced on creaking, rusted springs. The thick scent of must and decay filled his nostrils. A moth flapped against his cheek. Mark shoved out the shutter, every muscle within him rigid with tension. The vehicle traveled south, past Buckingham Palace and Belgrave Square. The district of Chelsea flew past in a blur. Darkness closed over the carriage as the city became villages, and villages became countryside. Eventually, Mark lost all sense of the

passing of time. Finally, wheels rattled, jerking him aware
with the distinctive sound of a bridge crossing. Another
few miles more, and the vehicle slowed.

He leapt down to the road, even before the carriage
had fully rolled to a stop.

A large brickwork gate rose from the earth. The sign
read THE CHELSEA WATERWORKS COMPANY. His conscious-
ness spanned out, searching the silent buildings and trees
and darkness for any trace of the one who had summoned
him. The air carried only the sound of rushing water and
the hiss of steam engines.

The location alone—waterworks—gave Mark cause
for concern. The works provided tens of thousands of
London citizens with water. But he also experienced an
electrifying sense of expectancy. His fingers curled into
his palms. Tonight he would share an audience with the
one who sought to wrest control of his deteriorating mind
for whatever dark purpose.

The Dark Bride.

The three fiends leapt down from a perch at the back
of the carriage and ran like excited children toward the
gate. Mark saw no evidence of a night crew or watchman.
A heavy chain and padlock hung to the ground, smoothly
cut. Side by side, they shoved the iron portal inward. The
metal groaned discordantly. With flapping arms, they ea-
gerly ushered him through.

Two enormous reservoirs spread before him, side by
side, and separated by a concrete divider. From either
side jutted a pair of arches, which he surmised served to
filter the incoming flow from the Thames.

Suddenly, the surface of the reservoirs flashed with the
appearance of what had to be at least a hundred scarlet
paper lanterns. They eddied about on the current, casting their glow against the water—creating the surreal
appearance of blood. Swept almost immediately against
the filters, some upended and were extinguished amidst a

tumble of crushed and sodden paper, while others twirled off to the side to sputter out a more eventual death.

Only then did he realize a shadowed figure stood at the distant end of the reservoirs, on the narrow division of concrete between. He perceived the outline of a head, and shoulders, and the long fall of a cloak. The fiends urged him forward.

"Be introduced," one urged.

"*Hurry*, she waits," the other hissed.

Mark followed them along the narrow path. As he grew closer, he perceived a foul scent on the air, like a carcass left too long in the sun—evidence that the Dark Bride was, without a doubt, a Transcending soul.

"You've come," she whispered.

The voice was not one he recognized. But then, she spoke so softly. . . .

Turned away from him, he could not see her face. The hood of her cloak covered the back of her head. "I've waited so long."

"Touching sentiments. Which are difficult to return when I've no idea who you are."

He scrutinized the Dark Bride's height and shape. Unfortunately, nothing distinguished her from the masses or identified her as anyone he knew.

"You know who I am," she responded teasingly.

"Tell me." He stepped closer.

The fiends blocked his path, but crouched low, with bent heads. They protected their mistress, but clearly did not wish to incur his wrath.

"I have told you many things . . . almost constantly . . . but you've chosen . . ." Her voice dipped low, taking on a vicious edge. "To ignore me."

That voice matched the one in his head.

"Turn and face me," he commanded.

Her shoulders went soft. She liked being ordered about.

She whirled, her cloak flying out in a dark circle. From the depths of the hood peered a white face, a porcelain mask, the sort one might see at a Venetian ball. The two eyeholes revealed only blackness . . . no glimpse of anything human. No whites, no pupils, no blinking flaps of skin.

"Did you like my presents?" she asked in her prior flirtatious tone, her breath hissing against the porcelain.

"You sent me . . . presents?"

"Yes, darling," she chided, sounding like any other normal, exasperated girl. "I had them delivered all up and down the river so there would be no way you could miss them."

"You killed a woman and cut her up."

"No, silly man. I didn't cut her up. That would be so . . . *messy*. I've got toadies for that."

"Toadies?"

She waved her hands in the direction of the crouching fiends. They grinned and nodded, happy hounds at the foot of their master.

"Why did you do it?"

"You know why. Think, darling, think. It's all right there in your handsome, immortal head."

"Tell me."

"I did it for you," she crooned softly. "For us."

The words in his head, spoken with such vicious, sensual fervor . . .

The dramatic presentation of the carriage and attendant toadies . . .

The lanterns on the water.

The Dark Bride had set the stage for a seduction. The dismembered arms and legs, and all the rest, hadn't been dropped into the river to taunt him or to lure him into battle.

The bitch was trying to woo him.

*   *   *

Mina awoke with a start. Something had awakened her. A sound.

She lay taut and aware, listening. Hearing nothing, she squinted across the room at her clock. Though she could barely make out the hands, it appeared to be nearly three o'clock. She'd been in bed for only an hour. It had taken that long for the house to settle down in the aftermath of the party, which had continued inside for the duration of the storm. After Mark had left—stumbling into the street—she'd retired to her room, pensive and concerned. Even now, she wondered: *Where was he?*

She'd been so suspicious of him, and of his interest in the scrolls. Now she ached for him. Ached to trust him. Everything within her shouted that he could be her safe place. Weariness dragged her back toward slumber, a relief because without him here, she didn't want to stay awake in the dark.

The sound came again—a scratching or sliding against her door, as if someone walked past and dragged their fingertips along the wood.

She lay very still, her stomach slowly turning into knots.

Brrr-usssh.

She sat up, pushing away the covers. Before she'd drifted off to sleep, there had been several rounds of voices and footsteps in the hallway. All the rooms were occupied by overnight guests. Perhaps someone was ill and needed assistance. She'd rather look and settle her mind than wait and imagine what the sound could be. She arose and drew on her dressing robe.

At the door she looked out. Midhallway, a small lamp on the table had been left on and provided a bit of light. She saw no one. A peculiar white haze curled up from the direction of the stairs. Her heart jumped. Smoke? Could there be a fire downstairs?

She rushed from her doorway. Nearer the stairs, the

stuff was thicker . . . but didn't smell at all like smoke. It seemed more like . . . fog.

She didn't care for fog.

There'd been a similar fog on the mountain that last night with her father. Of course there, at such a high altitude, the mountains pushed straight up into the clouds. But why was there fog inside the house? Panic tightened her chest.

Slowly, she descended the stairs, into the thick of it. A door shut behind her.

Her door?

She turned, thinking to go back . . . but a dense wall of white had closed in behind her. Her mind raced. This couldn't be happening. None of this made sense. She turned in a careful circle on the stairs, surrounded so thickly she couldn't see beyond her outstretched arm.

It was just a dream, she told herself, a surreal, nonsensical dream. Any minute she'd wake up.

Disoriented by the consuming whiteness, she felt her way up the stairs. She skimmed her hands over the wall and worked her way back to her room. All the while she expected skeletal, clawed hands to reach out and grab her.

She raked her hair and bit into her bottom lip. Something had indeed shut her door. Carefully, she turned the handle. Inside—there was only darkness. Slivers of moonlight streamed through the curtains. No fog. She glanced over her shoulder.

The fog in the hallway had vanished.

Veering inside, she shut the door behind her and turned the key in the lock. She lit a lamp. Trembling, she wrapped her arms around herself and turned back to the room.

Her father's satchel lay in the center of her bed. All around—on the bed, on the floor, on her desk—were the shredded remains of his papers and notebooks. Her hand flew to her throat but found only bare skin. She found the key amidst the destruction on her bed.

"Take off your mask, and let me see your face," Mark commanded.

The black holes stared at him, fathomless and unblinking. "Not yet."

"If you don't trust me, why am I here? What makes you think I am of any use to you?"

"You are to be the most powerful *brotoi* of all. The Messenger."

"The *Messenger*," crooned the toadies, bobbing between them, low to the ground.

Disgust rippled through him. The Messenger? *He* wasn't the Messenger. Jack the Ripper had been the Messenger, and when Archer had slain him, that had been the end of things—or apparently, it hadn't been.

He subdued the rage in his voice. "Was there another Messenger before me?"

Under the cloak, shoulders shrugged. "We never got on very well. I sent him several presents that he never acknowledged. I even buried one deep in the heart of his enemy—a sacrifice to thwart their efforts against him. Do you think he appreciated it? No. I think I'll like you so much better."

In the midst of the hunt for Jack, Selene's torso killer had deposited a dismembered and headless female corpse, bundled up in the material of a dress, beneath the grounds of New Scotland Yard.

"You serve . . . Tantalus."

Just speaking the name put a sour taste in his mouth.

Beneath the cloak her shoulders straightened. "You and I together shall serve him. Every sacrifice prepares the river for his arrival."

Mark's blood went cold. *Tantalus's arrival.*

"But there must be more sacrifices. So many more. I

need you, darling. Our toadies and I can't do it all on our own." Her voice cooled. "Yet I can sense your reluctance to join me. Really, love, you force my hand."

Mark hated to ask. "In what way?"

From the depths of her cloak, she produced a white balloon, about the size of a skull, filled with brown-yellow liquid.

She whirled and proceeded away from him, along the center concrete divider. The toadies fell back. Mark followed her between the next two reservoirs of water.

"Dark Bride." Really, what else was he supposed to call her? "What is that in your hand?"

"Do you know how these reservoirs work?"

He didn't answer her; he just followed. Listening. Watching. She moved quickly. Turning, she walked backward, perfectly balanced on the narrow path. "The Thames water comes into the reservoirs and runs through a series of filters." She lifted a hand and spoke in the pleasant, conversational tone of a museum docent. "In the first reservoir, there's gravel. Water sinks down through the gravel, and is carried by perforated pipes into this second pool to be filtered by smaller gravel and more pipes."

They crossed into the third and final undulating reservoir. "And then finally, in the third pool, there's a sand filter."

"Fascinating." Mark stared at the balloon.

"Once the river muck is filtered through those three processes, the clean and tasty water is carried through aqueducts to the city, and to all the lovely citizens of London."

Mark didn't know what was in her damn balloon, but he felt certain it didn't need to go in the water. He'd been divested of the ability to Reclaim her soul, but he tensed, prepared to—

"But I don't think those filters will work on this." She hurled the balloon high in the air over the reservoir.

Mark leapt.

Another arm unfurled, wielding a long-barreled pistol.

Crack. Liquid rained down. Crashing in, he diffused into shadow. He spread himself through the cool, green depths, attempting to catch the lethal poison as it drifted down. . . .

But there was no poison. There was only . . . ginger beer.

He broke through the surface. Rage welled up from within him, and he ground his teeth down on a shouted curse. He swam to the side. The Dark Bride peered down at him from a few steps away.

"Oh, darling, you take my breath away. The way you leapt in to save the citizens of London. Did you really think I'd kill all those people? I wouldn't do that. After all, if they are dead, who will become my toadies? I have big plans for this city. And for you. But obviously, you're not ready yet."

Mark climbed, drenched, onto the concrete ledge. He rubbed the water from his eyes. When he opened them again . . .

She and the toadies were gone.

Chapter Nine

Mark stared up at the front façade of the Trafford house. A few hansoms traveled the street, as well as early riders headed for the Row, but Mayfair, at this hour, still seemed to be rubbing the sleep from its eyes. He glanced down at his pocket watch again.

Eight thirty. It was early. Too early for a proper call, but he couldn't wait any longer. He could think of only one way to expedite a closer relationship between himself and Miss Limpett, and bring himself nearer to possession of the scrolls. He told himself that now, after all he'd heard the night before, he wasn't just seducing Mina Limpett to save his own skin. He was seducing her to save London. And England. Quite possibly, even the world.

A powerful *brotoi* prepared the damn River Thames with human sacrifices, in preparation for the arrival of the dark underworld lord, Tantalus. There'd never been a more valiant cause, a more noble reason, to seduce one lush, English virgin. *Yes, world. And I'm just the man to do the job.* His palms sweated, and his heart—he swore it skipped every other beat, an indication his emotions were tangled up in the decision more than he'd prefer. He rang the bell.

Mark's card in hand, the footman disappeared into the recesses of the house. A moment later he was led to his lordship's study.

His lordship strode in, wearing a silk dressing gown over his trousers. "You're out and about rather early this morning."

Mark stood, and the two men shook hands.

"Did you enjoy yourself last night?" Trafford inquired.

Instead of seating himself behind the desk, his lordship lowered himself to the chair beside Mark's.

"I did, yes," Mark responded politely.

"Can you believe that lightning storm? We're lucky no one was killed. All that racket and not a drop of rain."

"I think the storm only served to make the evening more memorable." The night had certainly been memorable for him. "I hope Lucinda is pleased."

"Yes," his lordship responded shortly, his lips pressed into a wan smile. "She . . . ought to be."

Mark began, "Well—I—ah—"

He swallowed hard. It wasn't like him to stammer.

"Yes?" His lordship's eyebrows arched up.

"There's a reason I've come this morning to speak to you. So early, so dreadfully early, I must apologize." Mark pulled a handkerchief from his pocket and swiped at his brow. Good God, he never perspired.

"No apologies are necessary. I'm an early riser and welcome the company." Trafford nodded and crossed his legs. His leather slipper dangled off his toes. "Tell me about this reason?"

Blast. He could barely catch his breath. "I've an important matter to discuss with you. A . . . proposal."

"A proposal. What an interesting choice of words." Trafford leaned forward and selected two cigars from the wood box on his desk. Taking up a small pair of gleaming silver scissors, he expertly snipped off the ends. Snip snip. One, two.

"I've found myself rather smitten by a young lady in your household."

"Oh, yes?" Pleasure warmed Trafford's features. In fact, he appeared downright giddy. "Astrid will be beside herself. The two of you, last night on the dance floor. *Perfection*. Everyone commented."

Mark smiled at the awkwardness of the whole situation. "I'm sorry, although Astrid is a *lovely, lovely girl*—"

"*Evangeline*." Trafford's eyes widened. "Even better. She's a remarkable conversationalist. A smart, sturdy girl."

"Actually, your lordship, I'd like your permission to ask for Miss Limpett's hand in marriage."

The cigars dropped from his lordship's hand.

Mina had not slept for the remainder of the night. She sat at her desk, fully dressed, staring at the satchel. She hadn't been able to bring herself to throw the hundreds of bits of pieces of paper away. Instead, she'd gathered them all up and placed them inside. First there had been the rose, discovered inside the locked satchel, and now this. Fragmented visions eddied about in her head. Glowing eyes in the crypt. The masked actor on the street, wielding the same breed of rose. Was all of it designed to drive her mad?

Someone attempted quite skillfully to frighten her. And *badly*. But who? A servant or someone from outside the home?

Or could it be a member of her own family?

She couldn't think clearly. The otherworldly memory of the disappearing fog made her question everything. Whoever had orchestrated these events *were* just *people* . . . weren't they?

She glanced at her untouched breakfast tray. As had become her morning habit, she gathered up a few bits into the napkin and left her room. She needed air. She needed sunshine. She needed to think clearly and decide what to do.

In the garden, a servant stood atop a ladder, removing lanterns from the trees. Here and there lay bits of crushed flowers, and the odd pearl or bit of trim. Tables and chairs remained, the lightning storm having made conditions far too dangerous to stow them the night before. She proceeded to the far end of the garden, and took the few steps down to where the shrubs lined the wall. She laid the napkin out, and backed away to watch from the steps.

The cats didn't appear. Perhaps they were a bit skittish after the party and the storm. She'd wait a while longer.

Weary, she rested her face in her hands. Perhaps she should talk to Trafford and tell him everything. She just didn't know, and there was no one to help her decide. Perhaps . . . perhaps Mark? She wished—

"They're gone, you know."

Mina looked up and found Evangeline on the steps behind her, dressed in a pink and white–striped dressing gown.

"Who are gone?" She stood.

"The cats. Lucinda had the gardeners put out traps. She didn't want them slinking around during her party."

"Traps?"

Evangeline murmured, "I'm sorry if you were fond of them. The gardeners . . . well, they make sure the cats don't come back. They kill them."

Grief tore through Mina, a blunt stab of pain. Her stomach turned. Her three little cats, dead. For a garden party? Misery, compounded with her earlier fears, combined to steal her breath. The sky, the flowers, the big grand house . . . everything turned gray.

Perhaps she should leave. Go somewhere far away, even to America. Somewhere no one knew her. She could take a job as a governess or nanny. She didn't have much money, just that from the sale of her father's small Manchester house.

But Mark . . .

"I was sent to find you," said Evangeline. "My father wishes to speak with you."

Mina nodded. Her arms hung limp at her side as together they returned to the house.

Outside the study, Evangeline added, "I think there's someone else in there with him, but I don't know who."

Mina knocked. At her uncle's call, she let herself in.

Mark stood up from a chair, holding his hat and gloves, his expression solemn. The sight of him paralyzed her. Not because she didn't wish to see him, but because all she wanted to do was race toward him and throw herself into her arms, and sob into his shirt over three silly little cats and a pile of shredded notes.

"Good morning, Lord Trafford," she said. "Lord Alexander."

"Come, Willomina. Please sit," invited her uncle. He moved to stand beside the mantel.

Mina did as he asked. On unsteady legs she lowered herself into the chair beside Mark's. He also sat. A sudden fear struck through her that they were here to confront her about her father. Her face . . . her scalp went numb. It was the worst thing she could imagine; that Lord Alexander, the man who had kissed her so sweetly, so passionately, would think of her as a liar—a deceiver.

Trafford's expression gave away nothing. "His lordship has come with a special request this morning."

"Oh, yes?" she answered faintly. "What is that?"

Mark stared at her intently. Her uncle seemed to be drawing something out. At the edge of her chair, she waited expectantly, her hands curled into fists.

"Lord Alexander"—his lips spread into a slow smile, and his eyes twinkled—"has requested and received my permission to ask for your hand in marriage."

"He . . . has?" They were all the words she could muster. Her mouth, her brain did not wish to function.

She looked at Mark. Intensity sharpened his features. He offered her a crooked, hopeful smile.

"Yes, I have," he confirmed.

This wasn't at all what she expected. Her lungs collapsed. She couldn't draw a breath.

"I—I don't know." Her face—her tongue and lips—felt swollen with shock. "We don't even really know each other."

Mark nodded. Looking to Trafford, he said, "Perhaps I could speak alone to Miss Limpett."

"Of course." Trafford bounded toward the door. "I shall check in on you shortly."

He closed the door firmly behind him.

"I know my proposal is sudden. I know it's completely unexpected." Mark grasped her hand. "But I've got to get out of here. Out of England, and I want you to come with me."

Mina smiled at him, and her eyes flooded. "You don't want to marry me."

"Yes, I do." A bemused expression overtook his face. "I can honestly say there's nothing I want more."

"Why?" she demanded softly, blinking at him through tears.

"Why what?"

"Why everything. Why do you want to marry me? Why do you have to leave England? Why now?"

"Because I want you. I need you. It's that simple. And we've so much in common, Mina. We share a love for the more authentic places in the world, and the discovery of ancient things. I know this city doesn't make you happy, just like it doesn't make me happy. There are too many rules, and too many intrigues. It's a soulless place, and I'm itching to get away and return to what has always been real to me. Come with me."

"You don't even know me." She shook her head. "I'm a mixed-up mess."

"No, you're not," he assured her, his voice low and persuasive. "And even if you are, then I must like it very much. Perhaps I am a mixed-up mess too."

"There are things . . ." She stared at their entwined hands. "Things that I should tell you, things about myself that I just *can't*."

"You think I don't have secrets? Shocking, terrible secrets?" He grinned ruefully. "I'm sure mine would blow yours out of the water." He shook his head. "We shall share them, when the time feels right."

"What about you? I don't know *anything* about you, not even the most simple things. Do you have family?"

"My mother and father died when I was a boy," he answered. "Within hours of each other. It was all very tragic and dramatic."

Now she understood the underlying darkness she'd sensed beneath his otherwise warm and roguish disposition.

"That's very sad. Is there no one else? No siblings?"

"I have a twin. We are estranged." He paused, squeezing her hand. "So you see? We're both very much alone in this life. Let's be together, and learn the rest along the way." He left the chair, dropping to his knees and his legs crushing into her skirts. He took both her hands in his. His hands were warm, and large and strong.

Her safe place.

"Just say yes."

"Where would we go?"

"Europe. India. Tibet. Wherever you wish."

Perhaps she could have adventure *and* her safe place. *Yes*, her heart whispered, *perhaps . . . perhaps Tibet.*

Mina stared into his eyes. His hands came up to brace her chin, one on either side. Bending, he pressed his lips to her cheeks . . . to her closed eyelids in warm, fervent kisses, banishing her tears.

"Say yes," he whispered. "Mina, please."

He kissed her mouth. All her fear and the sadness faded.

"Yes," she answered. "Yes."

"Thank you," he murmured between hot, gentle kisses. "Thank you, Mina."

He did not declare his love for her, and she didn't need it. Not yet. For now, this was enough.

"When?" he murmured against her cheek. "Next week?"

Mina grasped his upper arms, drunk on their closeness. "As soon as possible."

A knock came at the door.

Mark quickly stood, his hand resting against her shoulder. After a quick swipe at her eyes, she also turned. Trafford peeked in, his smile hesitant.

"Have we an engagement?" he asked quietly.

With a squeeze to her shoulder, Mark answered, "We do."

Trafford grinned, his gaze dropping to Mina, as if for confirmation. She nodded and smiled. Her uncle opened the door farther, revealing three more faces. All ashen. All unsmiling.

Lucinda pushed past him, into the room.

"Trafford, I can't believe you're supporting this," she scoffed, her voice thick. "They barely know one another."

Mina blinked, her joy in the moment summarily evaporating.

The earl lifted his hands. "What does knowing each other have to do with anything?"

"Miss Limpett, I'm exceedingly disappointed in you," the countess snapped. "You've only just buried your father. You've been in mourning a scant three months. What do you suppose people are going to say?"

Mark raised Mina from the chair. The firm support of his hand came to her back. "They won't say anything. We'll have a quiet, private ceremony by special license."

"Those are the worst kind." Her gaze veered between them. Pale ringlets bobbed on either side of her cheeks. "They get everyone to talking scandal."

"I don't care about scandal," Mark said, looking to Mina. "Do you care about scandal?"

"No," she whispered. She cleared her throat and repeated more firmly, "No."

Lucinda's eyes widened incredulously. Her breasts rose and fell beneath the fitted bodice of her blue sprigged morning gown. "You're thinking only of yourselves. The scandal will not only affect you, but all of us."

Trafford interceded. "Lucinda, you're exaggerating things."

Mark added, "Any talk will quickly die. And furthermore, we'll be leaving directly on our honeymoon, on the *Thais*."

"Well then, I guess it's settled, isn't it?" Lucinda looked around at all of them. At Mark and Mina. At Trafford. At the pallid-faced girls. In a softer, ragged voice she said, "I've got to go lie down. I've a headache now."

She rushed through the open door, passing Astrid and Evangeline, who hovered in the corner. They didn't speak, but their gazes swept condemningly to Mina. In tandem, they too quit the room.

Trafford rocked back on his heels, his arms clasped behind his back. To Mark, he said conspiratorially, "How fast do you think you can get the license?"

"Today is Friday. I think I could manage it by Tuesday."

Her uncle grinned. "She'll be fine by then."

*   *   *

Mark hated to abandon Mina to a house in tumult, but being that they would be married on Tuesday, he had much to do—starting with obtaining the special license. He prayed Lucinda, in his absence, would not do anything drastic to force Mina to change her mind. Last night when the countess apologized for her behavior at Hurlingham, he'd actually believed she was sorry. Had she always been so manic in her moods and behaviors?

A clock ticked off rapid time in his head. He prayed he would not suffer another spell before the wedding, because he sensed that with each assault on his mind, he became less able to fend off the malevolent influence of the Dark Bride. Her voice had been noticeably silent since last night at the waterworks, but he feared when she returned, she would do so with a vengeance.

His plan was twofold: First, he felt certain that once they were under way, he could fully gain Mina's trust and persuade her to confess everything, most especially the details of her father's location. Second, he suspected the distance would mute the Dark Bride's voice—at least long enough for him to gain control of the scrolls, translate them and locate the conduit. Restored to his full Amaranthine powers, he would return to London, petition the Primordial Council for reinstatement—and put an end to the Dark Bride.

But of course, the trip wasn't all about his sanity. He planned to make love to his beautiful new wife at least a thousand times along the way. He closed his eyes, remembering how thick the attraction had been between them last night, and even more so, this morning. He had lived and loved for centuries. Some loves stood out from all the rest.

A carriage rolled alongside the curb where he walked. His eyes narrowed with suspicion, and he glanced aside. Thankfully, no whirly-eyed driver held the reins. Instead, Leeson peered out from the open cab of a hansom.

"Your lordship." The vehicle stopped. "Come inside."

Mark strode to the vehicle and climbed in.

"How went your proposal? Are you successfully betrothed?"

The driver steered them off the curb.

"I am indeed. You have news, I suppose?"

"I do." Leeson took up a notebook and read aloud from some scribbled notes. "Today's discoveries along the river include a right foot attached to part of a leg. This discovery occurred at"—he peered down his nose through a round monocle—"Wandsworth Bridge. And then we've got a left leg recovered at Limehouse."

"All the way down by the West India Docks?"

"That's correct. Both were carefully wrapped in sections of clothing, and tied with string."

Mark nodded. "Have you been able to locate Selene?"

"No, sir. Wherever she's residing, she doesn't wish to be found."

Mark nodded. "What else do you have for me?"

"There's a postmortem viewing of the body parts recovered thus far scheduled for this afternoon at the Battersea Mortuary with police surgeon Dr. Felix Kempster. Dr. Kempster worked the Rainham dismemberment murder of 1887. Very thorough. Very smart. It will be a pleasure working with him again . . . ah, even if he does not realize we are working together."

Mark pulled out his pocket watch and assessed the time. With everything else he needed to do, he'd just have time to attend the postmortem. Certainly he would encounter Selene there. He needed to tell her everything he'd learned about the Dark Bride. Despite everything, he couldn't forget he was no longer a Shadow Guard. The Thames dismemberment mysteries, from the beginning, had been her official assignment, bestowed upon her by the Primordial Council. Whatever actions he undertook against the Bride upon

returning to London would have to be done in coopera-
tion with his sister.

He looked out the window, assessing their location.
"Thank you, Leeson. If we are finished, you can let me
out at the next corner."

"Actually, we're not finished yet." The little man put
his notebook aside and rubbed his hands together. "I've
got a surprise for you."

"I've got a busy afternoon."

"You must make time for this. I've already arranged
for the driver to take us there."

"You know I don't like surprises, so just tell me."

"I've found a house for you. A place I think will be a
haven, and . . . perhaps protect you to some extent from
these spells. From that voice working on your head. I
know the Transcension can't be stopped, but perhaps this
shelter might slow the effects when you're in your more
vulnerable state."

Leeson's description piqued his interest. However, if
his voyage went as planned, he wouldn't need any such
sanctuary. "That's very interesting, but I'll be departing
London on Tuesday and won't need a house."

"Just have a look," Leeson suggested, adjusting the
strap of his eye patch. "That's all I ask. It would be nice
to have a place prepared for your return with Lady
Alexander."

Mark supposed he was right. He'd never had a real
home, a true base of operations. He'd preferred the tran-
sient accommodations of the *Thais* or elegant hotels. The
idea of setting up house with Mina held a secret, satisfying appeal.

Yet Archer, Lord Black, had a monopoly on the best address in town, a massive mansion he'd constructed nearly
a century before around the only portal to the Inner Realm
existing in London. How could any other property come
close?

The carriage turned down a side road, conveying them to a small neighborhood south of Mayfair, not far from the river. From the windows, Mark saw they traveled along a densely overgrown, once-grand street. The houses, for the most part, had succumbed to disrepair.

The hansom rolled to a stop in front of a large manse. Leeson led him up a short walk toward an immense black door. Many of the windows were missing. Weeds and grass protruded from the earth, knee-high.

Leeson fumbled in his pocket, and produced a large, fancifully shaped key. "All I ask is that you see everything before making your decision."

Mark hesitated at crossing the threshold. "When you said you'd found a place where I might be safe—a place of protection—this isn't exactly what I imagined. I'm not a vampire, Leeson. It's not my style to lurk around in drafty old mansions."

"Come inside," the little man insisted curtly.

Mark followed reluctantly as Leeson led him from room to room. There were two drawing rooms, a library, a study and a ballroom, all grandly done up with stained and peeling wallpaper and sagging ceilings. Clearly some sort of large animal had spent at least a few days living in the kitchen. And recently.

"I hate it," he announced, covering his nose with his handkerchief.

He could never expect Mina to live here. Not only was the manse in extreme disrepair, but all the surrounding properties were as well. There was no telling what vagrant criminals would be their neighbors.

"Let me show you the first floor." Leeson went to the stairs. His foot crashed through. He tested the next one. "Wait until you see the master suite. Once we get the swallows out—"

Mark pulled off his coat. He was starting to perspire. "I'm leaving. With or without you."

"Fine." Leeson rolled his eyes. "I'll just skip to the heart of the matter. Come on."

His mood growing fouler by the moment, he followed the elder immortal to the back of the house. Leeson tromped outside, leaving a crushed path through the weeds. Patches of overgrowth punctuated the garden, along with several discarded barrels and even a sofa and chair.

"Come on. Step up." Leeson arrived at a low stone wall, one encircling a large gazing pool, and hopped up onto the ledge. Filled with clear, sparkling water, the pool apparently sourced from a healthy spring.

Mark rubbed at the crown of his nose. "You're right. This is a very lovely feature, but it's not enough to make up for the rest of the house."

Leeson glared through his one eye over his shoulder. "I said *step up*."

Mark complied, though he grew exceedingly tired of humoring the man—a man who claimed to be in *his* service.

Leeson produced a coin from his pocket. "Here you go. Make a wish."

"I'm not a child," Mark retorted.

"You're ruining the moment," Leeson snapped. "Could you please just do as I've asked?"

Mark's patience grew short and his temper hot. "So be it."

He snatched the coin. With a flick of his thumb, the small disc went airborne, spinning through the air. Its metal glinted in the sunlight. *Plunk*.

"Did you make a wish?"

Let me live. Mina's beautiful face flashed across his mind.

"Now watch," instructed Leeson quietly. "*Watch*."

The coin descended into the murky green depths, its polished face flashing on each revolution . . . growing dimmer and dimmer as it sank through curious darting carp.

Mark saw something.

He tilted his head and narrowed his eyes.

"Oh." He caught his breath. *"I see."*

Chapter Ten

After leaving the ecclesiastical court, where he put in the necessary paperwork for the special license, Mark instructed the hansom driver to cross the Thames and take him to the Battersea Mortuary.

He had left Leeson at the house, waiting to meet with the present owner. In fact, he'd given Leeson authority to negotiate the purchase of all the houses on the street. Their collective worth—at least on the mortal market—could never approach the value of the gazing pool. Once Mark defeated his state of Transcension and regained his status amongst the Shadow Guard, he'd return to London with Mina and oversee their renovation—taking the necessary breaks for Reclamation assignments, of course. He vowed that within two years the address would be the most exclusive in the district, one from which he would earn a tidy profit.

What were these thoughts inside his head? Optimistic thoughts of a future with Mina? The city passed by his window, and he smiled to himself. He did not know how long such a future could last, but he vowed to make it good.

After a half hour's travel, he arrived at the mortuary. He paid the driver and passed beneath the central archway. There, shadowed in dim light, he transformed into shadow. From there he followed the scent of death until he arrived at the mortuary room.

Dr. Kempster held court with two dark-suited gentlemen. Mark brushed against them, drawing forth their names: Detective Inspectors Regan and Tunbridge. Moving farther inside, he bumped directly into Selene's shadow. Sensing the sharp edge of her fury, he took a position on the opposite side of the room.

"Thank you for coming, gentlemen," said Dr. Kempster, a distinguished-looking gentleman with a mustache. "I suppose we should get on with our terrible business."

He moved to the center of the room, where a series of shallow metal tubs occupied a lengthy table.

"Prepare yourselves," he warned. "We've kept the recovered parts in spirits to slow their decay."

The room didn't smell all that delightful in the first place, but both detectives produced pocket handkerchiefs with which to cover their noses and mouths. When everyone had braced themselves, the police surgeon lifted the cover from the first container. The strong stench of spirits, underscored by decomposition, cut through the room.

Detective Tunbridge coughed.

Dr. Kempster didn't appear affected at all. Mark knew it wasn't the first time he'd viewed such vicious handiwork. "Come closer so you can see."

The detectives edged closer and peered into the murky liquid. Mark was already there. His sister jostled him for position. Given that the torso killer—the killer he knew to be called the Dark Bride—was Selene's assignment, he ceded the space and again relocated to the other side of the table.

"What *is* that?" asked one of the detectives.

The doctor pointed with his finger. "The thigh discov-

ered at Battersea. This is the upper section and this the
lower. Do you see here? There are four bruises that appear to have been made by fingers clenched into the skin.
I believe this would have occurred while the victim was
still alive."

The doctor guided the detectives through the remainder of the recovered body parts, opening and closing each
lid as they moved along. A trunk . . . a section of right leg
with attached foot . . . and finally a left leg.

"There's no head?"

"No."

"Just like the torso that was discovered at New Scotland
Yard last year, on the Thames Embankment in 1887?"

"That's correct."

"You can see here . . . the bruising. She wore a ring on
this finger."

"It must have been removed shortly before, or even
just after she was killed."

"Her hands. Her nails are bitten down to the quick,
but there are no calluses. They aren't worn from work. It's
clear she was not a manual laborer."

Even though Mark already knew the identity of the
killer—at least to the extent that she was the Dark Bride—
Mark felt he owed the woman his reverence, and his attention. After all, her body had been deposited along the
river in a bizarre act of homage to him.

The doctor returned the lid to the final tray. "I think
you'll be very interested to see the clothing she wore. I
do believe the scraps will help us identify her. There is
actually a name marked on one particular piece. If you'll
follow me."

The two detectives, shadowed by two invisible immortals, followed him to the next table. There, large sections
of fabric—pieces cut from clothing—lay spread out for
their examination, each bearing the faint stains of blood
diluted by river water.

Mark closed his eyes, then gritted his teeth. Two of the pieces—one cut from a dark ulster, and the other a square of brown linsey—matched the clothing worn that night by the girl on the bridge.

"Do you see the initials stamped into the waistband of this linen piece?" the doctor said.

"'L. E. Fisher,'" read Detective Regan.

Tunbridge scratched out the name into his report.

But Mark knew differently. The girl's name had been Elizabeth. Elizabeth Jackson. Likely, upon investigation, they would find her clothes were purchased secondhand and stamped with the name of their previous owner. Mark didn't want to look at her anymore. Yes, he had spent two centuries as a Shadow Guard, and during that time he'd seen corpses—so many of them, in the worst of conditions. But he'd looked into this young woman's eyes. He'd given her hope . . . and she had given him the same. That she'd been reduced by some monster into a puzzle of jagged pieces filled him with rage.

Leaving Selene with the officials, Mark hurtled through the hall. He swept into an empty office only long enough to transform into human form, and then he strode to the street. There, with his palm planted against a brick column, he inhaled the smells of the city, replacing the scent of death in his nostrils and in his lungs. Even so, the stench clung to his clothes and skin, just as strongly as her memory claimed his mind. She had been a simple girl, but she had not deserved such a horrible death. Was her blood on his hands?

He had helped that girl out of arrogance as a way to show the Dark Bride that *he* was in control. By doing so, had he marked Elizabeth for death? Yes, she'd been intent on killing herself, but certainly the Dark Bride had to know he would eventually learn the victim's identity. Could she send any clearer message that it was she who held the upper hand?

"Don't ever do that again."

Mark turned. Selene stared at him from the top step.

She wore a rich brown silk dress, and a fetching straw summer hat, luxuriously trimmed with orange and green flowers and ribbon. As always, his twin sister looked like a queen in even the most macabre of surroundings. Who else would wear something like that to view a corpse?

"I knew that girl," he retorted darkly. "Now I've a personal stake in this too."

"You don't have anything," she hissed. "Don't you *ever* step foot into my territory again. You're not even a Guard any longer, so you don't have the right."

"I'm not trying to steal your assignment."

"You couldn't if you tried." She gave him her bustle and stormed away.

He caught up, walking alongside her. "Do you even know who your killer is?"

She cast him a dark glare.

Mark said, "I met her last night."

She whirled to face him. The silver purse on her arm flashed. "Did you meet her whirly, bug-eyed little toadies too?"

Lifting her arms, she wiggled her index fingers over her eyes.

"The Dark Bride. She wishes to *meet* you," she mocked.

Selene had always been good at impressions.

Mark straightened, disappointed. "I see you've already met her."

"Fleetingly, and on several occasions. She's only after you because"—Selene lifted her hand beside her mouth, as if sharing a secret—"she doesn't like *girls*, if you understand my meaning. Oh, and you're also losing your immortal mind, which makes you prime manflesh in her eyes. I'm sure your pedigree and familial good looks don't hurt either."

"What do you know of her true identity?"

Selene answered sharply, "None of your blasted business." With her finger, she jabbed his chest. "She's my target. Mine. Not yours. You, of all . . . well, excommunicated Shadow Guards, should understand that the boundaries must be respected, unless you're too far gone already to remember."

"I'm not," he retorted. "And I do remember."

Jack the Ripper had originally been his assignment. After a personal request from Her Highness, Queen Victoria, Archer, her longtime favorite, had interceded in the hunt. The wholesale invasion of his hunting territory had stung.

Selene blinked, and looked off across the street. "I suppose that's all we have to say to each other, then."

"Not quite." He sidled around, bringing them nose to nose. "You're right. The hunt belongs to you. And I'm leaving. Leaving England. When I return, I'll be as good as new. Fully reinstated into the Guard. If you haven't Reclaimed her by then . . . I'm going to do it. Fair warning, Selene."

She snorted. "Have a pleasant mental decline. I expect you'll only see me again once I've received firm orders for your assassination."

Just then, an enormous black carriage, pulled by four monstrous team horses, rolled to the curb beside them. A polished crest gleamed on the door, a black raven at its center. Inside the shadowed interior, Mark perceived the outline of a tall man with broad shoulders.

"It's time for me to go," said Selene, backing away from him toward the vehicle.

Mark scowled in displeasure. "One of the Ravens, Selene?"

The Ravens were a specialized regiment within the Order of the Shadow Guards. They consisted of eight immortal warriors who, in the year 1066, had taken an oath to protect the kingdom of England from destruction and anarchy, and her ruling monarch from harm. Through the subsequent centuries, the Ravens had continually bumped heads with their fellow Shadow Guards over territory, favor and prestige.

"Good-bye, Mark," she responded firmly.

"You're certain, Lucinda, that you want me to wear your wedding dress?" Mina sat on the edge of her bed, staring down into the large, glossy box. Nested in pale pink tissue paper was the most beautiful gown she'd ever seen.

"I insist on it," said Lucinda pleasantly.

While still not particularly joyful about the morning's intended ceremony, Lucinda had softened considerably, and thrown herself into the task of making sure Mina had a proper wedding day.

"Thank you, your ladyship."

"It's by Jacques Doucet," the countess announced proudly, lifting it out by the shoulders.

She draped the gleaming silk satin across the coverlet. "The diamonds and pearls are indeed real."

Astrid and Evangeline moved closer to admire the gown as well.

There had only been two days to shop for Mina's trousseau. She had not, of course, gone to Paris, but the woman at the lingerie counter had assured Lucinda that the ready-to-wear corsets, chemises, corset covers, petticoats and *chemises de nuit* they'd purchased all bore a tag proving a Parisian origin.

"It's time," Lucinda said, pointing to the clock. "Let us help you dress."

Mina removed her dressing gown and stood in place while Lucinda, with the help of Astrid and Evangeline, lowered the skirts and the attached bodice over her ecru undergarments. Lucinda meticulously aligned the buttons, and the dress took its intended shape.

Lucinda stared over Mina's shoulder, into the mirror.

"It fits you perfectly. Well, almost." She dipped to her knees and adjusted the skirt. "If we had more time, I'd have the modiste take off a half inch."

She fluffed the hem out and paused. "Mina, what is this? Don't tell me it's your old petticoat." She pinched at a bit of lace.

Mina looked down. "It's my something old. Besides, I like it. I think it has a nice shape."

Lucinda stood. "I suppose we all have our own superstitions. It's too late for you to change anyway. Everything but your traveling suit has been packed into your trunks. Now sit." She pointed to the dressing table.

There, Lucinda lowered a veil of Brussels lace over Mina's hair. The countess dipped to peer into the mirror beside her face.

"You're a beautiful bride," she complimented. Yet she didn't smile.

A sob sounded behind them, and Astrid rushed from the room. Evangeline followed her, pausing at the door. "She's terribly envious. She cried all night, saying over and over again that it was our debut Season and that it should be one of us getting married today." She followed her sister.

"Oh, dear," said Mina with a frown. "I hadn't realized."

Lucinda touched her cheek. "Don't let Astrid make your eyes red and weepy on this, your special day." She again met Mina's eyes in the reflection. "Allow me to do that instead."

Mina stared back at her, stunned. "Why would you say something like that?"

Lucinda's eyes grew glittering and cruel. "I think you know the truth, Mina. You're a perceptive young woman."

Mina didn't speak.

The countess repaired some nonexistent flaw in Mina's

hairstyle. "Your handsome husband to be . . . well, we had quite the passionate affair. But I married Trafford instead. Mark is using you, Mina. He's using you to punish me for my choice. I want you to remember that today as you are standing beside him, taking your vows."

The countess drew back. At the bed, she folded the tissue and lifted the box from the coverlet.

Mina remembered Mark and their brief time together in the study after his proposal. She remembered his deeply passionate kisses and his earnest words.

Lucinda paused at the door, her face a mask of cold satisfaction. "I'll leave you to gather yourself for a few moments."

"No, I'm ready now," Mina answered evenly. She stood and squared her shoulders. She swept past the countess, her chin held high. "Ready and gathered."

Mark took the stairs to the Trafford house. Behind him, Leeson clambered down from the hired town coach and followed at a slightly lesser pace. The footman pulled the door open. Mina stood at the top of the staircase. His chest tightened, even hurt a little, at the sight of her lustrous beauty. She smiled, appearing every bit as joyful to see him, and flew down the stairs to meet him.

Given the expediency of their nuptials, he hadn't expected her to wear an actual wedding gown. Whether the gown had been borrowed, or purchased ready-made, the thick satin clung to her breasts, her narrow waist and flared hips, as if it had been designed especially for her. It was not until he took her hand that he realized Lucinda, wooden faced and pale, followed behind her, carrying a bundle of white roses.

"You've already got flowers," he said. "I didn't know, so I brought a bouquet as well."

He indicated Leeson, who held a huge spray of white orchids and lily of the valley, trimmed with lace.

She grinned. "I like yours better."

He'd also stopped by his banker's office and retrieved his mother's ring out of his safe box. The box presently burned a hole in his pocket. He hoped the gold band, which displayed an open lotus flower with a large turquoise stone at its center, would fit Mina's slender finger.

Leeson presented the flowers to Mina with a flourish along the length of his forearm.

Mark said, "This is Mr. Leeson. He'll be my official witness."

"Thank you for coming, Mr. Leeson," she said.

As Mark escorted her toward the drawing room, she whispered, "He looks familiar."

Within the hour the ceremony had been concluded and all the necessary papers signed and witnessed. They'd also enjoyed a small but elegant luncheon. Rather, he and Mina had enjoyed the meal, while Lucinda, Astrid and Evangeline sat rigid in their chairs, picking at their food. Trafford had appeared noticeably embarrassed. Mark opened up his immortal senses and picked up all sorts of envious and spiteful thoughts, most of them directed toward Mina, but Mina, for her part, appeared blissfully oblivious. Best yet, she couldn't stop glancing down at her ring.

The ladies' disregard for Mina inspired a sharp glint of anger in his chest, but all he cared about on this day was that she was happy—and that they got to the *Thais* early enough to make their way down the Thames before nightfall. If they could get out of the house without any confrontations, or any food being thrown, he'd count their wedding day a success.

He could not help but view with foreboding the window of time before they departed. There were too many things that could go wrong. If he suffered a spell, he would delay their departure. Leeson, who would accompany them on their voyage, had been given instructions to discreetly interfere and draw attention from any abnormal behavior on Mark's part.

At present, Mark paced the base of the stairs, waiting for Mina to come down. Trafford waited with him, attempting to make conversation. Servants had already carried down her trunks and at present Leeson supervised their loading onto the town coach. Finally she appeared at the top of the stairs, dressed in a black traveling suit. No one had ever been more beautiful in black, but he could not wait to spoil her with all the gowns and jewels and female accoutrements her loveliness deserved.

After a cordial round of farewells, Mark escorted Mina to the town coach he had rented for the afternoon. Leeson climbed into the bench beside the driver. Once the door closed and they were alone, Mark pulled Mina close against his side. All day he'd waited for this moment. The muscles along the sides of his stomach tautened in an awareness that extended into his groin.

"Lady Alexander." He pressed his lips to her temple. "I can't wait until we are alone tonight, in our stateroom, when I can pull all that luxurious hair from its pins."

Her dark eyes went limpid. "Mark . . ."

He lifted her chin and leaned down—

She drew back sharply, a distance in her eyes that hadn't been there before.

"What is it?" he asked.

"I must speak to you about something."

"Go on." He released her chin, but kept her close, within the possessive curl of his arm.

"Moments before the ceremony . . ."

"Yes?"

She swallowed. "The countess informed me you were marrying me only to punish her."

"She said that to you?" Anger stormed his cheeks, and his nostrils flared. "This morning? Just before we were married?"

He'd never suspected Lucinda to be so malicious.

"Is it true?" she asked solemnly. "I'm not going to cry or curse or hit you. I just need to know."

"No. It's not true. What is true is that she and I shared a flirtation last Season, before she was betrothed to Trafford. We kissed, but that is all."

She examined his face. "And that's all there is to her claim?"

"I swear it."

Mina reached out and touched her fingertips against the center of his chest. Her eyes went sultry. Grasping his tie, she pulled him close and kissed him full on the mouth, her lush lips staking their claim on his.

Turning her face slightly aside, she whispered, "What were you saying about tonight?"

All too soon they arrived at Cadogan Pier. The *Thais* gleamed in the sunlight, its hull freshly scraped and painted, and every brass and nickel-plated fixture polished to a brilliant shine. His newly acquired crew made ready on the deck. Mark led Mina along the boardwalk, taking pride in the way she easily walked the narrow gangplank, as if she'd done it a thousand times before. The new captain and ten crewmen, dressed in crisp white uniforms, awaited them. Introductions were made all down the row.

While Mina's trunks were being brought aboard, Mark took her on a brief tour of the ship. They began in the main saloon, an expansive room with emerald green walls, large mirrors, artwork and moldings.

"How many staterooms?" she asked.

"Outside of the crew's accommodations, there are six singles and four doubles. Enough to house fifteen to twenty guests."

"It's marvelous," Mina breathed. "I can't believe I'm here."

By way of interior stairs, he took her below deck to the master cabin.

"This can be your stateroom." Appointed in gold and white, the room, while intimate of scale, reeked of comfort and elegance. Two portals offered a view of the riverside scenery. "Or it can be . . . our stateroom."

Her brown eyes glowed in clear invitation. "Our stateroom, Mark. I didn't get married to have separate rooms."

He backed her against the wall, slid his fingertips into the thick hair along her nape and bent to kiss her. When she responded, he turned his face, deepening the intimacy. The other hand slid up her torso to cup her breast. She sighed and gave a small moan.

No doubt, at any moment, they'd be interrupted by a crew member delivering her trunks.

He pulled back, then placed one more kiss on her mouth. He ran his thumb over her damp lower lip. "I've been told there's champagne to enjoy up top as we make way."

Above deck, they watched from the rail as the *Thais* drifted away from the dock. Along the foreshore, two Thames River Police galleys dragged the river.

Mina frowned. "They are looking for the rest of that poor girl, aren't they?"

Mark nodded. On Sunday, just two days before, another of Elizabeth's thighs had been discovered within the ornamental railings of the private estate of Sir Percy Florence Shelley, the son of Mary Wollstonecraft Godwin Shelley—an author whose legacy included a dark piece of fiction about a creature fashioned from body parts stolen from corpses. The Dark Bride clearly had a morbid sense of humor.

Over the next two hours, they watched the Parliament buildings and Big Ben go by, as well as the Tower and all the rest of London's recognizable monuments. Behind them, a small table had been set between two high-backed deck chairs. The porter produced two crystal flutes and poured them half full of sparkling gold liquid before presenting them to Mark.

Mark handed one to Mina, and raised his in toast. "To this new adventure together."

Her brown eyes shone with anticipation. "Where are we going first?"

"I told you—that is your decision."

"Do you have maps?" She looked out over the water. "I'll decide by the time we leave the Thames."

Return to me. The voice exploded inside Mark's skull, and with it, a shattering explosion of pain. The air left his lungs.

The deck tilted. He seized the rail.

Mina looked up. The smile dropped from her lips. "Mark, what's wrong?"

He shook his head. "Nothing."

Nothing? the voice shrieked.

His champagne glass fell to the deck and shattered. Pain ripped through his brain and down into his spine, as if the poison in his head sought to invade the rest of his body. He legs weakened, and with all his strength he fought to stand.

"It's all right. Lean on me." Grasping his arm, she guided him to a chair. Leeson appeared and rushed forward to assist. Mina knelt beside him, pressing her palm to his face. To the porter, she said, "Could you please bring his lordship some water?"

Once the man rushed off, she said, "This has happened before, hasn't it? That night at the party. You are ill. Something you contracted on your travels? Is it malaria?"

Mark closed his eyes, unable to answer, or even nod. Already the next round of agony flayed his insides.

"You're so pale," Mina said worriedly. Concern lined her brow. "I'm going to take care of you."

Leeson hovered behind her, grim faced.

Mark pressed back into the chair, grinding his teeth against the pain.

You belong to me.

"It's getting worse, isn't it?" Leeson asked, but his words faded off.

Mark saw Mina speak his name, but he could no longer hear her voice for the scream inside his head.

Suddenly, the vessel jerked and vibrated. He felt the groan of the engines, up through the soles of his feet. The engines stopped, and the ship slowed.

A black plume of smoke poured out from the side of the ship.

Chapter Eleven

In the dim light of a solitary lamp, Mina bustled around her room at the Trafford house. She placed the leather bag that contained Mark's comb and his shaving articles on her dressing table. Admittedly, she had fantasized about his being here in her bed, but not under these circumstances—not stricken with some as of yet unnamed affliction. Thankfully, Trafford had escorted Lucinda and the girls out to a fete, so there had been no prying questions.

He lay on the bed, his hand pressed over his eyes. She proceeded to hang his coat in the dressing room. By the time the *Thais* had finally been towed into dock, it was already very late. For simplicity's sake Mina had instructed the driver to bring them here. There was no need to subject Mark to the ordeal of a hotel lobby and prying eyes.

"Stop busying about," he said from under the canopy. He lay in the shadows, watching her, propped on one elbow. "We're only staying one night. It's not like we're setting up house."

"I thought you'd fallen asleep," she responded.

"I have not."

He was so handsome, with his streaked hair messily tucked back over his ear. She'd always considered her bed to be inordinately large, but he lay diagonally across the mattress and his booted feet jutted off the end.

Mina sat on the edge of the mattress beside him. "Are you feeling better?"

"Embarrassingly so." He scowled. Clearly, he suffered a foul mood. She knew he was frustrated by the occurrence of his illness, and the delay to their trip. Perhaps his health condition had been one of the deep dark secrets he'd referred to in Trafford's study. But she'd meant her words—she would take care of him. He was her husband now.

She smiled. "I, for one, am glad the engine blew out. I know it will cost you a pretty penny to have repaired, but it's important that you see a doctor about these spells before we travel to an isolated area where there is no medical care to speak of."

He didn't respond. He frowned like a sullen boy.

"*Mark.*"

"All right. I'll see a doctor if it pleases you."

"It will please me. And afterward, we'll get back on the *Thais* and have our beautiful voyage. For now, it's late." She loosened and untied his necktie, feeling very wifely. "I know you've got to be exhausted. Let's get you to bed."

She unfastened the first button, the one over his throat, and revealed a triangle of firm, golden skin. She bit into her lower lip, and proceeded to the second button.

Abruptly Mark plucked *her* bodice, releasing the button at the center of her breasts. She looked down. The fabric gaped, revealing a glimpse of her linen corset cover, beneath.

"What are you doing?" she laughed softly. But of course . . . she knew.

"You need to go to bed too, don't you?" Dark mischief sparked in his eyes.

She unbuttoned his third. Mark plucked another of hers. His scowl lessened and he grew very intent on her bosom. Another volley of button plucking and both their garments hung open to the waist. Mina's breath came faster. Mark wasn't even touching her, but his intensity, his riveted, *hot* attention, awakened her still fully clothed body to every sensation . . . to the delicious abrasion of her chemise against her nipples, and the satin band of her stockings, tied round each thigh. Long, square-tipped fingers slipped beneath her chemise strap to caress the swells of flesh created by the stricture of her corset. Mina swayed toward him, dizzied by a feverish heat.

Mark knew Mina would be even more beautiful without her clothes than she was in them. She perched beside him, a mysterious gift, wrapped in layers and layers of fragrant, feminine packaging. He could not wait to divest her of every stitch. Every sinew in his body roared alive in anticipation of making love to her—*almost* drowning out the staggering realization that he was trapped in the city, a virtual prisoner of the Dark Bride. With a raging intensity, he wanted nothing more than to spiral into the mindless sensual oblivion of Mina's body. Hooking two fingers into the loveliest display of décolletage he had ever seen, he pulled her by the corset, down for a kiss.

Her mouth was soft, open and eager. Tilting his head, he deepened the kiss, his hunger ravenous and all consuming.

"I've wanted you . . . like this . . . from the start." Since the cemetery. Hell, since seeing her in that tiny drawing room in Manchester, six months before. That they should be together now felt something like destiny.

Taking her beneath the arms, he fell back onto the pillows, dragging her half on top of him. God, she was soft and lush—a willing, hazy-eyed beauty painted in black. Greedily, he thrust his fingers into the cool, smooth hair at her nape, and drew her down. He plundered her mouth, his thumb pressed against her full lower lip, more deter-

mined than ever to bind her to him, to have some measure of progress toward his ultimate goal.

"Mark . . . ," she whispered against his lips.

His fingers curled into the front of her corset. He
tugged the stiff fabric down. Freed from their confines,
her breasts spilled out. He paused in their kiss to boldly
glimpse down. They jutted, full and youthful, framed by
the constriction of her manipulated undergarments. Pink
raspberry nipples grazed his shirt.

"Do you know how beautiful you are, Mina?"

Seizing her by the torso, he lifted her and took one into
his mouth. He suckled, caressing the swollen peak with
three terse strokes of his tongue. She groaned and staved
her fingers through his hair.

"Mark . . . ," she breathed near his ear. "Are you sure
you're able?"

He rolled, caging her beneath him, reveling in the
crush of her breasts, so soft, against the hardness of his
chest. Braced on one arm, he plucked a pin from her hair.

"I want . . ."

He pulled another.

"My damn . . ."

And another.

"Wedding night."

He lowered himself for a kiss.

"Wait." She stiffened in his arms.

"No," he murmured, kissing her neck, tasting her skin
with his lips and tongue. "No more waiting."

She pressed the flats of her hands against his chest. She
forced his gaze to hers. Her eyes were shining; her smile,
dazed. "I have a special gown, just for tonight."

"That's not important." He was so hard, and so ready, he
could probably penetrate her through his damn trousers.

"It's important to me," she countered softly, sliding out
from under him. "I want things to be perfect. I don't think
you'll be disappointed."

She tugged her corset up to cover her breasts, but her bodice still sagged alluringly. He wanted to pounce.

He scowled, knowing he must be a gentler lover . . . at least tonight. "Very well."

"I'll be back."

"Hurry."

Her eyes sparkling, she disappeared into the darkened depths of the dressing room. Mark wrenched his shirt off his shoulders and tossed the garment to the chair. With his toe, he pried his boot off, and then the other. Collapsing back onto the bed, he closed his eyes and fended off thoughts of morbid reality, choosing instead to imagine how it would be, moments from now, deep inside his soft, welcoming wife.

How much time passed, he wasn't sure, but . . . something fluttered down against his bare skin. The scent of roses perfumed the air. Mark's eyes flew open—only to be covered by a swath of cool . . . dark . . . cloth. His necktie. The band tightened as unseen hands knotted the ends at the back of his head. She straddled him.

"Mina . . ."

"Shhhhhh." Her cool fingertip pressed against his lips, silencing him.

He did not probe the darkness, did not wish to see her with his mind. Rather he surrendered to the sensuality of her touch. Hands tore at the fastenings to his trousers. Aroused by her enthusiasm, he assisted her. Lips and hands pressed against his naked torso. Her tongue traced downward along the center of his chest, over his stomach.

Lower . . . lower . . .

Mark groaned and buried his hands in her hair.

Mina drew the brush once more through her unpinned hair. She doused the dressing room lamp and pushed the door open, thinking to find Mark on the bed just where she'd left him—handsome, smoldery-eyed and waiting to take up where they'd left off. But the room was dark, save for a shaft of moonlight streaming in through the open windows. Very romantic. After the disturbing events of the previous days, she'd been very fastidious in locking her windows, but she felt completely safe with Mark. The idea of making love to him on a bed strewn with moonlight held a definite appeal. She sniffed, detecting the fragrance of roses as well. Where would roses have come from?

A sound came from the bed—a groan.

"Mark?" she whispered.

He didn't answer. There was only the sound of movement . . . thrashing against the sheets.

Fear struck through her heart. What if he'd fallen ill again? She moved closer, her eyes adjusting to the darkness. The dark coverlet slid off the mattress to puddle onto the floor. In its absence were white sheets. Someone lay atop them, moving . . . writhing . . . becoming not one person, but two.

"Mina. *Darling*. Yes."

Shock jolted Mina through.

Could there be an *imposter* in her bed?

At the bedside table she struggled with the lamp, her hands shaking. At last, light streamed out. Mina stared at the bed. A blond woman, clad only in a thin chemise, crouched over her husband's—

"*Mark!*" Mina shrieked.

Lucinda threw back her head, flinging her hair in a brilliant arc. The sound of her guttural laughter filled the room. Mark stripped the band from his eyes.

His eyes widened, and his nostrils flared. He shoved her off. "*Lucinda.*"

The countess swung her face toward Mina and grinned. "I told you he was mine."

Like something out of a nightmare, her eyes rolled erratically in their sockets. Before Mina could even react to the impossibility of such a thing, Lucinda sprang, hurtling through the air, and slammed into her. Mina crashed backward. Her head struck the carpet.

She twisted—rolled and kicked—but still, her attacker clambered on top, straddling her shoulders, pinning her with extraordinary strength. Wiry, viselike hands seized Mina's throat—

Only to be wrenched off.

Mark dragged Lucinda away by the wrists. Mina scooted backward, retreating into the corner.

"You don't *touch* my wife," Mark seethed, his face a mask of fury.

"Ha! Your wife." Lucinda writhed and coiled like a snake, her legs and feet dragging and kicking. "Not for long. I'll cut her. I'll cut her to pieces."

With a curse, Mark hurled her against the wall. A framed oil crashed to the floor. Lucinda sagged, but she immediately sprang to life, bizarrely climbing up the wall on her hands and knees, to half crawl, half slither out the window. Mark leapt against the window frame, looking out. The muscles of his bare shoulders and back bunched with tension, and for a moment Mina expected him to leap out after Lucinda.

Instead he came to her.

"Mina." He crouched. "Are you hurt?"

Mina pressed back into the corner, flinching from his touch.

"Did she hurt you?" Mark demanded.

"Don't. Don't touch me. Please." Mina pushed his hand away.

She'd wedged herself against the corner as far as she could go. In the foray, the slender strap of her white satin gown had snapped. She clutched the garment in place over the swell of her breast. Dark tresses fell over her bare shoulders. God, he ached to touch her but . . . horror gleamed in her wide eyes, as if he were a huge arachnid with eight fuzzy jointed legs. Or worse, as if he were no different than one of the Dark Bride's bug-eyed fiends.

Of course . . . *his eyes*. They glowed bronze and his skin fluxed with heat, an effect of his turning, brought on by the skirmish with Lucinda. He would also be larger now, both in height and in muscled bulk. He again tried to touch her, to soothe her fear, but she raised her hands and arms defensively . . . fearfully . . . against him.

"I said *don't touch me*."

He backed away, his hands held level with his shoulders. His chest tightened, realizing the terror and disbelief she must be experiencing. This was not how he'd wanted her to learn the truth about him. "I won't hurt you, Mina. I would never hurt you."

Her thoughts screamed: *Betrayal. Fear. Loss.*

"What *are* you?" she demanded, her eyes filling with tears.

He was no longer "Mark" to her. He'd become a "what," not a "who." He turned from her, wanting to deny the revulsion in her eyes. She saw him as a monster, which of course, despite all his arrogance, wealth and power—was exactly what he was. He stared at the black blot of the window.

He considered rushing toward her and forcing his touch. Already, too much time had passed; soon, *lethe*, the power to make her forget, would become impossible. His colder, crueler self insisted he stand and accept her judgment, no matter the consequence. His duplicity revealed, he deserved no less than her scorn.

"You're one of them, aren't you?" The whispered question arose from the corner. "One of the beings my father sought to prove? An immortal."

He closed his eyes. "Yes."

Somehow, amidst all the turmoil and misery of the moment, he found relief in the confession.

"What is Lucinda?"

Like the toadies, Lucinda had been empty. She'd not given off any energy whatsoever, dark or light. Just . . . nothing. Was she the Dark Bride? He did not know. He turned from the window.

"Something worse. I've got to go after her, else she'll come back."

A tear streamed over her cheek.

"Go." She nodded, swiping it away. "*Go.*"

Mina jerked awake to stinging eyes and a sick heart. *Mark . . .*

For one hopeful moment, she told herself everything had been a nightmare. Of course it had been. There were no such thing as immortals, and Lucinda could not have—

Her eyes came into focus on the chair she'd wedged beneath the door handle. Slowly, she lifted the coverlet and discovered that yes—she'd slept in not one of her dressing gowns, but *two*, buttoned up tight to her neck. And her boots. Hearing a sound behind her, she froze. A low, masculine snore.

Rolling carefully so as not to shake the bed, she looked over her shoulder. Mark sprawled beside her, on his stomach . . . naked. One fist curled in the tangle of her hair. She could not help but wonder if the touch were purposeful or a simple coincidence of sharing a bed. How he'd gotten back inside the room, she didn't know. Her head thundered with memories of the night before.

There was so much she didn't know or understand.

The dim light revealed his shoulders, his back, his sculpted buttocks and legs. There were also faint tracings around his upper arms, his wrists and his ankles, healed scars. Just hours ago he'd been a glowing-eyed beast, but now . . . now he looked like a sleeping warrior angel. Which was the truth? Both, she suspected. Her father had told her of the ancient legends. Only then, she hadn't believed.

She ought to be amazed and out of her mind with delight at finding herself in the company of an immortal, something her mind still declared as wholly *impossible*. But she could find no pleasure within her fractured heart. She could only grieve the loss of the man she'd believed to be her husband. Her "safe place" had turned out to be the most dangerous choice of all—at least for her heart.

"Caught you looking," Mark growled sleepily, his blue eyes narrowed and smoldering. His arm snaked across her waist. Linen scooted under her buttocks and her shoulders as he dragged her across the sheet, underneath him, caging her within the prison of his arms and his legs. She pushed her hands to the bare skin of his chest. Heat and male scent enveloped her. God save her, but she felt every flex of every muscle . . . especially *that* muscle, long, hard and unapologetic against her stomach. Her body went to flames. His unsmiling face hovered above hers, so close that his hair brushed her cheek.

"Mina . . ." He drew the backs of his knuckles against her cheek . . . her throat . . .

She wanted to melt, to allow his touch, his kiss, his possession. But she couldn't. He sought to control her through desire. Certainly, he'd had plenty of practice with other women and even *other wives* throughout his existence. Her heart pounding, she shoved free—only, she knew, because he allowed it—and escaped from beneath the coverlet to stand on shaking legs beside the bed. Her mind imposed control.

"I'd rather assumed you wouldn't return."

"Why wouldn't I?" He clasped the blanket against his hip and rolled to his side. Lithe and muscular, he appeared a sensual, demanding emperor in her bed. His blue eyes blazed with heat. "You're not going to let a little thing like immortality come between us, are you? We *are* married, Mina."

"Don't say that," she hissed, her eyes widening. "We're not married. Not really."

Nostrils flaring, he pushed up onto one hand. The muscles on his abdomen lengthened and flexed. "Yes, we are."

Her mouth went dry as paper. She double- and triple-knotted the sash of her robe. "I married you under false pretense."

"What false pretense?"

"I was led to believe I was marrying *a man*," she retorted.

"I *am* a man." Danger lurked in the depths of his eyes. "I can prove it, too . . . if only you'll come back to bed."

Everything about him mesmerized her. The way he looked at her, the way he spoke her name. God save her, she burned for him.

"You stay *here*," she ordered.

She had to remove herself and fortify her defenses. She escaped into the dressing room, and silently—*frantically*—set about clothing herself. The memory of their passionate prelude to lovemaking the night before sent her blood scalding through her skin and her cheeks. She'd been nothing but strategy to him, strategy to get to her father and the scrolls. She didn't even know the man on the other side of her dressing room door. He was a stranger. She supposed she ought to be trembling—crying, destroyed and afraid. But over the past three months, she'd braced herself for anything. Even for this, it seemed. Once dressed, she took a moment to steel herself, before turning the handle. Emerging, she found him upright on the mattress, his arms crossed over his bent knees. The coverlet hung low across his naked hips. How was she supposed to think with him looking like that?

"Why didn't you dress?" she demanded sharply.

"You told me to stay here."

She indicated the dressing room. "In there, if you please."

"Someone's at the door." He cocked his head nonchalantly.

"I didn't hear anyone knock."

A knock sounded on the door.

Apparently he could see through wood . . . and probably through her clothes too.

She crossed her arms over her breasts. "Is it anyone I should be concerned about?"

A bizarre image sprang to mind, one of Lucinda waiting on the other side with spinning eyes and wild hair. Given the events of last night, she couldn't discount such a possibility.

A wry smile tugged his lip. "I believe it's coffee. While you were in there, I called down to the kitchen on the speaking tube. Damn convenient."

Mina wrenched the chair from underneath the handle and slowly opened the door. Just as Mark foretold, the upstairs maid held a silver tray, topped by a full coffee service. There was also a small platter of toast, bacon and sausages, which this morning, only served to offend Mina's stomach. The girl curtsied.

"Good morning and congratulations on your wedding, Lady Alexander. His lordship ordered coffee," the girl said. "I see you've already dressed. Would you be requiring my assistance with your hair? Perhaps his lordship would like a bath prepared?"

"No, but thank you, Jane." Taking the tray into her hands, Mina closed the door with the tip of her shoe. She set the tray on the escritoire.

"Are you hungry?" she asked blandly. Although she avoided his gaze, his eyes followed her every movement like twin beams of heat.

"No."

Perhaps he'd already eaten. Perhaps he'd eaten Lucinda.

"Mina . . . are you all right?"

"I'm fine."

He muttered a curse and arose from the bed, clasping the sheet at his hip. *"Mina."*

"What?" she answered, too sharply.

He closed the distance between them. The faint light coming in through the windows revealed every muscular cut and striation along his arms, his chest and stomach. Certainly, he realized his effect. Mina held her ground, refusing to retreat.

"I'm still me. I'm still Mark."

Her heart threatened to burst with all the emotion she sought to contain. At last, she met his eyes.

"Do you know that I never believed my father? Like everyone else, I thought him a fool in pursuit of a fool's quest." She gave out a rueful laugh. "But, my God, he was right to believe in the possibility of immortality. Just look. Here you are. You found me . . . you *married* me . . . because you wanted to get to those blasted scrolls."

"Yes," he said simply.

"Why?"

"My life depends on them."

"Your life? Your *immortal* life?"

"Yes, Mina." He nodded. "For centuries I have been a member of an order of immortals known as the Shadow Guard. Six months ago, while participating in the hunt for Jack the Ripper—"

"Jack the Ripper?" Mina gasped, covering her mouth with her hand.

"Yes," Mark answered. "In order to battle him on his own level, I entered into a deteriorative state known as Transcension. It's a slow, progressive disease of the mind, an affliction normally suffered by a small population of mortals."

"Mortals such as Jack the Ripper?"

"That's right."

"Oh, my God."

"The Guard hunts such souls, ending their mortal lives, and dispatching them to a secure underworld prison. I'm not a danger to you now, Mina. I swear it. But I don't know how long I've got before I change. Before I become one of the souls I once hunted."

His gaze held her. A frown turned his lips. Earnest. He looked so earnest. Yet his revelation terrified her.

"Your spells . . . they are a result of that deterioration?"

"That's right." He raked a hand through his hair. "Immortals such as I do not recover. But I will, Mina. I will. The scrolls contain the knowledge I need."

For a fleeting second, she saw desperation flicker behind the brilliant blue of his eyes.

Mina's mind blurred with the complexity of it all, trying to align prior knowledge and events with the present. She tried to sequence her questions into orderly and systematic categories, but one image haunted her: that of Lucinda, and her spinning *eyes*.

"How is Lucinda involved in all this?"

"I swear to you, I do not know." His blue eyes examined her face. "Our relationship was exactly as I explained it to you, no more and no less. Her appearance last night in this room was as much a shock to me as it was to you. I suspect, though, she was recruited by darker forces at work here in the city."

"Recruited? By . . . dark forces?" Mina raised a hand to her temple, feeling dizzy. "That sounds mad." But her mind presented all the peculiarities of the previous months, and suddenly, *dark forces* seemed a fully plausible explanation.

Mark shrugged. "There's a lot about the world that you probably don't wish to know about. Whether Lucinda was willing or merely a pawn to someone else, I cannot yet say, but I believe, in some way or another, she was selected because of her proximity to you. She was chosen to watch you. To find out what you knew about your father, and the scrolls."

Mina pressed a hand to her temple. "She's the one who gave me roses and destroyed my father's papers."

His cheeks tautened. "Roses? Destroyed papers? Mina, when did this occur?"

Mina pressed her lips together. She wasn't prepared to answer his questions. No. He should answer *her* questions.

"Is what happened to her . . . my fault? Would she have been left alone and . . . unrecruited if I had not come to live with the family? Did I bring her transformation on by my presence here?"

"I don't know," Mark answered. "Regardless, you can't blame yourself for the evil others do."

Mina shivered, remembering Lucinda's vicious hatred. "Did you find her last night, after you left?"

"Those things with the twirling eyes are . . . empty inside. They don't give off any emotions or thoughts, which makes them difficult to track." He shook his head, frowning. "I lost her out in the city."

A cold chill struck Mina through. "What if she's downstairs, even now, drinking tea and s-s-sliming marmalade on her toast, waiting for us to come downstairs?" Mina's stomach pitched. She pressed a hand over her lips. "What are we supposed to do? I just want to get out of this house."

Mark towered over her. "Let's go, then. I swear it, Mina, I am no enemy to you or your father. Tell me where he is. I implore you, as your husband."

"Stop saying that." She recoiled. "You're *not* my husband, and I can't."

"Why not?"

"My father is *dead*," she insisted.

Frustration showed in the flash of his eyes and the

tightness of his mouth. "There were only stones in that coffin."

Her eyes widened. "That was you in the crypt! You pulled my petticoat."

"I'd do it again too." He grasped her forearm. "And he's *not* dead."

She wrenched free. "*Well, he's dead to me.*"

"Why?"

"He told me to come back to London," she blurted. "To tell everyone he'd died on the mountain. I told him no. Whatever the danger, we needed to remain together. But he left me, Mark. He left me alone on that mountain in that damn whispering fog, and I don't know where he's gone."

Someone screamed. Mina froze.

More screaming . . . two voices now. The shrillness of the sound sent gooseflesh down the backs of her neck and arms.

Mark said, "It's coming from outside."

She rushed to the window and drew the curtain aside just in time to see Evangeline and Astrid race toward the house. Both looked over their shoulders in the direction of the garden fountain.

The fountain.

Mina's eyes riveted upon it. Pink water sloshed in the lower basin, and something bobbed on the surface.

A woman's headless body, clad only in thin linen.

She felt Mark beside her, felt his power and his heat.

"Hell," he said. "That's Lucinda."

Chapter Twelve

Mark followed Mina through the cadre of uniformed officers, his arm extended alongside her to prevent her from being jostled. Farther down the hall, Trafford's study was shut up as tightly as a crypt.

"This way, my lady, if you please." Assistant Commissioner Anderson of the Metropolitan Police extended his hand toward the yellow drawing room. After they entered, he followed them in and pulled the polished doors closed. Overnight, the sunshine yellow walls and draperies and upholstered furniture appeared to have taken on a garish hue.

Anderson held out a guiding hand, indicating an arrangement of chairs near the windows. Out toward the street, Mark glimpsed the row of police wagons, and a sidewalk already thick with bobbing black top hats and bowlers, the gathering curious. "Lord and Lady Alexander, thank you for your patience. It was, of course, important that we speak first to Lady Astrid and Lady Evangeline, who first discovered the body, as well as the unfortunate Lord Trafford."

Mark lifted an assuring hand. "It's quite all right."

What a lie. A goddamn lie. Mark wasn't quite all right. From the moment Lucinda's headless body had been discovered in the fountain, the house had deteriorated into a state of hysteria. Mina had veered between two incoherent, sobbing girls to a trembling, white-faced Lord Trafford, who had just returned from his morning ride on the Row when his wife's body was discovered.

Mark, for his part, had gone outside with a bedsheet and covered the countess's corpse and bobbing, severed head from the wide-eyed servants who gaped from the upstairs windows. Peculiarly, her body appeared—and *smelled*—as if she had been dead for weeks.

Next he'd summoned the authorities, because, damn it, he had no other choice, given the flamboyant disposal of her body. In the midst of all the madness, he hadn't had a moment to speak to Mina alone.

So it wasn't with the highest degree of confidence that he went into this interview with the *bloody* assistant commissioner of the *bloody* CID, knowing his wife might very well point to him as a *bloody* murderer. Since they'd left their room above the garden, she had not once met his gaze, and her internal thoughts had remained tellingly shuttered, as if she were afraid to trust anyone, most especially him.

Anderson instructed gently, "Please, please sit. I know all this must be exceedingly distressing, especially for her ladyship."

Mina nodded, her cheeks devoid of their usual vibrant color. "Thank you."

She lowered herself into an armchair. Her hands twisted around a linen handkerchief on her lap.

Mark situated himself behind her, his hand rested on the top of the curved chair back. "I prefer to stand, if it's all right."

The commissioner nodded. He too remained on his feet. "As I previously introduced myself in the hallway,

I am Robert Anderson, Assistant Commissioner of the Criminal Investigation Department, Scotland Yard. While I do not customarily participate in actual day-to-day police investigations, due to the rather high profile of this most tragic and disturbing death, I felt it necessary to involve myself on a more personal level. As you are both likely aware from reading the papers, there have been a number of unpleasant discoveries along the Thames over the previous week. Because of the . . . uncommon violence of Lady Trafford's death, we must be absolutely certain the two incidents are in no way related."

It was no surprise that Anderson would take a special interest in Lucinda's murder. His predecessor, Sir Charles Warren, had been forced to resign his post after having lost the confidence of the city's public for his handling of the investigation into Jack the Ripper's killings. Certainly Anderson had no wish for a similar murderer to run rampant on his watch.

The assistant commissioner spread his hands graciously. "That said, I hope you understand that this interview in no way implies you are under suspicion. Indeed, at this time we are not even certain we're dealing with a murder—and I shall explain that comment in just a moment. But in order to make an educated determination, we must speak with everyone present last night on the premises." Anderson crossed his arms. "It is my understanding the two of you were married only yesterday."

Mina nodded. "Yes, Commissioner, that is true."

Mark's gaze settled on the dark, glossy crown of Mina's head. At some point in the night she'd removed his mother's ring, something that wounded him more deeply than he might have expected.

Anderson continued. "Please accept my congratulations on your nuptials, but also my sympathies that such a happy occasion has been darkened by this morning's terrible discovery."

"Thank you," Mina responded softly.

Anderson had a polished, quiet way about him, but keenly observant eyes. No doubt the commissioner would make note of their every facial expression and telltale gesture. He would perceive the slightest inflection of their voices, and seek to translate any clues, no matter how slight, to attempt to discover the truth behind Lucinda's death.

"Now, if you could please share with me . . ." The commissioner's voice softened. "When did the both of you last see her ladyship alive?"

Mark answered, "Yesterday, at our wedding. It was a small, private affair—just family—here at the house."

Mina nodded. "We had luncheon after the ceremony, and then we departed on our . . . on our honeymoon." Her voice went husky on pronouncing the final word. Mark flinched inside. He could not—and would not—change how ruthlessly he'd pursued her, but he regretted the pain he'd caused her.

"Did everything seem well with Lady Trafford then?"

"Yes," answered Mark.

Mina nodded.

"No trouble between her and his lordship?"

"None at all," she responded.

Anderson's eyes narrowed. "Neither of you has heard any whispers of . . . gambling debts?"

"No."

"Infidelities?"

"No, sir," they answered in unison.

Commissioner Anderson picked up his notes from the mahogany sideboard and quickly scoured them. "I understand that, as you've just shared, the two of you set off on your honeymoon voyage yesterday, on board Lord Alexander's yacht—and actually, I know that to be true because your departure and pictures were in the papers this morning."

From beneath his notebook he produced a newspaper,

folded to frame several photographs. Anderson handed Mina the paper. Mark looked down over her shoulder. The photographer had captured her face at its most lovely and optimistic. The shadow of his hat obscured his face.

Anderson continued. "Obviously, as you got under way, some sort of mishap forced you to abandon your plans and return here to the house."

Mark supplied, "One of the ship's engines blew out."

Anderson scratched out a few lines. "What time did you arrive?"

"It was very late before the yacht was finally towed into dock," answered Mark. "We did not return to the house until perhaps . . . one o'clock in the morning?"

"Thereabouts," confirmed Mina quietly, "although I cannot specifically claim to have made note of the time."

"Upon your return, did you visit with Lord Trafford or her ladyship? Either of their daughters?"

"They had not yet returned home from their evening engagement." Mark rested his hand on the back of the chair. "We were greeted only by servants. My wife and I retired directly for the night."

"I am told your window overlooked the courtyard. Did either of you hear any peculiar noises in the night that might have indicated either violence or the disposal of a body?"

They shook their heads.

The commissioner rubbed his chin. "And did either of you leave your room at any time during the night? For a celebratory bottle of wine? A late-night trip to the kitchen? Anything?"

"Sir, if I may say something," said Mina.

Mark tensed, steeling himself for what she might say.

Commissioner Anderson nodded. "Of course, my lady. Please speak freely."

Mina's expression, though solemn, appeared utterly placid. Her gaze did not waver from the commissioner's.

"Last night was our wedding night. I'm sure you'll understand, when I say most emphatically, that my husband and I were together all night, and, for reasons you must surely understand, we were neither aware of anything going on outside our room, nor did we emerge until this morning when we heard the obvious sounds of the disturbance outside."

Did Mark imagine things, or did Anderson actually blush? Hell, he felt a similar warmth in his own cheeks, but one inspired by hopeful pleasure. Perhaps things with Mina weren't irreparably damaged.

Anderson tilted his head and raised his eyebrows to Mark in silent congratulation. He issued a raspy chuckle. "On that note, I believe our interview is concluded. Has either of you any questions?"

Curious, Mark inquired, "You mentioned a moment ago that you weren't sure the countess's death was a murder. I saw the body shortly after its discovery. What did you mean by that?"

Anderson pressed his lips together. "This is such a peculiar case. . . ."

He glanced considerately toward Mina.

"Please speak candidly," she encouraged quietly.

"Well . . ." Anderson's brow furrowed. "From the *condition* of her body, it appears she's been dead for quite some time."

Mina responded, "But we all saw her yesterday. She was the picture of health."

He nodded. "Dr. Bond, the police surgeon, will have to examine the body, of course, but I must say . . . given a lack of explanation or motive for a murder and the deteriorated condition of her ladyship's body, I'm starting to believe that what we have on our hands here is some sort of rare deteriorative disease. It's almost as if the bone and flesh of her neck had . . . *melted* away."

Mina coughed into her handkerchief.

Mark's eyes widened. "You think a . . . disease made her head fall off?"

Anderson nodded. "Have you ever seen chickens or geese that suffer from limp neck disease?" He twirled his index finger in the direction of his neck. "Perhaps this is some extreme human mutation of a similar nature." He crossed his arms and stroked his chin. "It's a frightful possibility, but certainly not contagious, else we'd have heard of other instances of similar deaths."

Mark assisted Mina up from the chair. "My wife and I had planned to leave the Trafford household today. Is that still possible?"

Anderson pulled a card from his vest pocket and extended it to Mark. "The less civilian traffic we've got here to muddy up the evidence, the better. We've asked Lord Trafford to retain only a minimal staff until then as well. Just send word to my office once you're settled elsewhere, in the event we must contact you for additional questioning."

There would be no evidence to muddy. Not a trace. Just a stinking, headless Lucinda. She had been beheaded elsewhere by an Amaranthine silver blade, and her deteriorating corpse purposefully deposited on the grounds. No doubt, it was his twin's skillful work.

Mina arose from the chair. "Thank you, Commissioner."

An hour later, after Mina had said her good-byes to the family, two officers pushed back a crush of onlookers who had gathered to gawk on the sidewalk in front of the house.

"Back away," one shouted. "Give room. Give room."

Of a sudden, Mina halted on the steps and stared into the crowd. Mark bent low, bringing his arm protectively around her shoulder.

"What is it?"

The slight touch against her elbow granted Mark a vision of a man—a handsome, dark-haired man with furious green eyes.

Mina's shoulders drew together, a slight but stinging rejection of his touch, and she continued toward the carriage. Mark peered over the crowd to see a tall, broad-shouldered man in a dark suit and top hat striding away. It took him a moment to identify as jealousy the sick, cold-water-in-the-veins sensation he experienced. Unnerved, he followed her into the vehicle and sank onto the squab opposite from her. Although tempted to demand she identify the man and his relationship to her, Mark shunned the role of jealous lover and spoke the second foremost question on his mind.

"Why did you tell the inspector we were together all of last night?"

She looked out the window. Soon the carriage rocked with movement, and the jumbled wall of faces disappeared. "You didn't kill Lucinda. You told me you lost her in the city. Unless you lied to me."

"No, I didn't."

"Who did kill her?"

"I have my suspicions."

"There are more of you out there, aren't there? More . . . immortals?"

"Yes."

"How many?"

He shrugged. "Not as many as there used to be. Most remain within the protected boundaries of the Inner Realm."

"The Inner Realm . . . ," she whispered.

"Another dimension of existence, here on Earth. It's beautiful there."

Looking weary, she pressed gloved fingertips to her temple. "But you are here, in this dimension, to . . . hunt souls? What did you call them before?"

"Transcending souls. Yes. Evil souls. Wicked souls. Dangerous mortals who deserve nothing less that an eternal death."

She gave him a level stare. "And if you don't find the scrolls . . ."

"That's right." He nodded. "I'll eventually become one of them. But that's not going to happen, because—"

"You shall have your wish," she interrupted quietly.

"What wish is that?" His wish, at the moment, was that she'd look at him the way she had before. Not in the cool, distant manner in which she presently considered him. Her dark, demure clothing taunted him, hiding the precise combination of pale skin and feminine curves he'd come to crave. In these close confines, her delicate fragrance teased his nostrils, taunted that he could only look, and not touch.

She reached up and repinned her hat. "I have no idea where my father is, but . . . I'm sure with you as enticement, he'll eventually make an appearance. Me, dangled by my toes above a fiery pit? No." She giggled, low in her throat, though no humor lit her brown eyes. "But you, yes. Never fear. I'm sure it's just a matter of time."

"And then what? Once we find him?"

She folded her hands atop her lap. "The two of you can both go off and do whatever you wish. Read scrolls. Recover artifacts. Save the world through your shared knowledge. Mutually admire one another. I don't care. Just so you both . . ."

"Mina—"

She shook her head, an indication she didn't want to hear anything he might have to say. "Just so you both leave me alone."

He stiffened and closed his eyes. "No."

"I've had quite enough adventure for one life, thank you, and I'm done with it. I didn't ask for this. For *you*. I just want . . . yes, a life. A dull, little happy life."

"I won't leave you alone," he answered harshly. "I married you yesterday."

A sudden rush of moisture brightened her eyes. "Don't say that."

Mark could only feel relief at seeing her tears—relief that she felt *something* for him, even if that something were misery. With an irritated frown, she blinked them away and jabbed a gloved fingertip at the corner of her eye. "Oh, drat, you've made me cry. I'm not the sort of woman who cries."

"Then why are you crying?"

"Just don't even look at me."

Mark sat rigid on the bench, his shoulders back and his hat in his hands. "You've every right to be angry, Mina. I lied to you."

"You misunderstand." She focused on the ceiling of the cab, just above his head. But then her gaze fell to his. "I'm not angry. How can I be? I've told my share of lies, so how can I issue judgment upon you for doing the same thing? I realize you wouldn't have made all this outlandish effort to get close to me unless the scrolls were very important to you."

"Then why won't you let me close?"

She exhaled and took several deep breaths. "Please understand that while I'm very . . . impressed by you"— she offered him a miserable, fractured smile—"dazzled even . . . but . . ."

"What, Mina?"

A solitary tear trickled over her cheek. "I lost my husband last night."

"No, you didn't." He lunged across the cab to sit beside her, so close his thigh crushed firm against hers, through silk and petticoats. His hat, discarded, fell to the floor. He raised his hand to obliterate the tear, to make it go away.

"*Don't.*" She jerked her face away, and with a push of her slender arms, fled to the other side, taking the space he'd just abandoned. Her black skirts twisted like a dark mermaid's tail around her legs.

He could make this right, make their time together enough.

"I don't deny it, Mina—I pursued you to get to your father. But I chose to marry you," he insisted, angry that even at this proximity, she slipped from his grasp. "Because I *want* to be married to you."

"But I don't want to be married to *you*," she insisted, her eyes wide and glazed over. "Not now. Not anymore."

Mark's windpipe tightened. Centuries-old memories tore like claws through his chest.

She whispered, "I want children. I want a husband I can grow old with. I want tombstones side by side that say 'Beloved Wife' and 'Beloved Husband.' Can you give me that, Mark? You might be immortal, but you can't give me forever. Not the sort of forever I want."

He stared at her. He could give her protection. Wealth. Sensual pleasure. But no . . . he could not give her the kind of forever she spoke of.

"So yes, Mark, do you see . . . I did lose my husband last night." Her dark, spiky-damp lashes lowered against her pale cheeks. "And I've been left with you instead."

Left with you instead. Her choice of words wounded too deeply. Mark's defenses came up in the form of a simmering rage in the pit of his stomach. It wasn't the first time in his life he'd been told he wasn't important enough, wasn't worth the trouble of loving. His own mother had chosen death to be with her lover over him. It had made no difference to a ten-year-old boy that the man had been his father. He'd spent his immortal existence working to smother the memory, and the pain. He'd found satisfaction in the arms of an endless blur of women—queens, courtesans and famed beauties—but he'd always, *always* left them with his heart entirely and coldly intact, to prove it was *he* who made the choice to leave. He'd be damned if he'd allow Willomina Limpett, a professor's daughter, to cast him off.

Mina watched the change in Mark's face, and for the first time, truly feared him. The gentleness left his features. His cheekbones and jaw took on taut, hard edges. His eyes cooled to a glittering, azure blue. Had her words struck so deep? Could it be possible that he cared more deeply than she imagined? How, when she could be no more than a blur in the passage of time for him?

The carriage turned, traveling in a brief half arc. Their bodies swayed with the movement. Mina blinked away the wetness in her eyes and glanced out the curtained window. She'd been so focused on their conflict, she wasn't aware of their exact location, but they appeared to be somewhere off the Strand, near the Thames Embankment. The vehicle rumbled to a stop in the shaded forecourt of a towering structure, concealed by scaffolding and heavy canvas drapes. Gray stone peeked from beneath. Exterior gardens and walkways appeared very new, as if they'd only recently been installed.

"Where are we?" she asked warily, imagining the place to be abandoned. But just then, a doorman, dressed in a pristine black suit, hat and gloves, strode out from the entrance.

"The Savoy Hotel," Mark answered coolly. "We'll stay here a few days until the house is ready."

"You have a house?" She'd believed the *Thais* to be his only residence.

"*We* have a house."

Her heart turned over, hearing his emphasis on the word. She quietly restated her previous decision. "I just told you, Mark. There is no 'we.'"

The door opened. Mark took up his hat from the floorboard and climbed out. Without looking at her, he extended his gloved hand to her. She stared out from the interior, and for a moment considered refusing to join him.

His nostrils flared, and his eyes narrowed. "You can walk in . . . or I can carry you in."

Mina's heartbeat quickened, and her scalp drew tight. Obviously the battle between them had only just begun, and she didn't doubt for one second that he would do as he threatened; the promise was there in his eyes. Without funds, she didn't have any other options but to return to the Trafford house, and she certainly had no wish to return there. Admittedly, she felt safe under Mark's protection—safe from everyone but him.

She gripped the silver chain strap of her purse and stepped onto the stair, firmly resting her hand atop his. Tilting her face upward in assessment of the building, she queried, "The hotel isn't even open yet, is it?"

Additional hotel attendants appeared, all moving in the direction of the wagon that held their trunks. The doorman barked out orders.

"Soon," Mark growled. He assisted her down until she stood beside him. His shadow swallowed her. He seemed to have grown taller. Bigger. More dangerous.

The idea of being in such a large building, alone with him, unnerved her. "Then why are we here?"

His brilliant blue gaze swept over her, unnervingly rapacious. "Because here, no one will hear you scream."

His hand open and firm on the small of her back, he led her up the walk. She had to lengthen stride just to keep up.

Heat stung her cheeks. "That's not funny."

Pulling open the narrow door, he held the panel with the flat of his back. He watched her predatorily as she walked through.

"I wasn't attempting to amuse."

To her relief, the interior of the Savoy did not consist of scaffolding or piles of construction rubbish. Together, she and Mark traveled over a sea of black-and-white tile. Everything smelled rich and new. Thick wood columns supported the high ceiling, which was highly carved and decorated with classical scenes in some places, and painted with murals in others. Shaded electric fixtures provided the ideal amount of ambient light. Most interesting, though, was the row of ten men in dress frock coats standing shoulder to shoulder, their hands at their sides, obviously awaiting them. A short-statured, bearded gentleman stepped out from the rest and rushed forward with open hands.

"Lord Alexander." He grinned slyly. "How thrilled I was to receive your note."

Mark nodded curtly, his expression no less treacherous than before. To Mina, he said, "This is Mr. Richard D'Oyly Carte, manager of the Savoy Theatre, and hotelier extraordinaire." Tilting his face toward the spry gentleman, he continued. "D'Oyly Carte, please allow me to introduce . . . my *wife*."

The man didn't seem concerned at all that Mark had growled the last two words. Rather, he beamed with pleasure and, wide-eyed and openmouthed, assessed Mina with as much enthusiasm as if she were the Venus de Milo come to life. She blushed at the intensity of his admiration, but she suspected he was well schooled in the art of paying court.

"A pleasure, Lady Alexander," D'Oyly Carte gushed, clicking his heels and bowing deeply. He extended a hand, and after she placed hers within it, he lowered his head to press a kiss to the back of her glove. "What a delightful surprise it was to learn that our favorite financier had married. No one was more shocked than I to see the news in the papers this morning. Seeing you, I can certainly understand his lordship's decision to end his glorious run at bachelorhood. Curse your ship's engine for giving out, but clearly you were intended to spend your honeymoon here at the Savoy." He beamed. "I, myself, can think of no grander location."

Given his cheerful demeanor, Mina concluded he did not yet know of the murder that would be in all the same papers the next morning. How *did* one share news of a murder? Of someone's head getting cut off? She decided to defer to Mark on that matter.

He said nothing.

"We'll be here for two or three nights only, until our residence is prepared." He frowned at the line of men, who still stood a few feet away, like a row of frozen, smiling penguins. "What is all this?"

D'Oyly Carte glanced backward. "We used you for practice. I had the doorman watch for you as if you were the Prince Regent himself. One press of the royalty buzzer and we all scrambled into place." He smiled proudly. "Don't they look exceedingly smart? We must be prepared. It's only a matter of time before His Grace strolls through that door."

Leading them forward, D'Oyly Carte introduced each staff member by name and position, and dismissed them to go on about their duties.

Mark asked, "Have we got César Ritz on board as manager yet?"

"He insists he's not interested, sir, but"—the hotelier winked—"your letter appears to have worked magic. He's agreed to come for the grand opening."

"He'll stay." Mark flashed a tight grin. "Have you a key for me?"

D'Oyly Carte fished a tagged key from his coat pocket and handed it over. Riveted, Mina watched the transfer. Mark curled his fist around it.

"Do you recall how to use the lift, your lordship, or should I call an operator?"

"I remember."

Without further pleasantries, Mark led Mina toward a wide row of descending stairs.

She licked her bottom lip, feeling like a gazelle being

dragged off to be mauled by a ravenous lion. She supposed she could throw herself on D'Oyly Carte's mercy, but given his apparent adoration of her "husband," she imagined he would only call in a crew of jacketed assistants to help in her abduction. She conceded also, at the heart of her concern, was that she did not trust herself alone with Mark. Her rational self panicked at the thought of leaving the safety of others—but her adventurous self was undeniably curious about what would come next.

A handful of stairs down, and they arrived in a grand entrance hall. Open elevator doors revealed the most wickedly extravagant ascending room Mina had ever seen, adorned wall-to-wall with red lacquered panels and accented by gold scrollwork. A sort of giddy panic shattered her pulse. Mark stood to the side, silent and watching . . . waiting for her to enter.

"That key is for a suite, is it not? I won't go up unless we have two rooms," she insisted quietly. "Separate sleeping quarters."

Even now, memories of his naked body, sprawled across pale sheets, assailed her.

Mark shrugged. "There is no shortage of rooms."

Mina nodded. She bolstered her courage, and marched in, taking a place against the back wall. He followed her inside. The door closed smoothly behind him, outlining him in crimson.

"But I didn't marry you to sleep in separate beds."

Chapter Thirteen

Her eyes flew wide.

"You're not *listening*," she insisted, in a firm, strong voice. "It's finished, Mark. This farce of a marriage is over."

"To new beginnings, then." His eyes held dark, wicked promise.

The gentle hiss of hydraulics sounded, and an upward pressure beneath her soles announced their ascension. She was trapped—trapped inside four iniquitous, scarlet walls with the most beautiful, tempting man she'd ever known.

"Come here."

"No."

But she *wanted* to. Like a flower, the entire front surface of her body awakened to him, as if he were a bright, sensual sun. She swayed backward, pressing her shoulders to the paneled wall as if by that mere effort, she could anchor herself from throwing herself into his arms. Because, curse her, she *wanted* to feel him pressed against her. She *wanted* to kiss him and see him naked—every last bit of him. She wanted to experience all his spectacular heat, and his strength and fiery desire.

She flung her purse at the center of his chest. "Blast you."

His eyes went blank, and his lips flattened.

She clasped her hands over her face. "Please. Don't do this. You're making me so miserable."

His footfall came against the carpet, and then a darkening as his shadow fell over her.

No . . . no . . . no . . .

Large, warm hands covered hers . . . tilting her face up, almost rough in their handling. The spice of his skin filled her nose.

"Don't you see? I can't stop myself," he rasped.

Between the triangular frame of their joined hands, his lips descended onto hers. Mina kept her eyes shut. It was easier that way, to pretend the moment wasn't real, that this was all some dark, forbidden fantasy.

Oh, yes, please. More.

Her lips parted on a gasp. His mouth slanted, and he deepened the kiss. His tongue moved over her lips and teeth in a hot, possessive caress. Everything inside her ached—rejoiced. Like a secret key, his words and his kiss unlocked her resistance, and her heart.

He'd hurt her.

She twisted away, pressing her feverish forehead against the cool panel. His arms, his shoulders folded around her, a smothering, perfect prison. Wet, hot kisses fell on her neck. The friction of his mouth and the faint morning growth of his beard wrought a seduction of their own, sending a swirling heat down through her chest, into her breasts and nipples. His tongue teased her skin, her nape and her earlobes. Instinctively, she pressed her buttocks against his groin. He slid the swollen ridge against her and let out a low growl. Mina's eyes rolled in pleasure.

Trapped between Mark and the scarlet wall, Mina moaned, hating him and loving his touch all at once. His

size and power overwhelmed her. The scent of his skin
and his breath filled her nostrils and her mouth, intoxi-
cating her. The achy, heavy spot between her legs grew
heated and damp.

He captured her wrists and pressed them on either side
of her head, against the lacquer. Deliciously, his hands
moved in tandem, down her arms, over her breasts in a
knowing, circular massage, through black silk and corset.
Skin hissed against silk. The sounds of their quick, mu-
tual breaths blended into a secret, elemental song. Long
fingers slid the top three of her bodice buttons through
their holes, and his hand deftly slipped inside to squeeze
one swollen, aching breast.

"I think . . . ," she rasped.

"You think what?" he murmured against her neck.

"I think I hate you."

She meant the words too. And, of course, she did not
mean them at all.

Again, by her wrists, he forced her around and with
the pressure of his body, his chest and his knee between
her thighs, fixed her to the wall.

"I can live with that." His taut features, haloed in
scarlet, filled her vision. The rest was sensation: cool
air against her stockinged ankles; his breath, warm and
sharp, against her exposed upper breast. He hooked his
hips against her, boldly presenting his arousal against her
thigh. She arched, matching her body against his, aching . . . wanting.

His hand cupped her face.

"Don't cry. Don't cry, sweetheart." His thumb brushed
through tears she hadn't realized she shed. "Let me love
you. I'll make things right."

He bent, dragging his lower lip against hers in a teasing, openmouthed invitation. She moved forward, accepting. His fingers scored into her hair, dislodging her hat.

She didn't feel the lift stop. She only heard the slide of

the door. And then . . . his arms were around her, lifting her off the floor, against the rigid wall of his chest.

The world spun into fragmented visions of a paneled ceiling . . . a long hallway of doors . . . and dim, electric light. He carried her like a medieval war prize, and oh, she allowed it; even liked it. She ought to be ashamed at falling so easily. But they were alone here, and there was no one to see; no one to chastise her for how wicked she'd become in the arms of an immortal who was not her husband, not really, despite all the vows and the clergy and the papers.

He unlocked the door, taking them inside a large, clean-smelling room. A blur of blue and cream and rococo. He set her to her feet, and she wandered a few steps on legs so shaky, she could barely stand. Late-afternoon light streamed through elegant red and white blinds. His arms came around her waist, and he deftly unfastened the final three buttons of her bodice, nudging her farther into the sitting room. Tugging at her cuffs, he slid the jacket off by its sleeves, and dropped the garment to the floor. Cool air kissed her shoulders, but her back burned with the press of his shirtfront. Again, his mouth found *that* place on her neck, and she turned into melted wax. She felt dazed . . . delightfully mauled. A tug at the back of her waistband, and her skirt gave way.

He suddenly pulled away. She heard the brush of fabric against skin. She glimpsed back. He tore the necktie from his throat. His expression was stark, and his cheeks hollowed by passion. His eyes, riveted on her, promised far more than the intimacies they'd shared in the lift.

Lost. You are lost, Mina. A slave to misery, unless you stop him now.

"Wait . . . ," she whispered, holding up a hand and wobbling backward.

"No."

He stalked her, dropping his coat to the floor. A skillful

manipulation of the buttons at the front of his shirt revealed firm, vital skin between gaping linen. She clenched
her fist at her hip, into her skirt, suspending the garment
in place.

"I want to *talk* some more first. Can't we talk? Please,
Mark?"

"Talking always messes things up." He tilted his head.
The edge of his lip jerked up. "Let's never talk again.
Starting now."

She laughed—a sharp-pitched trill that didn't sound
like her at all. Mark was so funny when he wished to be.
Funny and frightening and beautiful.

Her mind shrieked out that she had only one weapon
at her disposal, one distraction worthy of throwing him
off his current path of seduction, one that she alone was
powerless to stop.

"Do you . . . truly want me?" she panted between
parched, tender lips.

Releasing her grip on her skirt, she shoved the waistband down around her knees and stepped out from the
middle of the silken puddle. Standing in corsets, chemise
and petticoats, she backed toward the center of the room.

"Oh, yes." He followed her. His smile widened, lecherous and attractive all at once. "I truly . . . truly want
you."

She grinned. "I think I've got something you might
want more."

The backs of her legs bumped against something. Off
balance, she twisted to take a step, but fell onto her stomach across a large, rectangular ottoman. So like a little
bed. How convenient.

How *inconvenient*.

She scrambled, crawling on hands and knees. A large
hand closed on her ankle and dragged her back.

"Oh—" Her stomach, her breasts crushed against the
striped brocade.

Thud. Him, on his knees behind her. His hands crept up her legs, over her calves and the backs of her linen-covered thighs. He squeezed her buttocks with both hands.

"There's nothing—*nothing* I want more."

Mina twisted to her back, then propped on both elbows.

"Look under my petticoat," she gasped.

"Oh, yes, sweetheart." He chuckled wickedly, sliding his hands underneath, up her stockings. "I want to look under your petticoat."

"No, Mark," she breathed, desperate to make him understand, before she begged him not to stop all the wonderful things he was doing with his hands. She stiffened, as his squared fingertips brushed over the bands of her stockings, and higher, across the bare flesh of her inner thigh. Her back arched off the cushion "I mean *look*. Look under my petticoat."

His eyes met hers, glazed. He gripped the bottom lace edge of her top petticoat. Like most ladies, she wore two. His head disappeared under the quilted ecru linen.

"The bottom one," she instructed breathlessly. "Do you see?"

"Yes."

For a long moment, he didn't move.

She felt a yank, and felt the drag of her linen drawers down her legs.

"What are you doing?" she whispered, alarmed.

Hands gripped the tops of her thighs. Two thumbs dragged heavily along her damp center seam. Her body exploded with pleasure.

"I think that's obvious," came his muffled reply. Firm pressure coaxed her thighs apart, and the bump that was his head underneath her petticoat, dipped low.

Her hands twisted in the linen on either side of his head.

"But—but—it's Akkadian, Mark." Her head fell back at the first bold stroke of his tongue—an erotic and comical moment all at once. She laughed ruefully. "I—I—copied one of the—" He went deeper. She writhed. "*Oh, my God. I copied one of the scrolls onto my petticoat. Don't you see?"*

"Thank you," he murmured, his breath feathering against her most sensitive flesh. "Thank you, sweetheart, but it's too late. I can't stop. Right now, I want you more."

Mark sensed her surrender in the sudden pliancy of her thighs. They no longer clasped his head in a vise. Not that he'd minded, of course. But in that moment he realized something greater than sensual pleasure: He needed her. He needed to be close to her, to lose himself in her brilliance, if only for the night, and no one else would do.

"Shouldn't we go to the bedroom?" she whispered, breathless. "It's so bright here. The blinds are open."

He tore his shirt over his head, craving the crush of lace and corset boning and her soft skin against his bare chest. "No, this is perfect."

Besides, he couldn't risk losing her somewhere between there and here. A sensual urgency he hadn't felt in centuries—since he was a mortal man—ordered him to hurry. He pushed her petticoats up, hitching them above her oh-so-sleek thighs and buttocks. Yes, he'd intended to be more gentle, more romantic, but he couldn't wait. His sex lengthened. He groaned at the exquisite surge of blood. The hot, swollen tip edged above his waistband. He unbuttoned his trousers with one hand and gasped with relief as the swollen flesh fell heavy, against her thigh.

Her eyes widened, and her tongue darted out to

dampen her lower lip. "Yes, Mark . . . before I change my mind."

He rubbed his thumb along her pink, glistening center, spreading her. Grasping himself, he slid against her a few times, up and down, not entering, but then he full-on prodded. Ah, good. Such sensation . . . damp, tight heat, closing around him. An erotic first kiss.

"Now . . . ," she urged softly, lifting her hips. She stroked his chest and drew her nails along the tightly drawn muscles of his lower stomach. "Come inside me."

Her velvet voice. Her beautiful face and mussed hair, against the backdrop of blue stripes. His eyes rolled back. His hips jerked. He pushed between her thighs, but her narrow slit allowed him entrance only halfway. Oh, God, delicious torture, but the ottoman. The blessed, beautiful ottoman . . . why bother with a bed ever again? The tufted square provided the perfect plateau to lean into her. With his toes angled against the carpet behind, he cursed. He whispered and praised. Gravity pulled, and thrust by thrust, inch by inch, he sank inside her completely. When she arched, he seized her beneath her wadded petticoats. Hands splayed over her bare buttocks, he seized her. Pressing his cheek to her corseted breast, he thrust, over and over again, as she tightened her arms about his neck. Her thighs tightened on his waist. Slender, cool feet slid against his buttocks.

"Someone's . . . at the door," she whispered.

Oh, yes. Someone knocked. So far away.

"Let . . . them . . . wait."

He braced for leverage and bore into her, each frantic thrust taking him toward a brilliant edge. Narrow walls shuddered against his penis. She moaned, gripped his arms . . . cried out. Certainly, whoever was on the other side of the door heard, but Mark didn't care. He couldn't stop. The ottoman scooted a few inches through the deep-pile carpet, forcing him to readjust.

The shift in angle created a different, firmer friction. Behind each eye, a colorful prism burst into a thousand points.

"Oh, y-y-yes. *Mina*. Perfect."

His penis jerked, pulsed, throbbed inside her.

With a groan he slowly lowered himself between her legs. There wasn't enough room for them both on the ottoman. He rolled, dropping back first onto the floor. He dragged her down atop him. The movement flung her dark, silky hair across his shoulders. He scored his hands through, framing her face, and brought her down for a kiss. He lifted his head, groaning in sated pleasure, and filled her mouth with his tongue.

Collapsing back, he stared at the ceiling. "God, that was even better than I imagined."

Sprawled across him, she spoke between gasps. "I don't . . . think I'll . . . be able . . . to walk until . . . next week."

The sex had been delirious. Mind-altering.

But he'd not been her first lover. He had no right to the stab of regret, deep inside his chest. *Who?* He wouldn't ask. Perhaps, in time, she would tell him.

They lay for a while longer, kissing and talking nonsense. Pretending the world was normal. She felt perfect against his side, tucked beneath his arm, her head rested on his chest. If given the choice, he'd lie here with her on the carpet, beside the ottoman, for the rest of his days. He smiled.

Certainly that thought sprouted from the balmy afterglow of sex, but . . . he wished things were different.

Ticktock, ticktock. The clock kept ticking. He rolled out from under her and bent to kiss her shoulder. He stood, pulled his trousers over his hips, and helped her up by the hand.

"Let's have a look at that petticoat now."

Her hands went to the satin tie at the small of her back. Mina bent and tugged the undergarment down and off. "You weren't supposed to get me *and* the petticoat."

"Thank you anyway." He kissed her nose.

Despite the intimacy they'd just shared, he saw wariness in her eyes. She still did not trust him completely. Yet she handed the garment over and circled the room, gathering her clothing. He draped the petticoat over the top of a chair, and went to the door, where he looked into the hallway. The porter had left their trunks in a row against the wall. He grinned. Mina's hat sat on top. For the first time it struck him as comical that his trunk was bigger than hers, as if he were a peacock who required more clothes. More things. He wanted to buy her more. Silky things. Sparkly things. Expensive things. Enough that when they traveled, she'd need ten trunks, all larger than his. He knew clothes and jewels weren't important to her, and he supposed that was exactly why he wished to spoil her with them. He'd do it too, once he was done saving himself and the world. He'd be a legend then. She could be one with him.

Mark hoisted her trunk first and brought his inside second. Once she found her dressing gown, she joined him on the settee. It was then he told her everything, everything about how he'd pursued her and her father to India, but woke up three months later in London. He also told her about Elizabeth Jackson, and his introduction to the Dark Bride.

"I don't mean to terrify you," he concluded.

"No," she murmured, wide-eyed and pale. "I want to know everything. I'm glad you told me."

He spread her petticoat over the same ottoman where they'd just made love.

He squinted. "There's a bit of smudging."

"I've worn that thing for three months, remember."

"This is just one of the scrolls?"

"The first of the two my father had in his possession," she confirmed. "He marked them with a tag, one and two. I didn't have time to copy the second. You're aware there's a third scroll, located at the British Museum?"

He nodded. "I've translated that one."

Her eyes warmed with admiration. Mark's chest swelled. God love a woman who found the translation of ancient scrolls attractive.

"My father had hoped to do the same. He told me the papyrus was terribly deteriorated."

"It was a damn mess."

Mina looked down at the toes of her slippers. "He was so excited to get the ancient languages position at the museum and to discover the final scroll that completed the full set of three. He even considered donating his to their collection. His are exceedingly rare. Rarer than the museum's scroll, even."

"Because the tablets from which they were copied no longer exist."

"Yes." Her smile faded. "But things changed after the museum accused my father of stealing the original cuneiform tablet from which the first scroll was transcribed."

"Did he take the tablet?"

"I have to admit, at the time, I wasn't sure myself. When he left for his new employment in London, I remained behind in our Manchester house with the understanding I'd join him by midyear. But shortly after beginning the new position, he started behaving strangely. Secretly. And then suddenly, with only a cryptic telegraph to me, he departed for Bengal. When the accusation came out from the museum, I traveled all the way there to confront him about everything."

"Alone?"

Her shoulder came up. "The ship captain was a friend of Father's, and I knew him from prior travels, and so felt comfortable traveling alone. Knowing the city, I found my father rather easily. He was still there in Kolkata, provisioning up for an expedition."

"What did he tell you?"

"He assured me he hadn't stolen anything from the museum. Instead, he told me of a secret society of men who, like him, sought the secrets of immortality. But unlike my father, they didn't just wish to discover the existence of an immortal—they wished to *become* immortal. He feared they wanted the scrolls for nefarious purposes. That's all he would say. He told me it was better if I didn't know everything."

"Could he identify these men?"

She shook her head. "He didn't know who any of them were. He told me only that they'd been following him in London, and that they'd broken into his room at the boardinghouse, searching for the scrolls. I feel so terrible now, because I doubted him then." She bit her bottom lip. "At the time, I feared he was losing his mind. He insisted that I leave. That I return to England, but I refused."

"Why did he go to Bengal in the first place, and what happened there? When you returned to London, you carried a pistol in your bag."

A faint smile curved her lips. "You would know about that, wouldn't you?"

"What frightened you?" Mark asked softly. "And why did you decide to feign his death?"

Mina's eyes clouded. "We only started out in Bengal. Our expedition traveled into Tibet, to a temple near Yangpoong, at the foot of the Himalayas. My father requested an audience with the resident monks."

Mark interrupted. "What do Tibetan monks have to do with anything? The scrolls originated in the ancient library in Alexandria. They are copies of Akkadian tablets. These are artifacts from Egypt and Persia. You're on a completely different side of the map."

"I wondered the same thing myself." Mina rested her hands on her knees. "I went with my father to the temple, and he showed them the scrolls."

"What happened then?"

"Well . . ." She scooted forward in her seat, clearly excited at the memory. "First of all, they started up immediately striking their gongs. Over and over again. And then they gave him the scroll rods."

"Wait a minute." Mark squinted. "Scroll rods?"

"Yes. My father had two papyri. Two scrolls, but no rods. They gave him four ivory rods, two for each scroll." She drew her knees up onto the settee, and wrapped her arms around them. "And that, Mark, is when the trouble started. Our first night back in camp, a heavy fog settled over the mountainside. Fog is commonplace in Tibet, of course, but this fog whispered. The Bengalis we'd hired to convey our belongings up the mountain grew frantic."

"You don't have to convince me," Mark assured her. "I've seen stranger things. I believe you."

Mina touched her fingertips to her lips. "The next morning, we found the body of one of our Bengalis at the bottom of a ravine. Our English guide, Lieutenant Maskelyne, said he must have wandered off the cliff in the dark, but from what my father told me, the man's body was badly mangled. Too badly mangled for the injuries to have come simply from the fall. The next night, our native translator disappeared. Whether he abandoned us out of fear, or found some more disturbing fate, I doubt we'll ever know. The next night we lost more men."

"And so your father left you?"

She nodded. "He told me they'd found us. That he wouldn't risk my life any further, and so we had to split up. He told me to return to England and tell everyone he'd died on the mountain. He also told me I'd—I'd never see him again." Tears crowded her lashes. "Apparently he'd already considered the idea of disappearing under the guise of such a lie, because he gave me the name of a man in Kolkata who would provide all the necessary falsified documents."

"What happened then?" Mark prodded gently.

"I refused. I was upset. I stormed out of the tent. I didn't go far. Not far at all. But a cloud moved against the mountain." Mina shivered. Mark took her hand and squeezed it. "I tried to follow my steps back to the camp, but couldn't see anything but fog. I was afraid I'd fall into a crevice and end up like those men. So I sat, and I waited. I waited hours, almost until morning. At last the fog lifted, just enough for me to see I was right beside the tents. So close, I could have crawled a few feet and touched them. But he was gone. He and Lieutenant Maskelyne were gone."

Now Mark understood the mix of emotions Mina displayed for her father, the love, tangled up with anger.

She continued. "And so I made my way back to Kolkata. Alone. I waited a few weeks until my money had almost run out. And then, once I realized he wasn't coming back, I did what he told me to do."

"You were very brave." Mark slid his hand over her shoulder, to the back of her delicate neck. He pulled her close and rested his forehead against hers. "You had no other choice."

"I don't know." She squeezed his leg. "I lied to people. People who were nothing but kind and accepting of me. Trafford. Lucinda. I still can't help but believe she'd be alive today if I hadn't come here."

"We don't know that." He kissed her ear.

She pulled back, blinking, and dabbed at her eyes. "Find out for me, will you? When you figure all this out."

"I will," he assured her.

"Now, look at that petticoat and tell me what I wrote."

"I've already translated it."

Mina's eyes widened. "What do you mean you've already translated it? While we were sitting here talking?"

He shrugged. "I'm good. It also helps that your petticoat is in much better condition than that damn first scroll."

"What does it say?"

"That I've got to get my hands on an Eye."

Chapter Fourteen

Mina seized his arm. "My father spoke of an eye. He'd seen the character in the scrolls, but didn't understand the context."

Mark tilted his head toward the petticoat. "The scrolls speak in terms of prophecy. Of things that will come about in future centuries. I'm almost certain the eye the scroll refers to is a large mirror that eventually became the Eye of Pharos."

"Pharos . . . as in the lighthouse at Alexandria? One of the seven wonders of the ancient world?"

"That's the one," he affirmed. "Legend tells that the Eye, a large mirror, could be used with a special lens, not only to incinerate approaching warships, but to destroy advancing armies."

Her eyes widened. "Is that true? Would this mirror hold such power?"

Mark rubbed his chin. "I can't say for sure. I've never actually seen the Eye. By all accounts, the mirror was stolen from the lighthouse, perhaps as early as the first century AD, and was allegedly cast into the ocean. By whom, or why, has never been told. Perhaps, if its powers are real, that was done to keep it out of the hands of those who wished to use it for purposes of evil."

"Such as the men who were following us. But why would my father wish to uncover such a mirror? He has no wish to do harm. He's an eccentric, but gentle man."

"Perhaps he's trying to stop them. To keep the mirror out of the hands of these men."

Tears filled her eyes. "My father . . . a hero? He should have just told me. But then . . . I think he knew I didn't believe." She blinked rapidly and swallowed. "What about you? Can the Eye help you?"

Mark answered simply, "Yes."

There were conditions, of course. He'd have to deal with those when the time came.

"We've got to find it," she said.

"If your father hasn't found it already. He's got the other scroll with all the instructions about where to look."

"But I thought . . ."

Mark fingered the lace at the hem of the petticoat. "This is the third scroll, the one that tells how to use the Eye. Not where to find it."

She bit into her lower lip. "Remember when I told you my father gets things mixed up sometimes?"

"It's all right. This will be marvelous to know when the time comes." Mark stood, weaving his fingers across the crown of his head. He went to the window and stared out.

"I'm sorry." She approached from behind him and touched his bare back. "I know you're frustrated."

"A little."

"Mark . . ."

"Yes?"

"Who are you?"

He turned away from the window. "I'm me."

He bent. Kissed her lips. Stroked her waist.

"I mean, who are you? You're an immortal." She closed

her eyes. "I still have trouble believing. Where did you come from? How long have you existed on this earth?"

"I'll tell you later. We've had enough talking for now."

With his thumb, he hooked the edge of her dressing gown and tugged the thin fabric aside. He pressed a kiss to her neck and slid his mouth lower, licking and tasting the warm skin of her bare shoulder. Mina sighed and lifted her hand to the back of his head. With a gentle push, the shaped cup of her corset released her breast into his open palm. He sucked her nipple, hard enough to elicit a gasp. Drawing back, he admired the pink ring he'd left around her areola, and caressed the moist flesh with his thumb.

"What do you say we try out the bed?"

Late the following morning Mina awakened to the sound of male voices and a closing door. She lay naked atop sheets that were strewn every which way, their corners and edges no longer tucked beneath the mattress, the result of a long night of lovemaking. They'd done such things . . . wild things . . . wicked things. Every part of her body ached, as if she'd fought a mighty battle. She supposed she had. They'd wrestled, twisted and mauled each other until morning.

Get on top.

No, you.

On your hands and knees. Yes. Like that. Oh, how pretty.

She smiled, pushing away the melancholy ache of sadness inside her chest, the one that told her nothing had changed between them. Not really. Her heart remained locked away, safe and sound . . . but it rattled in its cage, discontent and complaining. When would she allow the tangle in her chest to *untangle* and simply fall in love?

Not yet. Not now. Not him.

Comforting sounds came from the sitting room. The pouring of liquid, and the contact of a teacup against a saucer. She threw back the covers and pulled on her dressing gown. Not bothering to look in the mirror or brush her hair, she ventured out.

Mark stood at the window, looking out over the Thames. In the distance, and visible over his naked shoulder, arose the Egyptian obelisk, Cleopatra's Needle. He wore only a pair of loose, striped trousers. Golden skin flexed over the taut muscles of his shoulders and arms, and tapered down to sculpted hips. Her mouth went dry. She knew how that skin felt—like warm, smooth perfection.

"Good morning." He turned to greet her. He looked like a big, mussed lion, holding a tiny teacup. He wore a pensive expression, but his eyes . . . his gaze warmed when he saw her. "I had the kitchen send up breakfast. There's tea for you, if you like."

A little zing of self-consciousness shot down her spine, into her legs. Things had been so easy between them in the dark. But here . . . now . . . she could not deny a sense of awkwardness.

"Thank you," she said, moving toward a brass cart, nestled amidst a solid bank of flowers. She poured a cup full of tea. "Where did all the flowers come from?"

"There's a stack of cards and telegraph messages as well, on the escritoire." Mark came to stand beside her. He set his empty cup on the tray. "The porter said they were brought over from Trafford's house. I haven't looked at the cards, but I'm quite sure that ridiculously huge arrangement in the corner is from my banker."

"At least there are no red and white–striped roses."

"I admit to thinking the same."

She pulled the card from the nearest arrangement. "Interesting."

"What does it say?"

Her eyebrows went up. "Just one word. *Idiot*. And it's underlined about twenty times."

He smiled. "That would be from my twin."

"Your twin. What is his name?"

"*Her* name is Selene."

"She seems delightful." Mina chuckled, returning the card to its place. "When do I get to meet her?"

"I'm certain she'll put in an appearance sooner than I prefer."

"Will we be going out today?"

"Much as I'd like to hole away here and make love to you for the foreseeable future . . . we've got to make contact with your father and find out if he's gained possession of the Eye."

Her brow furrowed. "Have you heard the Dark Bride's voice again?"

"No, and it's a relief, to be sure. But Transcension doesn't just go away. Even if Lucinda was the Dark Bride, it's just a matter of time before something takes her place. I've only got until the next wave of energy moves over London to try and make some sort of progress. I can't predict what sort of condition I'll be in afterward."

She nodded. "We'll start at the telegraph office. I know a handful of my father's closest associates. Contacts he must use in order to get around, from country to country. Geographically, they are so far removed from London and its society, I doubt they've heard word of his supposed death."

"Good." He bent to press a kiss against her shoulder. "I've a question for you."

"Yes?"

Mark's lips twisted. He appeared mildly abashed. "Who was that man outside Trafford's house?"

"What man?" She turned from him and pretended to look at the selection of jams.

"The one on the steps, when we were leaving." He tugged a length of her hair from the center of the back of her head. "Tall. Dark haired."

He pulled, a teasing, steady tension, until she tipped her head backward. He pressed a kiss to her nose.

She smiled ruefully. "I won't be able to hide anything from you, will I?"

"No. So don't bother trying."

She pressed her lips together. "He is Lieutenant Philander Maskelyne. I made mention of him last night. Remember? Before you told me you were tired of talking."

"He's the English guide your father hired for the Tibetan expedition."

She sipped from her cup and swallowed, licking her lower lip. "He's an adventurer. A well-known ascentionist. And yes. The last time I saw him"—she offered him a hopeful smile—"he was with my father."

Mark blinked. "So there's a chance the lieutenant knows where the professor is."

She nodded. "Either they parted ways or my father is here in London as well."

"All right then." Mark's nostrils flared. "Where can we find this Lieutenant Maskelyne?"

She planted her cup on the tray.

"That's the problem," she whispered, grasping his arms. "I've no idea. I'm so scared I botched things. At the time, his appearance on the steps caught me off guard. I didn't want you to know about him. Things were different between us yesterday morning. I wanted to find him myself and see what he could tell me about my father. So yes, now he's out there somewhere in this huge city, and I've no idea where. I'm so sorry, Mark. I suspect he'll try to make contact, I just don't know when."

Mark nodded. "It's all right. We'll find him."

"But what sort of time frame are we working on here? How long do you have until you . . . well . . . become . . ."

"A raving demon, bent on the destruction of mankind?"

She frowned, stricken. "Don't say it like that."

Mark pinched and broke the stem of a fat, pink rose from an arrangement. "Based on the frequency of previous Krakatoan waves, I'd say a week until the next. Maybe two, if I'm lucky."

"Then what?"

"Then . . . you won't see me anymore."

"Where will you go?"

Mark slid the rose over her ear. "To meet my assassin."

She gasped. "Your assassin?"

He shrugged, as if his revelation were nothing. "That's the way of things, Mina. The Shadow Guards won't allow me to become a true threat to them. They'll destroy me first. And I'll have to let them."

"Oh, Mark, no."

He looked at the flowers, then the coffeepot. "I want you to know . . . you're taken care of. If things go wrong, there will be a benefit to this short marriage of ours. You'll be the wealthiest widow in England and be able to make all your own choices."

"I like making my own choices, but I don't wish to be the wealthiest widow in England. I don't want you to die."

"It's all part of the risk I took when I crossed into Transcension, Mina. I knew it could happen. But know I don't intend for such a thing to ever take place. You'll be stuck with me for a good long while. I'm going to win this." His eyes glowed with fervor. "Despite everything that's happened, I've never been more certain."

Mina frowned morosely, and turned her attention to the stack of telegraph slips and calling cards. She found them to be a mix of congratulatory messages on their wedding, and notes of sympathy on the death of her aunt. And again, a card from Mr. Matthews. She paused at the next card in the stack.

Her heart jumped inside her chest. "Oh, Mark. Look here."

"What is it?"

She held it up. "It's Lieutenant Maskelyne's. He must

have come by the hotel and left it. On the back he's written the address of a boardinghouse."

Mark claimed the card and examined the scrawled words. "Get dressed, sweetheart."

Within the hour, they disembarked from a hansom in front of an aging three-story house distinguished from the other structures on the narrow street by its vivid green paint. Mark paid the driver to wait for them at the curb. As they delved down a shadowed corridor, Mina glanced at the peeling wallpaper. "Lieutenant Maskelyne can be rather snobbish. This place isn't at all to his standards. He must be in hiding, or have run out of funds."

Mark scanned the doors. "What was the door number again?"

She glanced at the card. "C2."

"This is it." He lifted his hand to knock. Mina reached up to stop him.

"Mark . . ."

"What is it?"

She considered him from beneath the brim of her hat. "Well . . . it's just that he might be angry."

"About what?"

Her lips twisted. "A lot of things."

"I don't care what he is, as long as he tells us where your father is." He rapped his knuckles against the wood. He leaned against the door frame, thinking it best to allow the man to see a familiar face first. The brass doorknob turned. The door scraped open.

A low, masculine voice murmured, "Willomina."

Mark scowled at the intimate tone.

Mina, peering inward, smiled brightly. "Lieutenant Mask—"

Hands grasped her by the wrists and hauled her inside. "Philander, *wait*—"

The door swung to almost shut. Mark halted the closure with the palm of his hand. With a quick shove, he pushed inside after Mina. There, he stood face-to-face with the man he'd seen on the street outside Trafford's house. Only now, instead of a suit and hat, the fellow wore linen trousers and a white undershirt. Lean muscles corded his shoulders, arms and neck. He wore his dark hair short, military style, a cut that emphasized the masculine angularity of his skull. Though the man was taller than most, Mark topped him by at least two inches. Still . . . he had to concede that Philander Maskelyne was disturbingly handsome.

Disturbingly because of the way he stared at Mina.

Mark's gaze narrowed on the man's hands, where he continued to claim his wife. *Burn. Burn. Burn.*

The lieutenant snatched his hands away, then stared at his palms. He blinked in disbelief.

He looked between them, lips curled into a sneer. "So this is he? Your rich viscount?"

Mina's expression went blank. Obviously, his bluntly worded greeting stunned her.

"I saw you on the street yesterday outside my uncle's house. I'm so relieved to see you safe here in England."

"Safe?" he laughed caustically. "Thanks to your father, I've got a target on my head. It's only a matter of time before those crazed immortality freaks find me. Don't expect me to cover for him either. I'll sell him out in a second. Bastard shorted me nine hundred pounds."

Newspapers littered the desk. Folded into a neat rectangle atop all the others was the feature about their wedding and honeymoon. There were also two pistols and a rifle, polished to a high sheen.

"I'm sorry you're in danger and shorted in pay," Mina responded, clasping her hands together. "But tell me . . . my father *is* alive?"

"Alive enough to pack up everything and disappear in the middle of the night."

"Where did you see him last?"

"In Alexandria."

"Egypt?" Mark interjected.

Maskelyne nodded curtly, his nostrils flared. "Whatever he was looking for . . . well, it wasn't there. I demanded he pay up through the next leg of the journey. The next morning, he was gone."

Mina asked, "What was the next leg of your journey?"

"I don't know. Bastard wouldn't tell me."

"Did he still have possession of the scrolls?"

"Damn well, he did. If I'd gotten my hands on them, I swear I'd have thrown them in the Nile. They're a bloody curse on all of us."

Mark warned, "Mind your language in front of my wife."

"Your wife." He chuckled. A lecherous smile cut the lieutenant's lips. "Want to bet I know your wife better than you do?"

Mark lunged, planting a fist to Maskelyne's face. He felt the satisfying crack of bone against his knuckles.

"You like the word 'bloody'?" Mark growled. "*Philanderer Masculine?* Go look in the mirror." He raised his fist again.

"Mark, *no.*" Mina's voice broke through the thick haze of his fury. She was on him, a blur of arms and skirts and orange blossom scent, both of her small hands gripping his wrist.

"You broke my nose," the lieutenant shouted. Blood streamed out of his nostrils, over his lips.

"I'm so sorry," Mina exclaimed. "Please send your doctor bill to the Savoy Hotel." Mina tugged at Mark's arm, leading him into the hallway. "We're finished here. Let's go."

With a shouted curse, Maskelyne slammed the door behind them.

"Why did you *do* that?" she hissed. "Was it the voice? Did the voice tell you to do that?"

"The voice?" he growled. "You're damn right it was a voice. *My voice*. He's the one, isn't he?"

"The one, what?"

His cheeks went taut. "You know what I'm talking about."

Mina flushed and her mouth fell open—and snapped closed. "That's none of your business."

Mark lunged toward Maskelyne's door.

Mina wedged herself between him and the wood. He stared down into her face, his jaw rigid and his eyes reflecting the violence of emotion within.

She gripped his shoulders. "I'm sorry, darling. I didn't realize *you* were a virgin when we married. I should have been more gentle with you that first time."

His head jerked. "What did you say?"

"Was I *your* first?" she demanded sardonically.

"Of course not."

She smacked his shoulder. "Then you've no business throwing punches at anyone."

"He *seduced* you."

"No, he didn't." Her face crinkled up with impatience. She stormed down the hallway. "We seduced each other. I was curious. And for your information, completely willing. Stupid, but willing."

"Did you love him?" he called after her.

"Don't be ridiculous."

Pursuing her, he grasped her arm. *"Did you love him?"*

She pulled his hand and flattened it to her temple. "You tell me. You can do that, can't you? Read my emotions? My thoughts. Yes, yes, I've sensed you prodding around in there, especially last night when we were . . . well, *you know*. Anyway, have at them. I'm an open book."

He snatched his hand away and fisted it into a ball. "I want you to tell me."

"I didn't love him," she declared. "And for your information, I don't love you either."

"You don't?" He lifted his hand toward her temple.

She smacked him away and scrambled down the stairs, into the street. With a hitch of her skirts, she clambered into the hansom. On entering, she spoke to the driver.

Mark climbed in after her and dropped down beside her. His weight sank the bench, and Mina bounced into the air.

She snorted. "You're jealous. I like it."

"I'm not jealous." He *wasn't* jealous. He didn't get jealous.

Oh, God. He *was* jealous. His head buzzed with hatred for another man, all because that man had . . . oh, his thoughts blurred over the whole horrible picture of the two of them together in some dark mountainside tent while her damn father snored, oblivious, in the next tent. Like an ill-behaved, pouting boy, he wanted to grab either side of his top hat brim and pull the whole blasted thing down over his head and smother himself on his envy. He hated the weakness. He hated the whole damn idea of her with someone else. God, he'd never acted so stupidly before.

Women. Pah. Who needed them?

He did. Dammit, he needed her.

"Where are we going?" he asked sullenly. His hand slid to her thigh. She smacked him again.

"If my father's run out of money, he may very well have returned to London. And if he has, I think I know where he might go to get more."

"Where?"

"There's a man in the East End. He collects things."

"Things? What sort of things?"

"You'll see. If he's still there. I don't know. It's been a long time."

He sat beside her, rigid and silent. Her hand curled over the rail at the side of the bench. Tension radiated out of her. He'd made her angry. Of course he had. He'd made himself angry as well. The hansom clattered through traffic and a dense haze of dust and heat, halting and stopping at least a thousand times before at last the vehicle drew up in front of a warehouse.

"You can wait here if you like," said Mina.

"I'm not letting you out of my sight."

"Just keep your hands in your pockets, if you will," she instructed, unlatching the door, and climbing down without waiting for the driver. "No punching anyone."

He followed her around the back of the warehouse, and up a staircase to a second-floor entrance. She pushed a little black buzzer. They waited in silence, but no one answered. She jabbed the buzzer again. Nothing.

"I don't hear anything," she said. "Maybe the buzzer doesn't work."

Mark pounded on the wood with his fist. That didn't bring anyone either. Twisting the knob with both hands, Mina gave a stiff shove. A look of surprise lit her face when the door opened.

"Let's go inside."

"Oh, I agree." His eyebrows went up. "I like going uninvited into strange East End warehouses where no one answers the door. The only things better are abandoned houses and crypts, both of which, as a matter of fact, I've visited over the last several weeks."

She glanced at him, amused, which Mark took as an exceedingly good sign that she would forgive him for pounding on Maskelyne. Now, if he could just keep himself from hitting anyone else or losing his mind to Transcension, he might have a chance at more lovemaking tonight.

"Oh, yes," Mina breathed. "This is still Mr. Thackeray's warehouse."

Mark's eyes widened. Ancient Doric columns leaned into the corners—five of them, from different periods and locations about the world. He could tell by their sizes and

textures. Mr. Thackeray apparently also had an interest in
exotic animals. As they made their way toward the center
of the warehouse, Mark tapped a stuffed polar bear in its
chest. He wiggled the yellowed fang of a mountain lion.
More animals perched on shelves all around the warehouse. Two flying machines, with wings and motors and
flaps, dangled from the ceiling.

Mina pointed into the shadows, toward a huge white
and gilt carriage. "That was always my favorite. I used
to pretend I was a princess while Mr. Thackeray and my
father worked out whatever business they had."

Mark stooped, lifting the lid of a battered sarcophagus.

Mina continued on. "Mark? Are you coming?"

"Just looking to see if it's anyone I know."

Suddenly, a sound drifted out from the darkness . . . a
low, tortured moan.

Mina froze. "Did you hear that?"

"I did." He did. And he didn't like it. He sidled past a
barrel full of horseshoes to reach her side.

She called, "Mr. Thackeray? Is that you?"

Something flew at them from the darkness—a huge,
openmouthed ghoul. Mark grabbed Mina and shoved her
behind him. A skeleton veered over their heads, pedaling
a bicycle.

Skeletons. Severed heads. Dammit.

Heated blood fluxed beneath his skin. His eyes
turned.

"*Willo-mi-na Lim-pett,*" bellowed a talking severed
head, high on the wall. "Welcome to my *phant-as-magori-
ummmmmm.*"

"Wait a minute." Mina gripped his arm from behind. "*I
recognize that severed head.* That's Mr. Thackeray."

She bounded past him, toward a wooden partition.
A suspicious sliver of light emanated from between the
hinged panels. Mark pursued her. If Mr. Thackeray were

indeed a talking severed head, he might have to go back on his vow not to punch anyone. Mina sidled into a box formed of large mirrors.

"Mina," Mark warned.

But then he saw them. Two booted feet jutted up, attached to skinny ankles, which were only half concealed by droopy red stockings.

"Mr. Thackeray?" Mina inquired.

"Could someone help an old man up?" a voice shouted.

Mark patted his pockets until he found his spectacles and quickly slid them up his nose. He clambered forward, and pulled—yes—an old man out from a padded box cut into the floor.

The aged fellow's hair, however, remained a rigid gray flag atop his head, the unfortunate effect of gravity and too much grooming ointment.

"How'd you like the show? I purchased the entire inventory of an old Cheshire phantasmagorium and have only just now got the magic lantern to work. Thing didn't come with instructions. Unfortunately, I've got to be upside down for the image to appear right side up."

"Please allow me to introduce you to my husband, Lord Alexander."

"Oh, good gracious. You've wed." Thackeray squinted. "Congratulations." He bussed her on the cheek and reached for Mark's hand. "Congratulations. Er . . . what's wrong with your eyes, young fellow?"

"Nothing serious, just a . . . sensitivity to light."

"Ooooh." His lips squished together, and he pressed his index finger against them. "I've got some special spectacles that might do a better job than yours. Come along. Come along."

They followed the old man through leaning stacks of dusty encyclopedias. Mina turned back to Mark. She tapped at her eye.

What is it? she mouthed.

He slid the spectacles down his nose. Her mouth fell open.

Oblivious, the old man trundled along. "I buy lots of things. Lots of interesting, valuable things. Things people don't want anymore. Like the phantasmagorium. What fun! But young people these days just aren't impressed by such outdated technology. They're always off, onto the next flash in the pan."

He led them into an office, crowded wall-to-wall with boxes. A mountain of papers in every shape and color obscured the desk. He pulled a drawer and rummaged.

"No. Not here." Sinking to his knees, he crawled under the desk. "Ah, here they are. Come here, young man."

He held up a narrow wood box, open on both ends. Eyeholes had been cut into the front, and were covered in green glass and vertical slats. He murmured, "Ingenious. An ingenious invention."

Mark wondered if he ought to balk. Refuse. Even run. He glanced to Mina, and she smiled encouragingly. Apparently, she thought it best to humor the man, and he supposed he ought to trust her. He did, after all, wish to please her after he'd gone and made such an utter buffoon out of himself over Maskelyne.

Thackeray's gray hair-flag wobbled as he went up on his toes and lifted the box *up up up*. . . . Mark closed his eyes and bent at the knees to facilitate the bestowal of the dusty contraption onto his head.

Just like that, everything turned a soothing green.

"I believe if you wear these spectacles for the next . . . oh . . . four to five weeks, your sensitivity to light ought to be repaired. I wouldn't even take them off to bathe or to sleep, if I were you."

Mina covered her mouth with her hand. Her eyes sparkled with . . . well, something beyond amusement. *Mirth.* Mark's tension eased, and he smiled as well.

"Thank you so much, Mr. Thackeray," Mina said tenderly. Mark could tell she held a real affection for the man. No telling what bizarre contraptions she'd been forced to suffer in the past. "I suppose you're wondering why we're here at all."

"Well, no . . . I hadn't really. It's nice to have visitors every once in a while, for no reason at all."

"I do have a reason." Her expression grew serious. "I've come to ask if you've heard from my father."

"Your . . . father." He scratched his chin.

"Yes." She bit into her lower lip. "I wondered if he might have come here trying to sell anything."

He waggled his eyebrows. "That would be difficult being that he is deceased, wouldn't it?"

Disappointment weighed like stone in Mina's chest. "Yes, I—I suppose it would."

Mr. Thackeray hummed a tune. He searched his desk, finding a pencil and a sheet of paper. He scratched out a few words. He held them up, so that they both could see.

Yes. Yes. Yes. Alive and well. Selling things. Lots of things.

Mina smiled, relieved to her toes. She and Mr. Thackeray had played this game when she was a child. He would tell her one thing—such as *I don't believe little girls should have sweets*—and then he would write out silent instructions on where to find the candy. She also suspected the game was a method of getting around whatever vow of secrecy her father had sworn him to. Mr. Thackeray smiled at Mina, perhaps a bit guiltily.

He disappeared, again, under the desk. When he arose, he held a wooden box, which he ceremoniously opened: a dark, leathery thing nestled in blue velvet. Mina leaned closer. A mummy's hand.

Across the desk, Mark's shoulders drew together in a wince, and he rubbed his wrist.

Mina took up the pencil and scribbled, *Where is he?*
More scratching.

Don't know. London. Somewhere.

"Well, then, since you *haven't* seen him, I suppose we should go and let you return to perfecting your phantasmagorium display."

They made their way across the warehouse.

"Come back soon," Thackeray called as they made their way down the stairs. "I'll run the whole show for you."

The door shut.

Mark followed her down the stairs. "Do you think he's watching from a window, or can I take this thing off my head now?"

Mina snorted behind her gloved hand. "We'd better go all the way to the hansom. You don't want to hurt his feelings."

The driver stared at him, wide-eyed.

"It's all right," he called to the man. "They are an *ingenious* invention."

Once they'd climbed inside, the driver tapped the horses, and the vehicle got under way. Mina turned to him. She lifted the box and stared into his eyes. For a moment he thought she'd kiss him, but . . . she didn't.

"Thank you," she whispered.

"Thank you for what?"

"For being so sweet with him."

He grinned. "I don't know about you, but I'm coming back for the full phantasmagorium show." His smile faded. "Provided I last that long."

Why had he said that? He hadn't lost confidence, hadn't lost hope.

Mina patted his hand. Her patting disturbed him. Mothers patted. Sisters and fond friends patted. Lovers did not pat.

"You are going to last that long. My father is here, Mark. My father is here, in London, with the scrolls. We're going to find out everything you need to know about that conduit of immortality, and then we're going to get you fixed right up. Righter than rain. We've just got to remain visible, so he can find us."

The rest of the afternoon was spent in the West End, in Mayfair, with Mina's grieving uncle and cousins, who conveyed that the authorities wished to retain Lucinda's body for further postmortem examinations. Given that the police surgeon leaned toward a final conclusion of disease, in the interest of science and public health, Trafford had agreed.

Due to the circumstances, and his lordship's wish for privacy, there would be only a private memorial chapel service for the countess, for attendance by her immediate family. Because the girls were still too distraught, Mina assisted her uncle in writing letters to their relations and friends, near and far, relaying news of his wife's death. Trafford also shared his plans to take the girls to his Lancashire estate for the three weeks following the service. The city, and all its attentions in the wake of his wife's death, proved too much for him to bear.

Mina, for her part, could not shed the lingering guilt that she'd brought the misery upon the family, that she was to blame for Lucinda's recruitment and death. When evening drew on, she and Mark returned to the Savoy, where they arrived to more flowers, and more messages. They read through them over a supper of cold chicken and salad, sent up from the hotel kitchen.

Mina frowned over the stacks of cards and torn envelopes. "There's nothing here from my father."

Mark closed the newspaper. There'd been no mention of more body parts being discovered along the Thames.

"Don't fret," he murmured. "News of our wedding came out in the paper only yesterday, and Lucinda's obituary is there today. He's going to see everything. He'll make contact. What sort of father wouldn't?"

Mina smiled hopefully. "You're right, you know. I've

been so angry he abandoned me on that mountain, but . . . he only did what he thought he had to do to keep me safe. I don't think he ever considered they would come after me."

"I don't either," Mark responded, but his thoughts were already on the darkening sky outside their window. Instinct compelled him to go out into the city, to spend the night on the streets, sending out his feelers in search of the professor, or taking stock of whatever evil he could find. Once the house was finished, tomorrow perhaps, he could leave Mina under Leeson's protection. But for tonight, left with no other interesting options for passing their time . . . his internal male clock counted the minutes until he could seduce her into their hotel bed.

A knock sounded. Mark stood up from the table and answered the door. A handsome youth in full royal livery stood on the other side.

Mark returned to Mina with a large square envelope, and a broad smile. "Delivery by equerry."

"A *royal* equerry?" Mina jumped up from the chair to touch his arm. "Open it. What does it say?"

Mark lifted the flap and removed a thick card from inside. As he read, a slow smile curled his lips.

"What is it?"

Betwixt two fingers, he rotated the card toward her.

Her eyes quickly scanned over the Royal Arms . . . *Ascot . . . admit Viscount and Viscountess Alexander.*

Chapter Fifteen

Her eyes widened. "The Prince of Wales has invited us to Ascot?"

"Not just Ascot, darling," he murmured. "To the royal box."

Her face lit up. "Do you know the prince?"

He shrugged. "I suppose."

"You *suppose*." She squeezed his arm. "Is it acceptable for me to attend? I'm in double mourning now. For my father, and for Lucinda."

"So am I. I'm your husband. But people go to Ascot in mourning. Just don't make a spectacle of yourself, dear." He grinned.

She bit her lip. "If you're certain. I would love to attend."

"We can't get more visible than the royal box at Ascot. We're certain to be mentioned in the papers."

"You're right." She touched her fingertips to her hair. "But I've got to get a nicer hat."

"I'll buy you whatever you want," he promised huskily.

"I'll go to the shops tomorrow. And actually . . . I'll

send a note to Astrid and Evangeline, and invite them to go with me."

Mark made a face. "Why, when they've been horrible to you?"

"Not horrible. They're just spoiled. They'll need additional mourning clothes before they travel to Lancashire. I'm their married cousin and closest female relative. It's only right that I see that such details are attended to."

"You're too kind." He came closer and rubbed his hands along her arms. "But that's what makes you special. That and you're so damn pretty."

"I'm glad you think I'm pretty." Her cheeks brightened. She wavered somehow. Ultimately she crossed to the table where she picked up her book. "I think I'll read for a while."

Read? Mark frowned, bemused. Who wanted to read when there was *bed*?

Flipping the cover open, she said, "Mark. I hate to tell you this."

"What is it?"

She turned the book toward him. "I think the hotel has mice. They've eaten half the pages of my story."

Ah, damn. Selene had been here, nosing about. Just his luck she had decided to feed her word fetish as well.

One step carried him to her. "I'll talk to D'Oyly Carte.

"Since your book is ruined . . ." He stroked her cheek, then tilted her face up.

She exhaled . . . and turned her face aside.

"Mina . . ."

He'd sensed her reluctance. He had known something was wrong. She shook her head, and backed away from him, until her shoulders touched the wall.

"Don't, Mark. Not if you care for me." She smiled, but her eyes welled with tears.

"Why?" Displeasure turned his lips down.

"Because I'm *this much* away from being in love with

you." She held up her index finger and her thumb, spaced a half inch apart. "Very close, you see. I'm not saying last night was a mistake. It wasn't. Everything was beautiful. A dream. But don't make me love you. I'll hurt too much, too deeply when you leave. And you *will* leave me, one way or the other. If I loved you . . . I don't think I could survive it."

Mark stood rigid, numbed by her words.

"Good night, Mark."

He nodded. She disappeared into the bedroom. He stood, fixed to the center of the carpet, and listened. He tortured himself with the sounds of her dress and undergarments being removed, her skin brushing against the sheets. Eventually she grew silent and still.

Mark crossed the room and unlatched the fastening for the balcony door. He stepped out onto the narrow ledge and gripped the iron rail. Air. God, he needed air. Canvas drapes shifted on either side, snapping softly in the wind. Desire ate him up inside, desire made infinitely more complex and terrifying by the simple need to be close to her. One woman. Mina Limpett. It took every ounce of his resolve to respect her request. To stay away.

Cleopatra's Needle arose from the edge of the Thames Embankment, just a long stone's throw away. He couldn't explain why, but he always felt stronger near the object, although the obelisk, one of a trio of such needles, held little connection to his mother. Formed of red granite, they stood some twenty meters in height, and had been in existence centuries before the Egyptian queen walked the earth. She had, however, ordered their removal from the city of Heliopolis, and their relocation to the Caesareum in Alexandria, a temple she'd built in honor of his father, Mark Antony. Centuries later, politics and new world powers had seen this one brought to London. The others were located in Paris and in New York.

"Alexander."

He glanced to the balcony above him. Long, dark hair rippled in the wind. "Hello, Selene."

"What did you receive from the equerry?"

"An invitation to Ascot. The royal box."

A foul curse drifted down. Mark chuckled.

"I've been trying to snare an invitation for . . . well, for the last century," she complained.

"I'm sorry. Maybe next year."

An extended silence passed. "You didn't have to marry that little girl to get to those scrolls."

"I realize that."

"Does she know?"

"That I'm an Amaranthine? Yes."

Another long silence.

"Would you like me to come up there?" Mark asked.

"Just shut up. I didn't even come here to see you. Just the view."

"I love you, Selene."

A drop of moisture struck his hand from above.

The next morning, Mina moved about the suite, fully dressed. Mark sprawled across the settee. Just the sight of him, sulky and shirtless, with his trousers half unfastened, made her mouth go dry.

"You didn't have to sleep out here," she chastised softly.

"Yes, I did." He rubbed his neck.

"Is your neck sore?"

"My neck isn't the only thing that's sore." His eyes burned on her.

Mina blushed. She'd slept fitfully herself.

"I don't like to sleep without you," he grumped.

She smiled. Not too broadly, though, because she didn't want to tease or encourage. "When have we ever *slept* together, for more than a half hour?"

He rubbed his eyes with a flattened palm. "Tell me I don't have to do it again."

"I just told you that you don't have to sleep on the settee."

"You know what I mean." Again, two carnal beams of blue light seared through her clothes. She knew exactly what he meant, but she didn't want to talk about it.

"The girls will be here soon," she said lightly. "I sent a note offering to take a carriage to collect them, but I think they wanted to see the hotel and our suite."

Mark stood. "I'll dress."

"You don't have to go with us. We're just going to a modiste shop on Tavistock Street. You can go check on Leeson and the house."

"I don't want you to go alone. I don't want you to go anywhere alone, until all this with your father and the scrolls and—and—" He waved his hand.

"And the dark forces."

He pointed at her. "Yes, until all that's settled."

He dressed and shaved. Just as he came out from the bathing chamber, a knock sounded on the door. Mina answered.

Astrid burst in first, dressed head to toe in black, followed by Evangeline in a similar costume. Their faces glowed with excitement, but Mina perceived a telling redness in their eyes, and dark shadows beneath.

"Oh, Willomina, do you know whom we saw in the lobby downstairs?" Astrid gushed.

Evangeline blurted, "The Devine Sarah. The *actrice*, Sarah Bernhardt. Mr. D'Oyly Carte introduced her to us. She's come to look at a suite."

Astrid giggled. "They say she used to sleep in a coffin, so she would better understand tragedy for her roles. Can you imagine the morbidity of waking up in a coffin?"

Evangeline whispered, loud enough for anyone within

three city blocks to hear, "They also say she's the Prince of Wales's mistress. Do you think it's true?"

"She is a very handsome woman," Astrid affirmed.

"I suppose she is that. For someone of her age."

"Girls," Mina interrupted, feeling as if she were fifty years older than either of them, when in reality only a few years separated them in age.

Their eyes flew to Mark. Both blushed deeply.

Astrid murmured, "My apologies, your lordship. It's just that the hotel is so beautiful, and we've been confined to the house for days."

"Only one day," whispered Evangeline.

"Well, it *feels* like days."

Mina showed the girls around the suite. Mark remained in the sitting room, tall and silent, his hands thrust in his pockets. Afterward, they all went downstairs. The Trafford carriage conveyed them the brief distance from the Savoy to the modiste's shop.

Behind an expanse of polished windows, an elegant reception room waited, done up in rich blue carpets and gold draperies. Mahogany tables displayed all manner of fabrics, trim and accessories. Other shoppers, mostly female, crowded the floor. Assistants and shop girls darted about. Within moments, the proprietress appeared from the back rooms, measuring tapes draped over her shoulders. She led them behind a screen to view two tables full of accoutrements for mourning, out of sight of curious eyes. On one table lay purses and shawls, gloves and veils, and on the other, rolls of various silks and bombazines and all manner of acceptable trims.

"Come, Cousin Willomina." Astrid clasped her hand and drew her closer. "Give me your every advice for looking lovely in the midst of mourning. My debut Season may be ruined, but who's to say the summer can't end with a proposal? After all, black seemed to work well for you."

"Order a few things." Mark stood behind her, tall and protective. She savored the deep timbre of his voice. "Some dresses. Something fine for Ascot." He waved his fingers toward the table. "I like that one, the bolt of black that has the purplish sort of reflection."

The modiste smiled. "A perfect choice. Our finest silk paduasoy."

With flair, she lifted the bolt and unfurled the silk for Mina's perusal. In the next moment she presented a leather-bound book of fashion plates, while an assistant offered a similar book for the girls to view. With Mark grunting and gesturing at the pictures over her shoulders, Mina made three selections.

"I've got to go for measurements."

"I'll be here." From his scowl, it was clear Mark hated being in the shop at all. But like an impatient mastiff, he settled into an armchair.

In the dressing room, Mina allowed an assistant to help her remove her dress.

"It will just be a moment, my lady," the girl said, hanging her dress and shawl on a peg.

"Thank you."

Mina stood in her undergarments. With nothing else to do with her time, she stared at herself in the mirror. What did he see in her? She touched her hair.

His scent filled her nostrils, exotic spice and masculine skin. Warm breath brushed her cheek.

She'd imagined it. But then . . . Mark had been invisible in the crypt.

A hard wall of warmth embraced her from behind. Mina gasped. Her hands came up, searching, but touched nothing but her own skin.

"Mark?" she whispered.

Yes . . .

His voice answered inside her head. Linen slid and crushed against her skin as unseen hands and fingers moved over her arms, her shoulders. A warm mouth pressed against her neck.

She closed her eyes. Exquisite. His every touch was exquisite.

"Mark, please . . . ," she whispered.

Please, what?

Pressure rippled over her hips . . . her waist . . . her corset. Sensual and electrifying. A hand closed over her breast. Another crushed her petticoats and stroked against her thigh.

Mina looked to the mirror, and saw nothing—nothing but a flushed young woman in disheveled undergarments and plump, crushed breasts.

She licked her lips. How wonderful. How erotic. How sneaky of Mark to use this talent against her.

"Please stop."

Abruptly, he released her. Her petticoats dropped into place. Mina swayed.

The modiste breezed in.

"My lady?" The woman rushed forward to steady Mina. "Are you ill?

"No . . ."

Your cheeks are flushed and you appear faint." She urged her assistant to go for a glass of water.

Ah, but she ached. Ached for more.

When you're ready, Mina. When you're ready, come to me.

Two days later, Mina walked in Mark's shadow through the crush of an enormous crowd. The sky spread above them, an endless canopy of blue. The weather was beautiful—warm without being hot. They moved along the center of the Royal Enclosure, having been escorted through by Lord Coventry, the Master of the Royal Buckhounds, himself. The grandstand loomed over the crowd, festooned in flowers and greenery. Onlookers crowded the windows and roofs. Flags of all colors whipped in the wind.

"My mother used to tell me about going to Ascot, but I never imagined anything as impressive as this."

They'd managed to coexist amiably for two days. Mina had held to her decision to keep their marriage out of the bedroom, and Mark had not pressed her, although a constant frisson of sensual tension electrified the air between them.

"It's really something, isn't it?" He drew her closer to his side, sheltering her from the jostle of the crowd. "They've made improvements recently, even enlarging the Royal Enclosure, though you wouldn't know it from this ridiculous crush."

Mina caught only glimpses of white rails, and beyond that, brilliant green turf. "There are so many people, how can anyone see the course or the horses?"

He grinned. "Most aren't here to watch the race."

Several gentlemen called out greetings to Mark. Surely she imagined it, but it seemed an echo spread out from around them, one formed of whispers and murmurings.

"Point in case." Mark's head dipped low, his lips near her ear. "They're all talking about you, sweetheart."

Mina touched her hat, feeling like a stray ink blot on an expanse of white linen. All around her, ladies wore diaphanous creations of silk, chiffon and lace, in the vibrant colors of summer. Mark had paid an additional fee to guarantee the timely delivery of her new dresses and hats, and she'd chosen the best of them to wear today. She felt pleased by the expert fit of her bodice, and the narrow cut of the sleeves, but as far as ornamentation, there were only a row of jet buttons along the center of her breasts and a bit of pleated satin trim at her cuffs and hem.

She supposed she looked as fine as one could while wearing mourning garb. Best of all, she wore a badge that proclaimed her to be the Viscountess Alexander. She had no wish to preen over her status, but she knew she'd always remember this day. Perhaps years from now she'd pull the badge from a special box of treasures and gift the memento to a granddaughter.

The thought put a little ache in her chest, because Mark, of course, would be the centerpiece of any such memory. Mina could not help but take a secret, heart-swelling pride in him. He was not only handsome and dashing, but also intelligent and utterly capable of . . . well . . . *everything*, so far as she knew. She cautioned herself against whole-hearted admiration, knowing such feelings would only compound her grief when they inevitably parted. She would simply enjoy this day and hold it dear once he was gone.

Voices rose all about them, and a surge of excitement traveled through the crowd. Nearly everyone turned in unison toward New Mile.

"It's the royal procession." Mark led her toward the rail, where they found only enough space for one. With a hand on her back he brought her in front of him. He stood very close behind her, his legs crushed into her skirts. She resisted the temptation to lean against him.

To the applause of the crowd, an open barouche rolled past, with the bearded and smiling Prince Albert Edward inside, and beside him, the elegant and serene Princess Alexandra. Four more carriages followed, crowded with elegant personages. The entourage proceeded up the center of the course.

With royalty out of sight, the throng disbursed, if only slightly. Mark guided her to the center of the grand-stand. At the base of a narrow tunnel of stairs, an official checked their name against a list, and with a courteous smile, sent them up. The scene that greeted them nearly overwhelmed Mina. Amidst the recognizable faces of the nobility, there were also politicians, artists and actresses. A long buffet table occupied the back wall, covered with smoked salmon, cheese and fruit. A silver plate fountain, surrounded by glistening, faceted crystal, spouted streams of champagne. A familiar face appeared from out of the crowd: Mrs. Avermarle, the woman from the stationery shop.

"Lady Alexander." Mrs. Avermarle reached out her hand. Her acquaintances followed close behind, their eyes wide with interest. The same sympathetic smile turned all their lips. "How is your dear uncle? Grief-stricken, I am sure. We are all simply shocked at the news of Lady Trafford's death. Come, come, you must tell me everything."

"Alexander," a voice boomed.

Mina glanced over her shoulder. Prince Edward gestured to Mark from the rail overlooking the track. His Grace waved off a few gentlemen, an obvious request for privacy. Mina turned back to Mrs. Avermarle and forced a smile.

By necessity, Mark abandoned Mina to the ladies. He sidled through four rows of gleaming white chairs.

"Your Grace." He bowed.

"A fine day for racing, eh?" The prince slid his hand into his front coat pocket. He wore a polished black top hat and an exquisitely tailored gray morning coat and trousers. A gold chain draped across the portly swell of his vest, ending in a pendulous gold watch. "These things take forever to start. I sometimes take the opportunity to dispense with a little Crown business."

"Business?"

Edward leaned close. He grinned slyly and murmured in a clandestine tone, "To think . . . all the parties. The card games. The routs. I never suspected you were one of them."

Chapter Sixteen

Mark held his gaze.

Edward grinned. "Her Majesty sends her greetings. Well"—he chuckled—"her *chastisements*. She's been in a high temper, unable to reach that other Guard, Lord Black."

"I see," Mark responded. He hesitated to inform the prince of his present state of banishment from the Shadow Guard. He imagined such a confession would be the fastest way to get himself and his pretty new wife tossed down the stairs, and hell, likely escorted out of the country. "I'll convey that along to his lordship."

Perhaps when Archer arrived to kill him.

Archer had always been Victoria's favorite. The aging queen staunchly refused to communicate with any other Guard. It was she who'd insisted that Archer replace Mark in the hunt for the Ripper.

"As you well know, the monarch grows . . . *older*." Edward whispered the word, as if even here, so far removed from Balmoral, Victoria might overhear. "More and more of the Crown's affairs fall to me." He tilted his head at a jaunty angle. "After the nasty business of last fall, we're quite concerned with these severed female body parts that have been recovered along the Thames." His eyes narrowed on Mark. "There won't be more, will there?"

Mark skirted any direct answer. "The Guard is presently working to ensure that."

Edward nodded and waved a hand in acknowledgment of the crowd below. "We wouldn't want another one of those bro-bro—by God, what do you call those nasty creatures?"

"*Brotoi.*"

The prince gave a little shudder. "Far too close to Bertie for my comfort. We don't want another *brotoi* on the loose, causing a recurrence of widespread panic."

Mark crossed his arms over his chest. Truth be told, he didn't know if there was still a *brotoi* on the loose. "I understand your concern."

The prince drummed his fingertips against the rail. "Along those lines, we've authorized the commissioner to finalize Lady Trafford's cause of death as due to disease."

Mark's eyebrows lifted. "I'm certain the Primordial Council would agree with that decision."

The prince clapped him on the shoulder. "I'm just damn pleased to be dealing with you on this matter. I'm not opposed to a little new blood, and shaking up the present ranks."

Mark's lip jerked in pleasure. "I'm pleased to hear that."

The prince would indeed be a valuable contact for the future, once Mark's immortal life returned to normal. Just then, Edward's eyes fixed on something across the room. Mark glanced over his shoulder to realize the prince's attention had settled on . . . Mina, at the center of a society Inquisition.

"The young woman in black," Edward murmured. "She's your new viscountess, is she not?"

Pride diffused through Mark's chest. "We were married just last week."

His Grace nodded. Slowly his eyebrows lifted. "You . . . er . . . travel a lot, don't you?"

"No." Mark scowled at the notorious womanizer and narrowed his eyes. "Hardly at all, anymore."

The prince took hold of Mark's shoulder and walked him toward the ladies. "Care for a glass of champagne?"

That evening, after races and all their associated festivities had ended, a rented carriage conveyed Mark and Mina toward London. She dozed against his shoulder, exhausted by the day's activity. A bump in the road jarred her awake and she glanced up. A telling tension drew the skin tight at his temples and jaw.

"You don't feel well."

"No."

"Are there voices?"

"Only one."

"What can I do?" she whispered.

"Nothing, Mina. There's nothing you can do."

Mark reached up and grasped the bellpull, a signal to the driver. Through the speaking tube, he provided an address unfamiliar to Mina. By the time they coursed through a neighborhood just south of Mayfair, night purpled the sky. The carriage turned down a short avenue, lined with immense homes. Heaping piles of wood beams and rubbish lined the pavement, as if every house on the street were under renovation. Eventually they slowed in front of the largest. Light spilled from the front windows.

"Where are we?" Mina asked as Mark assisted her down the stairs.

"Home." He led her up a paved walkway. "At least for the night."

His discomfort had intensified, as evidenced by the

gaunt draw of his cheeks and the shadows under his eyes.

Mr. Leeson, whom she hadn't seen since the eve of their failed departure from London, clambered down the front steps. "You're here. Why didn't you send word? I'm not ready."

"Show Mina the house," Mark rasped, his voice like gravel. "See that she has whatever she needs."

Realization flickered across the older man's features.

"Oh, sir. Yes, of course."

Mark took off across the lawn.

"Where are you going?" Mina followed him, trotting alongside him to keep pace. Her petticoats and skirts thrashed about her legs.

"For a walk."

"I'll go with you." She reached to touch his arm.

"You can't."

With a dig of her soles against the grass, she veered forward and planted herself in his path. "I don't want you to be alone."

He stopped, grasping her by the shoulders hard enough to make her wince. "But I *am* alone in this. No matter how I want things to be different, I have to do this *alone*. You were right when you said we were too different, Mina. I should never have brought you into this. Not in the way I did. I just thought, in all my arrogance, that I could make it work. For now, I just want you to be safe. I want you to go into the house with Leeson and stay there until it's all over. He will protect you."

"Why are you talking like this, Mark?" Mina blinked away a rush of tears. "As if we are saying good-bye? What's different now?"

Mark pressed a curled fist against the side of his head. "I can hear her, louder and more furious than ever before. I can smell her rancid scent in my nose."

His words pained her—tortured her. He hurt, and she

wanted to stay with him. "I'm not saying good-bye to you like this. I won't go in that house, and I won't stay there, not after everything we've—"

He lunged, seizing her face between his hands, and kissed her. Suspended there, her toes barely touching the grass, Mina felt the intensity of his emotion and his adoration for her pour through her lips, her throat and into her chest. With a groan, he pushed her away.

"*Stay.*" He backed off, giving her the flat of his palm.

"Mark . . ." She followed.

"Damn you, Mina," he bellowed. "I said *stay there.*"

The shouted words shocked her, sucking the air from her lungs. Stricken and pale, she stood fixed in place, paralyzed, as he retreated, to vanish around the corner of the house.

"It's best that you do as he says, child," counseled a gentle voice. Leeson stood a few feet behind her.

"Is he gone? Forever?"

"Surely not. Don't fret."

His words did not assure her. Had Mark lost his hope? Numb, she followed Mr. Leeson up the stairs and into the house. Even at this late hour, carpenters sawed and hammered. They cut wood moldings and fit them into place. Painters slathered the walls in a smooth coat of white. Leeson led her from room to room, chattering about wallpaper and carpet selections, and how the house was a blank slate and she could pick anything she liked. The entire structure had been refitted with gas illumination, so in every room he twisted the valves, as if to prove to her they worked. But no matter how valiantly he tried to distract her, she did not care about the house. Mina could think only of Mark.

Leeson urged her up the center staircase. "Once all is right in the world again, and your mind can turn to thoughts of pleasant things, we'll go across town to his lordship's warehouses and make whatever selections you like."

"He has warehouses?"

His mustache quivered into a smile. "He's got three, filled with furniture, artwork and every delightful thing you could imagine. Vases. Plasters. Urns. Old and new. It's almost as if he's been waiting all this time . . ."

"Waiting for what?" Mina whispered.

"For a home."

Tears surged into Mina's eyes. They surged into Mr. Leeson's eye too.

"Oh, dear. Look at us," she moaned.

He tugged two handkerchiefs from his pocket and handed her one.

"Thank you," she sniffled, dabbing her eyes.

He mopped his face, even plucking the eye patch up to swipe underneath. "You're very welcome, dear."

"I just don't know how to help him."

"Things will work out. You'll see. He's a strong one."

Mina paused on the third-floor landing. "The house is lovely, but I don't wish to see any more tonight. I think I'd just like to be alone for now." There were so many doors down the length of the hall. "Is there somewhere I could lie down?"

"Of course. This way, come along." Mr. Leeson guided her along the corridor. Horizontal patching striated the walls, evidence of the new gas lines. "Certainly, we'll cover all this mess with wallpaper, when you're prepared to make those selections."

He turned the knob and pushed in the door.

"Oh, my," Mina breathed.

Whereas the rest of the house might be incomplete as far as furniture and décor were concerned, the master suite had been finished to perfection. Wood-paneled walls gleamed. Dark blue drapes hung from the windows, and massive furniture occupied each part of the room, perfectly arranged. The air smelled of wood and polish.

"You're welcome to replace anything you don't like," he said.

"It's perfect. I wouldn't change a thing. You're very talented, Mr. Leeson. I hope someone tells you that at least a hundred times a day."

The diminutive man smiled proudly. "We'll have your trunks brought from the Savoy, then?"

"Yes, thank you."

"I'll dispatch the wagon for them now. I'll knock once they've arrived."

When he was gone, Mina removed her hat and her Ascot badge and entered the cavernous dressing room. A number of boxes lined the shelves. Green boxes, the same kind used by the modiste shop where they'd purchased her new mourning frocks. Tugging a ribbon, she lifted the lid of the first box. And then the second. And the third. They were gowns. Beautiful gowns, each in a different vibrant color. Blue, scarlet and green. In the final box she discovered a profusion of filmy, lacy undergarments and a card.

With devotion. M.

Mark. Clasping the card to her breast, she crossed the room to the window, and peered down into the shadowed garden. *Devotion.* He offered her devotion, even when she'd held him at bay.

Something slithered over her toe.

Mina blinked. *Slithered?* She could think of nothing that ought to slither inside the walls of a bedroom.

She searched the carpet. The dark colors and the pattern of twining leaves and flowers almost concealed the narrow black tail as it disappeared under the armchair. Mina gasped. Her pulse surged. A snake. She'd seen snakes before—mostly in India. One had even surprised her in her bedroll one night.

She could call for Leeson's assistance, but certainly in the brief absence required to summon him, the serpent would disappear and they wouldn't be able to find the creature again. How could she rest in this house, knowing a snake—possibly a poisonous snake—was on the loose? Where had it come from? Heart pounding, she bent at the waist and pulled off her shoe. Muscles drawn with tension, she wrapped her fingers around the toe so as to utilize the hard, narrow heel as a cudgel.

Advancing on the chair, she knelt and peeked beneath. The snake, dark and shining—an asp, she believed— darted out on the opposite side in the direction of the bed. She leapt up and scrambled after the serpent, then raised her arm—

"No, no, *noooo*."

A woman's voice. A hand seized her wrist, halting its downward swing. A swirl of dark skirts blurred Mina's view of her prey.

Mina scuffled away, the backs of her legs bumping against the mattress. She blinked, eyes wide.

Tall as a man, and standing as proud as a queen, the woman glared at her. Dark hair, as deep and glossy as mink, fell over her shoulders, all the way to her waist. Ivory pins held a heavy braided coil at her crown. She wore a cinnamon-colored gown, fashioned of rich, weighty silk. A garnet the size of a cherry glimmered on her finger.

"Where did you come from?" Mina whispered.

"What were you intending to do with that little shoe of yours?" Black eyes snapped with displeasure.

Mina lowered the shoe, breathing hard. "Well . . . there is a snake, and he's in my boudoir. I was going to smash him. Who are you?"

"I'm Selene. The Countess Pavlenco. And the snake is not a he," she sniffed. "She's a *she*."

Mina pressed a hand to her chest. "That must have gotten by me somehow, in all the excitement."

She stood only as tall as the countess's nose. "You're Mark's sister."

"Well, of course I am," she responded archly. With long-legged strides, she hurried after the snake and scooped it up. She cooed, "It's all right, Mrs. Hazelgreaves. That wicked little girl won't hurt you."

Little girl? Indeed she was, in comparison to this Amazon.

"Mrs. Hazelgreaves?"

A dark brow slashed up. "Named after a friend."

"Mrs. Hazelgreaves is an *asp*," Mina accused. "Asps are poisonous. Were you trying to kill me?"

"*Nooo*." Selene tucked the serpent into a velvet pouch at her waist. "I was just hoping for a little screaming and dancing around. That's all. I swear it." Her lips broke into a wide grin. "All in good fun."

Mina did not return her smile. "I'm sorry my reaction disappointed you. Why are you in my room?"

The smile evaporated. "Because he still hasn't told you."

"Told me what?"

"Who he is."

"He's Mark." Mina straightened her shoulders. "That's all that's important to me."

"What a perfectly darling response." Selene clasped a long-fingered, well-manicured hand against her breast. "You're curious though. I know you are."

The female Shadow Guard sauntered toward the chaise by the window. She sat and reclined against the pillows. Layers of lace-edged petticoats frothed around decidedly feminine ankles and polished black kid shoes. The weighty fabric hissed with her movement.

"Mark's true name is—"

"No, don't tell me—"

"Alexander Helios."

Mina crossed her arms over her chest and exhaled. "I think it would be best if you left."

The countess only smiled, and sank deeper into the cushions. "You don't recognize the name, do you?"

Mina hesitated. "Should I?"

"Cleopatra and Mark Antony were our parents." She turned her chin over her shoulder. "Do you see the resemblance? To the kinder depictions, of course. Mark looks more like our father."

Mina swallowed down her disbelief. If Selene's revelation was true, that would make Mark nineteen centuries old.

Still, she shook her head. This just wasn't right. "Please stop there. I think I should hear all this from him. Whenever he's ready."

"He'll never be ready." Selene examined a fingernail.

"That's up to him."

"You know the story, and yes, we were there. Our mother deemed it an honor for us to witness her suicide."

Selene's revelation took the air from Mina's lungs, and the argument from her lips. "That's . . . terrible."

Selene shrugged. Her silk skirts reflected the warm glow of the gas light. "Intrigue. Betrayal. Political murder. Such events were the cornerstone of our family—if you can even call what we had, that." Though the countess held a pose of nonchalant languor, her eyes glittered as black and hard as onyx. "We were ten years old. Not yet Amaranthines. She had the power, you see. She could have made herself immortal. As Octavian and his army advanced on Alexandria, the Primordial Council granted her the power to do it. But once she learned of Antony's death . . . she lost her mind. Raved and screamed. She made Mark and me immortal instead."

"To save you from Octavian?"

Selene rolled her eyes. "Not at all. We were to be her

weapons, her Trojan horses after death, if you will. She made us promise to carry out her vengeance against Octavian."

She shifted and adjusted the velvet pouch at her waist.

"What happened then?"

A certain amount of guilt accompanied the question. She shouldn't ask anything; shouldn't be so curious. Not with Selene making all the revelations.

Selene looked about the room. "Do you have any books?"

"Not in the room. I'm sorry."

Her aquiline nose scrunched in irritation. "Well then . . . to understand, you'd have to know that when children are granted immortality, they must mature into their prime age—the age at which they are physically and mentally at their strongest. So yes, for years we had immortality in our blood, but none of the related powers. We were helpless, and at Octavian's mercy. We became prizes of war—as Cleopatra must have known we would. Octavian returned us to Rome." Her voice grew hushed. "He had us bound in gold chains so heavy we could barely walk, and paraded us through the streets. The citizens jeered. Threw rancid rubbish and worse."

"Mark has scars. . . ."

Selene pushed the cuff of her sleeve and held up her wrist, revealing scars identical to Mark's. "As a final insult, Octavian turned us over to the care of his sister—the very wife our father had abandoned, to take up with our mother. As you can imagine, that made for a pleasant upbringing."

"I'm so sorry," Mina whispered.

A dark brow slashed up. "Don't pity me, little girl. And certainly don't pity him. The experience only made us harder. More ruthless. More determined to blaze a path toward our own legend as opposed to becoming a footnote to our parents' historic—and in my personal opinion, exceedingly cowardly—demise. It's why we gained the notice of the Primordials, as suitable candidates for the elite order of the Shadow Guards." Her eyes narrowed. "Looking back, I wouldn't change a thing."

"Why have you told me all of this?"

"You tell me the answer."

"To help me understand him better?"

"Stop the violins." Selene held up a hand and gave an arch laugh. "Wrong."

Heat stung Mina's cheeks. Lord only help her if she ever had to pass a holiday with this woman.

"Then why?" she queried brittlely.

"To tell you, in the plainest of terms . . . to let him go. You're not worthy of his pain or his legacy. Run and run now, as fast as your little mortal legs will take you." Selene stood. "Do you need some money to go away? I've got lots."

"No," Mina answered firmly. "I won't leave him. We're married."

Married. The intensity of her conviction startled her. They *were* married. Mark was her husband, and she was his wife.

"Married," Selene scoffed. "Lots of people are married. It doesn't have to *mean anything*." Selene sauntered close. "You're only a distraction for him on this, the eve of his greatest battle."

"He'll stop the Dark Bride."

She snorted. "I'm not talking about the Dark Bride. I'm talking about me. When you see him again—*if* you see him again—tell him the portals opened long enough for my orders to come through."

Her image wavered. Dissolved. Just before she disappeared . . . her smile faltered. But then she was gone.

Mina gave a shriek of frustration. She stormed the length of the room. What a horrible woman. What a horrible story. *Mark*. She went to the window and looked into the night. He was out there. Alone. Yes, she'd seen the frightening creature he could become. But she'd known another side of him as well.

Something lay in the middle of the lawn, something that looked suspiciously like a top hat. Her mind worked, clicking and whirring with thought. When Mark had heard the Dark Bride's voice, he'd come here for a reason—certainly not only to deposit her in a half-finished house with Leeson.

The moment he'd left her, shouting for her to remain behind, he hadn't returned to the carriage. He'd gone in the direction of the garden. Mina exited the bedroom and descended the service stairs. She managed to avoid Leeson, and after going room to room, eventually found a door leading to the garden-facing side of the house. Yes, his hat. And farther on, his coat, as if he'd discarded them along the way. The two items led her as far as a small alcove of trees.

A raised stone wall, just a foot or so high, circled a gazing pool. There was nothing else. No secret path or magic tower. She put down his things on the stones and sat, disappointed.

A gentle breeze rippled the surface of the water, momentarily warping the reflection of the full moon. Orange and silver ornamental carp twisted below the surface, their scales glinting in the moonlight.

Her reflection peered up, a sympathetic confidante.

"What am I going to do?" she whispered, her heart swollen and tender. "I love him. Oh, yes. I do. And I'm miserable without him."

Her mirror image smiled, appearing to bare teeth. Absently Mina touched the back of her head and found her hair, though mussed from the day, still pinned in place— nothing at all like the long, dark hair that swirled below.

A hand sprang from the water and *jerked* her by the wrist, toppling her face-first into the black water.

The shock of cold forced the breath from her lungs. Instinctively she inhaled. Air, not water, invaded her mouth and her nose. Hands on her wrists pulled her down . . . down . . . down. The moonlight grew faint. Mina struggled. Writhed. Kicked to free herself.

A pale face hovered. A sharp, *painful* pressure—teeth—clamped down on her nose, ending with a ripple of dark hair and a flash of silvery scales. Two hands pushed her and jostled her through a hole—a tunnel. Her feet found purchase on solid stone. Stairs. Eyes wide, she reached for an orange, wavering glow.

Mina burst free of the water. She collapsed, gasping, onto a flat expanse of a mosaic floor. She embraced the blue and white tiles. Her hair. Her skin. Her clothes. Completely dry.

Mark crouched over her, unsmiling. "What are you doing here?"

Chapter Seventeen

"She *bit* my nose," Mina exclaimed.

His eyebrows went up. "I see the teeth marks." He pried away her hand and smoothed the padded tip of his index finger over the tender spot. "She didn't break the skin though."

"What is she?"

"She's . . . a woman." He shrugged, nonchalant. "In the water."

Mina pushed up to sit. "I expect a better explanation than that."

He stood. "She's an outcast Nereid, biding her time until she can go home."

"A *Nereid*," she repeated in disbelief.

But of course, she did believe.

He extended his hand and hoisted her up. "For the time being, she's the keeper of this spring. She's not supposed to let just anyone come down. She must have liked you."

A cavern of close-set stone blocks spread above them. Two multitined candelabra lit the darkness. The tiles under their feet formed a large octopus, its coiling tentacles spread out in all directions. Against the wall lay a narrow pallet, strewn with blankets. The mineral scent of springwater filled her nose.

"What is this place?" Her voice echoed faintly.

"A Roman bath, long ago covered over by the city."

"Can you hear the Dark Bride's voice down here?"

Mark smiled tightly. "Not so much."

Mina gasped, her heart burgeoning with hope. "So you can stay here, protected, until the wave is finished?"

"Something like that."

She wouldn't talk to him any more about her father, the Eye or the Dark Bride. There was nothing more to discuss. When the wave was over, he would hunt. And as a result, he would either live or die.

"You're not angry with me for coming here?" she asked.

"Not as angry as I ought to be." Candlelight reflected off his jaw and the hollows of his cheeks.

Mina moved into his shadow and touched her hand against the center of his shirt.

"Don't, Mina." He backed off a step.

She dropped her arms to her sides. "I came looking for you for a reason."

He shook his head. "You shouldn't have."

"I wanted to be with my husband."

He looked down and closed his eyes. "You were right when you said one day . . . one day I'd have to leave." The muscle in his neck moved as he swallowed. "I don't stay, Mina. I never have. I could never be the husband you deserve. Even if I come through this, eventually I'd have to go. It's not right that I keep you from all the things that will bring you happiness."

"Happiness." She smiled, and her vision blurred with tears. "This moment . . . being with you, brings me happiness. It's enough."

Mina backed toward the pallet. With trembling fingers she unfastened the buttons at the front of her bodice.

"Alexander Helios, son of Cleopatra and Mark Antony, be my husband. Be my safe place now, tonight, and let me be yours."

His lips parted on a breath. "You . . . know."

She nodded. "Your vexatious sister, whom I'm afraid I don't care for all that much, paid me a visit tonight and told me everything." Mina pushed the garment from her shoulders. "She wants you to know she's gotten her orders to kill you."

Mark didn't so much as blink. Instead he watched, fixated as she removed her bodice and untied her skirts. "I'll concern myself with her tomorrow."

Held within his hot gaze, she barely felt the chilled air of the underground chamber.

With a soft curse, he closed the distance between them and seized her by the waist, lifting her against him, carrying her to his bed. She curled around him, inhaling his scent and burying her hands into his hair. Gently he knelt and laid her atop the blankets. He tore the shirt from his shoulders.

"My wife. My beautiful wife." Braced on rippling arms, he lowered himself atop her. "You're the only one. In all my life, you're the only woman I've ever loved. The only woman I've ever wed."

"Wake up, sweetheart. It's morning." Mark lay propped on his elbow, looking down at Mina's flushed, sleeping face.

Naked, she buried her face against his neck. "Can't we just stay here?"

"You know we can't." He bent to press a kiss to her temple.

The time had come for him to leave Mina and go out into the city. They dressed in silence, each helping the other with the fastening of buttons. A moment later and they stood at the edge of the stairs. Black-blue water rippled and slapped against the stones. Mina's nervousness was obvious.

"Here." Mark pressed a coin into her palm. "Give her something shiny on the way up. She likes pretty things."

With a squeeze, he led her down the steps. "Are you ready?"

Mina nodded.

"One. Two. Three."

Together they sank beneath the surface. Familiar with the narrow dimension of the tunnel, he guided and pulled her through. Once inside the column of the well, they ascended. Early-morning light revealed the Nereid's lithe outline against the gray stone. Like an ancient princess, bound forever to a watery tower, she circled them, stirring the water with her silvery tail. Yet her eyes were wide, and she shunned Mina's proffered gift. Instead, she pointed upward.

Mark looked. Mina's hands clenched on to his shoulders.

On the surface above, a face peered down, a black patch clearly visible.

With a strong series of kicks, Mark conveyed Mina to the surface. She grabbed on to the ledge, and he hoisted her up. Leeson's open hand reached down. Mark gripped the palm, and with a press of his boots against the stone, climbed out. Water sluiced off his clothes, his skin, leaving him dry.

"Your lordship, you've visitors," Leeson announced.

"Dangerous visitors?" Mark inquired darkly. "Or visitors with whom I should like to . . . visit?"

"Both, I'd say."

Mark's curiosity aroused, he took Mina by the hand. For the first time, he took his wife into the house he had hoped they could share as man and wife. A house in progress. One with many improvements to be made.

"Where?" Mark inquired.

"He's in the study."

Mark drew Mina aside. Leeson waited near the study door, his gaze focused toward the entrance hall of the house. It was early yet, and no workmen had arrived. The hallways and rooms lay silent.

Mark drew his fingertips along Mina's jaw. "Thank you."

It was all he could say. Bigger, more daring words skidded to a halt at the back of his throat. She nodded.

He bent, kissing her sweetly along the corner of her mouth, and then full on. A possible good-bye. She realized it too, he saw, for she blinked away a sudden glaze of moisture in her eyes.

Mina left Mark with reluctance. She feared at any moment he would be gone, and she would be left with only memories. Upstairs she washed. Their trunks had been delivered from the Savoy. Fixed on tasks of normalcy, she stood in her undergarments in the expansive dressing room and put away her things. When she reached for one of her black mourning dresses, she paused. No. Today she would wear the blue gown Mark had purchased for her. Fighting colors. The color of his eyes. Once dressed, she returned downstairs.

From the study came a volley of shouted curses. The wood, the chandeliers, shook with their intensity. Something crashed against the door and fell with a secondary shatter. She flinched. Was she to simply stand here and listen? Should she attempt to intercede?

A young woman appeared from the direction of the kitchen. Dressed in a smart, dark blue traveling suit, she carried a round silver tray with tea service. An easy smile lifted her lips. "You must be Lady Alexander."

Slightly shorter in stature than Mina, the woman was, quite simply, beautiful. Pale hair twisted in intricate coils at the base of her neck. Ringlets gleamed, perfectly turned, at either side of her face.

Crash. More bellowed cursing.

She didn't so much as flinch. Instead she asked brightly, "Would you care for a cup of tea?"

Mina followed her into the drawing room, directly across the entrance hall from Mark's study.

The smaller, blond woman lowered the tray to a table. With a turn of her shoulders, she greeted Mina again. "I'm so thrilled to meet you. Mark, *married*? You can't be just any woman, to have captured his heart."

Mina smiled. She had captured his heart. After their night together, she had no doubt of that. Days after their marriage ceremony, they'd without a doubt truly become man and wife. Despite the pending danger, the glow of love arose warm in her cheeks.

She drew closer to the woman. "It's clear you know who I am, but I'm afraid I'm a bit in the dark as to your identity."

She laughed. "Of course. How impolite of me. I am Elena, Lady Black. Lord Black is my husband."

"Lord Black." Mina tensed. Mark had mentioned the elder Guard on a number of occasions, always with the understanding that when he returned from the Inner Realm, it would be to assassinate him. Selene had already claimed orders in that regard. Were they all circling now, like vultures?

"Oh, dear. I can see I've upset you." Elena's smile dropped. She lowered herself onto the settee and patted the cushion beside her. "Please sit."

Mina did sit, but only because the room spun so wildly about her. With a frown, she met the other woman's eyes.

"Why are you and Lord Black here?"

"Because they're going to help me," Mark said from the door.

Another man appeared behind him, just as tall as Mark. His hair was darker than night. Intense, gray eyes settled on Mina. A chill shot through her as if by that mere glance, he assessed her completely, inside and out.

"Fine choice, Alexander."

Mark winked at Mina.

Mina frowned, perplexed. "What do you mean, they're going to help us? You've always told me Archer was to be feared."

Archer elbowed Mark. "You said that? I'm flattered."

Mark rolled his eyes.

Elena touched her hand. "Archer petitioned the Primordial Council to delay Mark's assassination orders. They refused and granted Selene's request."

"I think it's terrible," Mina said, scowling, "that a sister would volunteer herself to assassinate her own brother. Her twin, no less. She came to the house last night just to taunt me with her vicious orders."

Mark interjected, "But we as Shadow Guards are expected to be vicious. Fearsome. Ruthless. I understand the challenge and bear her no ill will."

Archer nodded in agreement, and held up a piece of parchment stamped with a triangular, black seal. "However, due to special circumstances, they've granted Elena and me permission to offer whatever assistance we can to Mark." He deposited the document onto a side table, and moved to stand in front of the bay window.

Mina's gaze veered between her husband and the darker Guard. "What special circumstances?"

"Because six months ago, Mark sacrificed himself to Transcension in order to save Archer," Elena revealed in a soft voice. "Not only Archer, but his sister and me, and the entire city of London. He sacrificed himself for the good of many."

"You're exaggerating greatly," Mark retorted. His cheeks flushed a ruddy, masculine shade.

"I'm not exaggerating," she murmured to Mina. "If not for your husband, Archer would not be here today and neither would I. The Council, despite their caution, is grateful. Archer persuaded them to reward Mark with this final chance."

Mark drew closer and touched his hand against the back of Mina's neck. "The chunks of missing time . . . they were caused by the Primordial Council. They utilized focused waves of Amaranthine power to debilitate me during the times when I'd grown most vulnerable to the Dark Bride, effectively preventing me from being used toward her dark purposes. They've delayed the effects of my deterioration."

Archer nodded. "Because they want you to survive."

"Then why the order for his assassination?" Mina blurted angrily.

She stood and went to the table, where she retrieved the parchment Archer had left behind moments before. She lifted it to read, but the characters blurred . . . and disappeared. She blinked and in the split second after she opened her eyes, glimpsed the bold, dark strokes again, but just as before, they vanished too quickly for her to examine them. Turning over the page, she brushed her fingertips over the wax seal and the deeply imprinted image of three lotus flowers. She turned back to her companions. "Tell me, please—why?"

Archer explained in a patient tone, "Because beyond all else, they must protect the integrity of the Inner Realm. They can't take the chance this final effort to save Mark will fail. Selene is aware we are here on Mark's behalf. She'll be watching and waiting until the last moment possible to execute her orders."

Mina pressed a hand to her forehead. "I don't like that woman."

"She's an acquired taste," Elena assured her. "I think under different circumstances, you'd come to love her as I have." Her lips broke into a smile. "Have you met any of her pets?"

Mina nodded. "Mrs. Hazelgreaves, in fact."

"Darling," Archer interjected, "we've no time for chitchat."

Elena pressed her lips together. "He's right. We've got to find your father. All of our Amaranthine intelligence shows he's here in London, searching for the Eye."

Mina sighed, relieved. "So we know for certain the Eye is here?"

Mark responded, "That's right, sweetheart." In a quieter voice, he added, "Your father, unfortunately, has been used."

Mina's face drained of warmth. "What do you mean?"

Archer's expression became stark. "We've made certain observations from the Inner Realm. Traced the paths of individuals through history, and found disturbing patterns. This Tantalyte movement has been ongoing in stealth for quite some time."

"But my father . . . you say he has been used. How?"

"It's like a game of chess, played out over the surface of the earth," he responded. "But with people and powerful artifacts."

Elena added softly, "This has gone on for centuries, beneath the awareness of the Primordial Council."

"Is he . . ." A sudden tightness in her chest cut her off.

"Evil?" Mark supplied. "Not at all. His motives are pure. But like a long line of others, he's been targeted because of his strengths and interests, and insidiously presented with information. Without knowing, he's acted on behalf of Tantalus."

Archer nodded. "He's a puppet. Tantalus manipulated a long succession of events—again, over centuries—to put those scrolls in his path. Tantalus needed a mortal to translate them and lead his followers to the Eye."

Mina stared at Mark. "In his desire to uncover the truth, he's actually been helping to execute some centuries-old strategy?"

"That's right," Mark answered evenly. "In this world there exist relics of phenomenal power. Relics that, when brought together in a precise fashion, can be used toward good or evil."

"And this Eye is one of them," she surmised.

"That's right," he confirmed. "Clearly, the mirror didn't start out in London, but somehow, over time, it made its way here. Archer tells me the Primordials are still trying to determine how. At any case, we're not sure what the ultimate intent is here, but it can't be good. We've got to find your father before they do."

"Then what are you waiting for?" she urged, curling her hands over his and squeezing. "Go."

Archer smiled grimly. "It's time we go out into the city. We'll divide the districts amongst us. Elena, though not a Shadow Guard, can help in the search as well."

"Elena's not a Guard?" Mina asked.

"I'm an Intervenor." Elena smiled. "I am skilled at healing, and when appropriate, I intervene when mortal lives are unfairly threatened with an early demise."

Archer continued. "Between the three of us, we'll find him. There's mention in the *London Times* today that city workers discovered a portion of the old city wall by Ludgate Hill, near Little Bridge Street. Roman in origin. I want to investigate the wall. You never know, the Eye might have been concealed there centuries ago."

Leeson entered, carrying two large black cases. Mina observed Mark's gaze go to the cases with fierce, intense longing.

Archer looked to Mark. "One more thing. I'm authorized to convey that for the next twenty-four hours, the Primordial Council rescinds its order against your possession and use of Amaranthine silver." He smiled, but his eyes and his lips were hard. "You may hunt fully armed. If you find the Dark Bride before Selene or I do, Reclaim her. She'll do anything to preserve Tantalus's increasing hold on this city. He wants London for his throne."

"Why London?" asked Mina. Her head ached with the enormity of all she'd heard.

Mark explained, "London has, by far, the greatest concentration of poverty, but also excess and vice. We believe the volume of misery, that deterioration of the mortal soul, has attracted him here. Once he arrives, he would have access to thousands upon thousands of recruits for his army of toadies."

Archer's brow lifted. "Toadies?"

Mark nodded. "I've never seen anything like them before. But they attend to the Dark Bride. They don't put off a sense of evil. They're just empty."

"We've observed the proliferation of such servants," Archer revealed. "They are humans who've had their souls subdued while their moral defenses were in a weakened state. During a fit of temper, or a rage of jealousy. They are damn difficult to track."

Mark's lips turned down. "But what if my deterioration advances? No matter how much I want it . . . I should not bear the power of Reclamation. Not when I, if fully consumed, might turn the power against you."

Archer edged toward him, so they stood nose to nose. A small smile pulled his lips. "Do you hear her voice now?"

"Not at the moment."

"It's not because she isn't talking, and trying her damnedest to turn you against us."

Mark tilted his head. "What are you saying?"

"That same focused power the Primordials employed to debilitate you—to protect you—is now being exacted across the city to mute her commands. But they've only got enough stored up, to utilize to this degree of intensity, through tomorrow. Hence, the aforementioned twenty-four-hour limitation."

Mark grinned. "Then let's get started."

Mina hovered at the edges of the room for the next half hour. The three immortals strategized, drew weapons and prepared to depart. A certain excitement, even optimism, electrified the room.

At last Mark came to her. "This isn't good-bye."

"I know it's not." She smiled up at him. "I wish I could go with you, but I know that's not possible."

"Stay with Leeson." He bent to press a kiss to her lips.

Her hands slid over his shoulders, and curled into his linen collar. She drew him closer for a second, more fervent kiss. In its aftermath, she whispered, "Come back to me, husband. I'll be waiting here for you."

A full thirteen hours later, night darkened the earth. Mark continued his search, methodically examining districts along the Thames. Frustration dimmed his earlier optimism. He'd found nothing. No professor. No Eye. No Dark Bride. Not even a blasted toadie. The hours whipped past all too quickly. Thirteen hours. Eleven hours left.

The Savoy rose up before him, her beauty still cloaked in canvas drapes and scaffolding. Cleopatra's Needle shone luminous against the backdrop of the clouded sky. Four colossal stone sphinxes guarded the corners of the site. The still evening air carried the sound of carriage wheels clattering on pavement. Bells tolled from distant ships. But here the Embankment was deserted. His gaze slid up the granite obelisk. For the first time he realized how his mother must have felt as Octavian's armies closed in on her.

Hurry. Hurry William. Before they find you.

Mark heard the mortal thoughts, as clear as day.

His pulse quickened. With a lunge, he rounded the monument. A shadowy figure hunched in the even-darker shadow of one of the stone sphinxes. A relief, greater than he'd ever known, washed like sunshine through his veins.

"Professor Limpett."

The man lunged up from his crouched position and stumbled away. He wielded a hammer and a chisel. His expression bore the intense strain of fear.

One of them.

"No, I'm not." Mark held his stance and shook his head.

"I remember you. Your face. We met in . . ."

Thirty years ago, his thoughts echoed.

"At Petra, yes."

"But you're . . . you're . . ."

"I'm what you've been searching for." Mark smiled. "And I've been searching for you."

The professor's jaw fell.

"I'm one of the immortals you've sought to prove. And the scrolls you possess, the Eye you seek . . . it's imperative that we find them, and quickly."

"They want to hurt people."

"So let's stop them."

The professor eyed him warily.

A snarl came from the darkness. A shadow leapt through the air, toward the professor. With a twist of his hand, Mark issued forth his sword. His skin, his eyes, *changed*. Amaranthine silver flashed.

Mark lunged and slashed. The toadie slumped, headless. The foul stench of its sudden deterioration clouded the air. The professor crouched on the pavement, gasping. He stared at the remains.

"Must I convince you of what side I'm on?"

"Oh, no," responded the professor. "That's quite sufficient for me. Have you another of those swords for me?"

"The silver would burn your hands. The blade is formed of primeval silver, and fire."

"Wonderful," the old man marveled.

"I must inform you, I've married your daughter."

"*You!* I knew from the newspaper announcement that she had married, but your face was blurred."

"I'll take you to her later." Mark jerked his head toward the tools the professor still clenched in his hands. "Why are you here? Do you have the scrolls?"

The professor nodded. "But scrolls be damned for the moment. Let's get the Eye."

The Eye.

Mark curled his fists. Concentrating, he conveyed the news to Archer. *Cleopatra's Needle. Come now. The Eye.*

Limpett pointed the hammer. "We've got to pry out those bored holes on either side of the Needle."

"Bored holes?"

Gray eyebrows rose. "You'll see them when you look. You pry one out." He offered a chisel.

Mark lifted his sword. "I'm covered."

"I'll get the other."

With a press of his fingertips against the surface of the granite, Mark did indeed discover a circular hole in the base of the needle. He wedged the point of his sword against it. The bore popped out. On the other side, Limpett struggled to make headway on his.

"Stand back," Mark ordered. When the professor moved, he dispatched that bore with the same efficiency.

"Now what?"

"Just watch." The professor drew aside his coat. There, strapped to his sides, were four ivory scroll rods.

Another growl came from the darkness, and then a low hiss. Two toadies bounded toward them, faces leering, arms outstretched. Mark blocked the professor, then swung the sword. Heads flew and bounced off the concrete before rolling into the grass.

"Damn it, William. Hurry."

Chapter Eighteen

Leeson leapt up from the armchair. "Someone's coming to the door."

Mina set aside the newspaper she hadn't been reading. "Do you know who it is?"

His eyes narrowed. "It's your uncle—Lord Trafford and his daughters."

"Oh, my goodness." She pressed her hands to her cheeks. "It's been days since I've called upon them or corresponded."

"We're not letting them in," he said firmly. He crossed to the drawing room door and peered into the entry hall.

A knock sounded on the door.

Mina bit her lip. "I can't just let them stand on the steps."

"Of course you can."

"All the lights are on. They know someone's at home."

"I'll extinguish the gas now."

"*Mr. Leeson.*"

"Oh, all right." He weakened visibly. "Just speak to them through the door."

"Which one of my relatives are you suspicious of?" Despite the tension of the day, Mina chuckled. "Trafford, or one of the girls?"

"At present, all of London is suspect. Especially with all those new soul mutations—*toadies*—lurking about." He drew his shoulders in and feigned a shiver. He grinned. "Just crack the door. Tell them you're ill. Typhoid always works well to send them scurrying back to their carriages."

As if to enforce his decision, he slid behind the door. He turned the key and twisted the handle. He allowed her—yes—a crack.

"Good evening," she said. She'd never been good at feigning illness, even as a child.

The door burst inward.

"The house is lovely," gushed Astrid, rushing past.

"*Grand*," agreed Evangeline, squinting into all corners. She pursued her sister. "You must give us a tour."

From behind the open door, Leeson let out a frustrated groan. The girls—two blurs in black bonnets—raced from room to room.

Trafford stood sheepishly on the threshold, a calling card in hand. "I'm so sorry for the intrusion. We're leaving for my northern estate in the morning, and we wished to bid you adieu. The gentleman at the Savoy gave us this address."

"It's quite all right," Mina answered. "But I'm feeling a bit under the weather and wouldn't want to give the girls a nasty bug."

He nodded. "Let me just gather them. Without Lucinda here, they've become rather impulsive. *Oh*—" He held up a finger, as if remembering something.

"Yes?"

"There was another gentleman at the hotel making inquiries about you." He turned to glance over his shoulder. "I told him you were my niece. I hope that's all right. He says he was an acquaintance of your father's. I think he may have followed us over."

Mina's heart sank. Sure as fire, Mr. Matthews, wearing a black bowler, rushed up the walk.

Trafford stepped through, onto the tile.

"Miss Limpett." A smiling Mr. Matthews clambered up the stairs.

"Mr. Matthews." She forced a smile.

Again, from somewhere behind the door, Leeson gave out a little squawk.

"I'm so pleased to finally find you here at home. I've been desperately attempting to pay my respects. I'm mortified to have missed your father's funeral service, but was out of the country on museum business."

"Thank you, sir. Your sentiments are deeply appreciated."

He strode boldly past. She glanced to Leeson. His cheeks were red, his lips flat with displeasure. She swung the door closed.

A scream came from upstairs, from one of the girls. Mina bit her lower lip. She could not help but recall the last time she'd heard the girls scream.

"What was that?" Mr. Matthews queried, spinning on his heel.

Trafford rushed out from the drawing room. "Did I just hear one of the girls?"

"It's all right." Mina lifted a hand. "Perhaps it's just a—a mouse." Or a snake. "The house is old, and the renovation might have gotten them stirred up. I'll bring the girls back down."

With a hand in her skirt, Mina climbed the stairs to the first floor. She found Astrid and Evangeline in the first bedroom, gripping each other by the hands. The room had yet to be furnished. There was only carpet, and an open door that led into a shadowed dressing room.

"Is everyone well?"

Evangeline giggled. "I'm so sorry, Willomina. Astrid frightened me, wicked girl. She said she saw a face in the window and grabbed hold of me, so I screamed."

Astrid stared at the night-darkened pane. "I *did* see a face. A white face. One that looked like a mask."

A chill scraped down Mina's spine.

Suddenly the gaslight that lit the room flared with a sudden hiss . . . and died.

Mina blinked into the darkness. Moonlight streamed through the windowpanes, but weakly.

"Willomina? The lights—," said Astrid.

"Over here," she instructed as calmly as her pounding heart allowed. "Come with me."

A dark figure hurtled out of the darkness, nothing more than a shadow but for the white mask it wore as a face.

Too late, she saw the flash of a long silver blade.

Mark heard Mina's scream inside his head. Panic tore through him so violently, he almost dropped his sword.

The professor mumbled, "Blast. Those two didn't work, not together anyway. You see, there are two holes, but I've got four scroll rods. It's all about finding the right combination."

Archer. Hurry. Cleopatra's Needle.

Only a minute away, Archer replied. *Delayed by toadies.*

"I've got to go," said Mark.

"Go?" William's eyes widened in alarm. "What if there are more of those things about?"

"It's Mina."

He paled. "Then go. Yes, go. I'll finish here and rejoin you at your residence. Yes, yes, I know the address. I have not always been the perfect father, but I love my daughter dearly and have kept myself informed of her situation and well-being."

"Another immortal will arrive momentarily. His name is Archer."

With a grim frown, the professor nodded and wedged a scroll rod into the narrow hole. "Give her a kiss from her papa. Tell her I'll explain everything soon."

Mark transformed into shadow. Light flashed past in brilliant streams as he bounded, twisted and soared over cobblestones, houses and carriages. He pushed himself, *strained* his power beyond any prior extremes.

Within three minutes, he'd arrived at the house. Fear twisted, deep in his guts. The windows were black and the door hung open. With an agonized growl, he materialized and delved inside.

"*Mina*," he bellowed.

"They took her," Leeson's voice shouted from the drawing room. "Bloody bastards."

Mark found the immortal's headless body at the center of a blood-spattered carpet.

"Over here. Over here."

His head lay behind the settee. Mark crouched over him and turned his chin so they looked eye to eye. "Who took her?"

"I'm not sure." Leeson's bloodstained lips moved. One eye wavered, seeking focus. The patch remained in place. "It was either Trafford or that Matthews fellow from the museum who cut me."

Mark seethed. The cult of immortality he'd originally suspected began to take shape. "Where? Where did they take her?"

A voice answered, "There's a note pinned to his chest."

Mark whirled. Archer bent over Leeson's body.

"Oh, dear." Elena rushed past to claim Leeson's head. "A decapitation. A difficult injury, but don't worry, my dear little man. I'll have you fixed up in no time."

"I told you to go to Cleopatra's Needle," Mark bellowed.

"We did." Archer's eyes flashed. "We found nothing but a gaping hole in the base."

"What of the professor?"

Archer shook his head. "He wasn't there."

"Bloody hell," Mark cursed. "What does the note say?"

"It's an invitation." Archer stared levelly at him. "It's for you."

Mark snatched the square card from the other immortal's gloved hand. A familiar foul stench offended his nose.

Frantic over Mina's disappearance, he skimmed the words, which were typeset in glossy black.

> *The Dark Bride*
> *requests your presence*
> *at the marriage of herself*
> *The Dark Bride*
> *to*
> *Jack the Ripper*
> *tonight*
> *at midnight*
> *Westminster Clock Tower*

Except disturbingly, a thick black X had been drawn across the words "Jack the Ripper." In round, childish handwriting, Mark's name had been substituted beneath. At the bottom, she'd added, *P.S. Come alone.*

"That's an hour from now."

"Then we'd better strategize on the way."

They paused only to help Elena with the positioning of Leeson's body on the settee. They left him there, cursing and complaining at being left behind, his neck thickly bandaged.

Mina awoke to darkness and a man's shout. Blindly, she pressed her hands about. They'd locked her into some sort of closet, with only a crack of light visible beneath the door.

Her lips were dry and tasted and smelled of chemical. Someone stepped on her.

"Ouch, ouch. Stop." She gripped a calf and steered the offending boot away.

"Willomina?"

Her heart leapt at the familiar voice. "Father?"

He collapsed halfway atop her, and after a moment, they found one another's arms. Oh, yes. She inhaled. Ink, paper and tobacco. She touched his face. Whiskers. Craggy nose. He did the same.

"Have they hurt you?" he asked.

"No."

"I'm so sorry. I sought only to protect you."

"I know that now, Father."

"I thought myself so clever, avoiding them this long. But once I uncovered the Eye, they closed in. There were so many of them. Too many for me to escape."

"You found the Eye?" She gripped his arm. "And now they've got it? Oh, no. No, no, no."

"They want it for evil, Mina. But don't worry. He'll find us."

"Who?"

"Your immortal husband."

She laughed and sobbed at once. "You met Mark?"

"Yes—again. I met him long ago, actually. Didn't realize what he was then, of course. Can't say I'm certain how the two of you will make a marriage work, but I couldn't hope for a more interesting son-in-law."

"Oh, Father." She laid her head against his chest. Tears stung her eyes. "I missed you. I was so worried about you—that they'd get you, and now look. They've got us both."

"Child, who brought you here?"

"Trafford and Mr. Matthews."

"Your uncle? And Matthews?" he repeated incredulously.

"They abducted me. I'm certain they're part of the group that's been pursuing you."

His narrow frame stiffened within her arms. "God forgive me, I sent you right into danger."

"It's not your fault. How could you have known?" She moaned softly. "What are they going to do to us?"

And what would happen to Mark?

From the shadow of the House of Commons, Mark peered up at Big Ben's illuminated face.

He hissed, "What do you mean, you can't scale the walls?"

Elena interjected, "Stop bickering, gentlemen. We're all here for the same purpose."

Archer scowled, then exhaled sharply. "The tower's emitting some sort of repellant energy. You know as well as I that even in shadow we don't have the ability to simply shoot up straight into the sky and through the windows. We've got to have some sort of traction or grip. Even the door is barricaded with the same stuff—I can't even shadow through. Likely they'll allow only you inside."

"Damn it," Mark cursed.

"I suspect that just as the Primordials are exerting their power tonight in support of this battle, so too is Tantalus."

"It's five minutes until midnight. I'm going to have to go in alone."

Archer stared into the darkness. "Do you know if Leeson still has that balloon?"

"That's a *stupid* idea."

Archer's brow slashed up, the only indication of a flare in temper.

Mark muttered, "But it's better than any idea I've got, and we've no more time for strategizing."

"The warehouse isn't far."

"All right." Mark nodded. "But I'm going on up. I'll try to delay things as well as I can, a half hour at best."

"What's going to happen once you're up there? What did that third scroll say?"

Mark stretched his neck, attempting to ease the tension in his muscles. "That any use of the Eye is a bloody one-shot deal. For instance, the conduit couldn't be used repeatedly by one person to move back and forth between mortal and immortal states."

"So what is your plan?"

Mark laughed darkly. "I don't have one. But I've got to place my hands on the Eye in order to reverse my Transcension. Once I manage that, I'll Reclaim the Dark Bride before she has any opportunity to transform herself into an immortal. I'm sure the bitch is waiting to do the honors during the ceremony." Mark paced a few steps. He didn't mention the worst-case scenario; he didn't want to acknowledge its possibility himself. "I need you up there, Archer. Do whatever you must to get Mina out."

"Trust me, Mark. I'll be there. Anything else I need to know?"

"You know the order of things. If things go bad . . . if *I* go bad, do what you have to do. Slay me if you must."

Mark closed his eyes and thought of Mina. *Please God. Let her still be alive.* He'd do anything to save her. Give anything.

Archer reached out a hand. "Well then, it seems as if we do, indeed, have a plan."

Mark accepted, and they clasped hands. "Whatever happens to me tonight, take care of her."

"We will," responded Elena.

He left them, two shadows in the darkness, and rushed toward the tower. No sentries stood watch. Though he heard the clatter of carriages on the nearby streets, the tower and the adjacent Parliament buildings appeared deserted. Abandoned. Dead. The observation filled him with foreboding.

He pushed through the doors. Warmth, heat from the furnace in the basement, touched his skin. He traveled through the various apartments, and at the shadowed doorway to the staircase, he paused to listen. He heard no sound.

Was this all a trap? *Most certainly.*

He delved up the oblong shaft. At the top of the first flight, he rounded the corner to ascend the next.

He froze. Faces met him, gray and leering, their eyes whirling. There were costermongers and prostitutes, and gentlemen and ladies. They lined the stairs on either side, the Dark Bride's toadies. His heart raced. There were more than he'd ever imagined.

"Relinquish the sword," the nearest one commanded.

"Part with your blade," said another.

God, their whispers . . . their fetid breath filled the staircase. He could slay them all, but the Dark Bride certainly held Mina in the belfry above. He could not endanger her life with so reckless a reaction. With no other choice, he flung open his palm. His sword lashed out, a searing flash of metallic white. Shouts of admiration echoed off the walls, almost sensual in fervor. With reverence he lowered the weapon to the stairs. A smile curved his lips as he plunged up the narrow space between the crush of toadies.

The horde gestured, laughed, goaded and cursed. Hands reached out to touch him. In his wake he heard hissing sounds, and yowls of pain from those who'd dared touch the Amaranthine silver. He climbed. Two hundred ninety-two bloody steps in all. At last, he reached the final stair and stepped out onto the platform. The four great faces of the clock hung like enormous opals, illuminated by gas burners and segmented by cast-iron framing. A pianoforte had been placed at the base of the northern dial. Here the air seemed heavier. A foul odor clouded his nostrils—sulfur and decay, the distinctive stench of a *brotoi*.

A quiet tick broke the silence, and repeated every other second.

Tick.

"I am here," he bellowed. "Let's get this wedding under way."

Tick.

From the shadowy corners, five men in head-to-toe shrouds appeared. He glimpsed their faces. Matthews. Trafford. The others he did not recognize.

And then he saw *her* . . . the Dark Bride.

Not one woman, but *two*.

Evangeline. Astrid. They smiled mischievously, wickedly, and drew impenetrable black veils down to cover their faces. Unease scratched down his spine. But there was only *one* Dark Bride. Their footsteps clipped against the wood floor.

"Lover. *Husband*. You've come, as I knew you would." The two girls spoke in unison, their voices twined in an eerie dual-toned harmony. They joined their black-gloved hands and circled each other. The hiss of their dark skirts filled the shadowed chamber. Before his very eyes the two merged and blended into one.

Mark had seen many strange things . . . but at this, his eyes widened in amazement.

Of course. It was why he hadn't sensed their deterioration at Hurlingham or Trafford's house. They were *brotoi* only when joined together.

The Dark Bride slid onto the pianoforte bench and ran her fingers over the keys. The discordant notes echoed through the cavernous space.

"I always like a bit of music to set the tone of an evening, don't you?" she asked.

But after only a few stanzas, she leapt from the bench and strode between him and the men in the shrouds.

With a dip of her head, she flung back her veil. She wore the same white mask as before, but she'd applied cosmetics: a slash of greasy red across the mouth; kohl, in dark scribbles, around the eyes.

"Let's go to the belfry." She pointed toward an incline of steps. "The lighting is better up there. Perfect for a wedding."

She scampered up. Her shoes clattered against the metal. "Hurry now," she urged in a low, seductive voice. "Don't linger overlong."

Mark followed her, eager to see Mina, to confirm she was alive. The five men came up behind. Darkness claimed the belfry. If not for his Amaranthine sight, he'd not have been able to see even the colossal bell at its center. One of the latticed window coverings had been removed to provide a clear view of the Thames. There, on a wooden stand, lay the Eye, a flat, circular mirror the size of a barrel lid. Moonlight illuminated its surface. Mark spied something else. Through the window, at a distance, he saw the tip of Cleopatra's Needle in perfect alignment with the Eye.

It's like a game of chess, played out over the surface of the earth, but with people and powerful artifacts.

A blur of movement drew his attention. In the opposite corner, a cluster of toadies appeared, dragging Mina and shoving her father.

"*Mark,*" cried Mina.

The Bride whispered, "Her sacrifice will be your wedding gift to me."

Mark clenched his teeth down on a shout. He could not chance displeasing the *brotoi*. Not until Mina was safe.

"Come now, darling." The painted, expressionless face tilted and considered him. "It's not really a sacrifice unless it hurts, now, is it? As a show of my commitment to you, I'll sacrifice someone too."

She flung an arm toward the row of men. Trafford coughed and issued a series of strangled noises. More toadies appeared from the shadows to capture him. He struggled. The shroud slipped from his head.

"I was promised immortality," he shouted as they dragged him past. "Matthews demanded I give up the girls for the cause. This has all got out of hand."

Someone cackled. Matthews. The toadies abandoned Trafford and backed away.

The Dark Bride twirled around the earl in a circle. He stood frozen, as if paralyzed by fear. She chuckled, a dark, wicked sound.

"I'm your *father*," he whispered.

"But, Papa," she cooed, "you gave us to Tantalus for the creation of a Bride for his Messenger."

He trembled and wrapped his arms around his waist.

"Surprise!" she snarled. "The girls don't live here anymore."

She flung her arms over her head. A blast of wind shot through the belfry. Trafford groaned and doubled over. He collapsed to the floor. *Thud*. Mina screamed.

Mark strode forward and bent over the earl, pressing a hand to his throat. His lordship was dead. The dark realization occurred that if the Bride could kill him with such ease, she could kill Mina as well if he displeased her.

A chime sounded loudly, and then another—the quarter chimes at each corner of the belfry. The familiar song drifted upward and dark birds fluttered on the rafters above. A moment of silence passed, and then Big Ben's enormous hammer lifted and dropped hard against the bell, tolling midnight. Wind and sound crashed through the belfry.

"Come forward, my love. It's time for us to be joined. Time for us to be married. We'll continue the sacrifices afterward." The Bride approached the Eye. "Give me your hand."

Her intention to enact his worst-case scenario became clear. She wanted a joining, a *true* joining, so their souls—her *brotoism* and his Transcension—would become intermingled. They'd both become more wickedly powerful from the sharing.

With a tug, she pulled the glove from her hand, revealing gnarled fingers and knotted joints. She spread her palm above the surface of the Eye, not yet touching the glass. Once she touched the mirror, the conduit would be filled with her evil, and as long as she remained enjoined, he could not reverse his Transcension—he could only draw evil from the Bride and share his own deterioration. His heart felt ripped in half.

Either he could back away and refuse to touch the Eye, risking Mina's instant death—and likely the deaths of thousands if the artifact were some sort of weapon of mass destruction when aligned with the Needle—or he could use his energy, his *stronger* energy, to take all of the Bride's evil within him, effectively bleeding her of power. He would remain in control of himself long enough to die by Archer's Amaranthine sword.

He looked at Mina—his beautiful Mina, his wife—and realized there was no choice at all. He'd do anything to save her. He loved her, far more than he'd ever loved his damn arrogant self.

Walking toward the mirror, Mark stared at Mina. *I love you, sweetheart*, he told her in silence, wishing he could shout the words, wishing he could say them, just one time, with his lips pressed to hers.

"No, Mark. Don't." She sobbed into her hands.

The Bride grasped his wrist. "No turning back now."

She was stronger than he'd expected. She pulled his hand closer . . . closer. . . .

With the proximity of their touch, the mirror emitted a bright green, hypnotic glow. He no longer tried to break free.

A different noise filled the air, a repetitive, deep *whoosh . . . whoosh . . . whoosh.* Closer . . . and louder. Shadows rippled over them both, and across the surface of the mirror. All along the perimeter, toadies shrieked and shouted. Footsteps sounded on the platform. Matthews bellowed in obvious agony. Yet Mark couldn't look away from the mirror. The light mesmerized him.

"I am here, Brother." A woman's voice.

The Dark Bride shoved his wrist. Contact. At the same moment, a hand thrust between them to press against the mirror. With a scream, the Bride flew backward, disappearing from view.

Selene, his twin, had taken her place. Mark stared into her eyes, and for a moment was returned to a time when they were ten years old again, with no one left but each other.

Her lashes fluttered and her eyes rolled . . . then again focused on his. "Go now. Save your girl."

Before he could react, she shoved him free. He staggered backward as she collapsed to the floor. What had she done? Light. Light moved under his skin. Warmth. Awakening. He stared at his hands, knowing . . . *feeling* that something was different, that the deterioration of his mind and his soul had ceased and reversed. But there was something else.

The Bride whirled, lunged for him—reaching. Furious that his sister had sacrificed herself, Mark planted his boot against the center of the *brotoi*'s chest. She flew back and crashed into the wall. The mask fell. He flinched at the sight of her misshapen head, mottled skin and sightless, black-hole eyes. She roared, revealing row upon row of jagged yellow teeth. She jumped up, over Selene, and wrenched the mirror free from the stand.

"Stop!" Mark lunged, but too late. She hurtled the Eye into the night. The glowing disc flew . . . flew . . . and descended over the river. The surface of the Thames flashed as bright as lightning, before instantly fading.

"Mark!" *Archer's voice.*

He pivoted. Through the narrow belfry window, Mark glimpsed the balloon, manned by Leeson and Elena. Archer leapt onto the platform.

"Reclaim her." The Guard cast him a long, gleaming dagger; and on its heels, a second. Mark caught them by the hilts. Heat ripped through his palms. The sensation bewildered him. He hissed and clenched them harder.

The Bride flew at him, a purple-faced cloud of black. He plunged the blades deep into her chest. She screamed—a wretched sound. Archer lunged forward, sword leveled. Mark ducked. The Bride's head hurtled across the belfry, over a tall, dark-winged warrior clad in black leather, who wrenched a sword out of Matthews's chest and stepped out from within a circle of slain toadies. The Ravenmaster. Mark now understood how Selene had arrived in the belfry.

The Bride staggered a few steps, a walking, headless corpse, and disintegrated into a heap of black sand—volcanic sand, the final demise of a *brotoi*.

Mark dropped the blades and stared down at his palms. Welts blistered his skin—his *mortal* skin. His sister had taken his Transcension upon herself, leaving him immortal. The conduit had instantly perceived immortality as his existent state—and turned him mortal.

"Mark!" Mina threw herself into his arms. He wrapped his arms around her, torn between euphoria and grief. He had prepared himself to say good-bye.

The Ravenmaster crouched on the floor, his dark wings spread wide. He held Selene in his arms. He leveled a cold, green-eyed stare at Mark.

Mark drew Mina along with him, and they knelt beside her.

"Reclaim me," she whispered. "Reclaim me too."

"Why did you do this, Selene?" Mark demanded, raw with grief.

"Go, Avenage." She shoved at the Raven's arms until finally he gently released her to the floor and backed away.

She lifted her head, and gritted, "Because the Bride was *my* target. *My* assignment. It must be I who makes the sacrifice." Her nostrils flared. "And Mark . . . oh, Mark, you've got something to live for. You and your girl." Her glance slid to Mina. "A mortal lifetime of love is better than no love at all. Our mother knew that. You know it too."

He felt the touch of a hand on his shoulder. Elena's face, serene and luminous, smiled down at him. She too knelt beside Selene, her dark skirts pooling on the floor around her.

"Can you save her?" he asked.

"No. But I can protect her until we learn how."

Hope. It was all he could wish for.

"Elena," Selene whispered, grasping the Intervenor's hand. "Friend."

Elena's palm moved over his sister's wide, dark eyes, and soon the tension in Selene's limbs eased. Her head rolled to the side.

Mark joined Archer at the window overlooking the Thames.

A circle of water glowed . . . and faded.

Three days later, Mark and Archer sat in the Alexander drawing room. Leeson entered the room, a large silver tray and tea service suspended in his arms.

Mark held a newspaper. He read the front page headline aloud. *"Lord Trafford and two daughters go missing."*

"And they shall remain missing. Forever." Archer stood and went to the front window. "What are the ladies up to? There's a wagon. And Mr. D'Oyly Carte is here."

Mark joined him. "It's a delivery from the Savoy."

"What is it?" Archer squinted.

"Ah . . . well, a piece of furniture from our suite at the Savoy." Mark shrugged. "Mina liked the piece. So . . . I had it sent here."

"You seem very happy, Mark." Archer gripped his shoulder. "Very content at the prospect of life as a mortal."

Mark smiled. Truth be told, he was happier than he'd ever been. He'd always thought himself a hopeless puzzle—one that only glory and recognition would complete. But Mina was his missing piece. His sweetheart. His girl.

Life would be perfect once they recovered the Eye from the Thames, and determined how to save Selene. He'd insisted on watching over her, but the wishes of a queen had superseded those of a brother. After hearing of Selene's sacrifice, and of the pivotal role she played in protecting the citizens of London, Victoria had insisted his twin remain under constant protection in the Tower of London. At present, his sister was being guarded at all times by not only the Ravenmaster himself, but by all eight Raven warriors.

Archer leaned forward. "What happened, Mark? What happened to all the arrogance and the bravado? The determination to be the greatest immortal legend in Amaranthine history?"

"I *am* immortal." Mark smiled. "Immortal in the only way that matters to me. I'll live on in the hearts and the minds of my wife, and my children and their children. It's enough, Archer. It's more than enough."

"Then you've succeeded in this life." Archer clasped his hand, gripping him hard. His brows went up. "But you don't think a little thing like mortality will keep you from doing your part . . . do you?"

Mina walked past the door of the study and took to

the stairs. She smiled, hearing Mark's boots on the carpeted steps behind her. Glancing over her shoulder, she returned his smile. In their room, she considered their delivery from the Savoy.

"A gift? For me?"

"For us." He grinned.

"Whatever could it be?" She tore at the brown paper, revealing the ottoman on which they'd first made love.

"Such a thoughtful gift."

Mark bent to press a kiss to her lips. "I thought you'd enjoy it."

"I think we should put it to use immediately."

"I concur, sweetheart." With another kiss, he eased her down onto the striped brocade. "I wholeheartedly concur."

Read ahead for a sneak peek
at Kim Lenox's next novel,

DARKER THAN NIGHT

Coming from Signet Eclipse in April 2010.

The discordant moans, formed by a host of voices, grew louder until they transformed into a thin, unified scream. Selene shuddered. The tiny hairs along the back of her neck stood on end.

"In all my life, I don't believe I've ever heard wind like that before," she murmured low in her throat. "It's almost disturbing."

Reclining on the sofa with her bruised and sprained ankle bandaged and propped on a large, square cushion, she stared out the stone-framed window. Intermittent flashes illuminated a roiling purple sky and the distant crags. She shuddered again.

"You're cold."

"I . . . suppose I am." Amaranthine blood flowed in her veins, and because of this she'd never been sensitive to changes in temperature. But this was not the only change in her normally infallible constitution. She prayed the effects of the vaccine would soon subside, and that she would find herself returned to perfect health. Vulnerability was not something she did well.

Bracken rose from his place beside the fire, a leonine

tower of leather knee boots, trousers and a white linen shirt. In one elegant movement he claimed the folded blanket from the high back of his chair. The fire blazed behind him. Other than the sharp angle of his jaw, his face was blacked out by shadow.

She welcomed the weighty drape of wool around her chilled shoulders—and the pleasant wave of spicy male scent that accompanied his movement. Inside its slipper, the toes of her unsprained foot curled with girlish pleasure, a reaction she had not experienced in ages. The only thing better than a blanket would be if he—Lord Avenage, a man who had never been more than a looming shadow atop the Tower of London—sat beside her. Without a doubt his lean warrior's body would be hard all over and deliciously warm. The perfect cure for a bone-deep chill and a near-shattered heart.

He backed away as quickly as he had come. His gray gaze flicked over her, his eyes bringing to mind those of an enormous wolf she'd once observed skirting along the edges of a desert encampment. Eyes that had conveyed both interest and feral mistrust.

"More whiskey?" He lifted the bottle from the table.

Anything to draw him close again. "Yes, please."

A moment later, still woefully alone on the sofa, she swirled the amber liquid in her cut-crystal glass. The wind groaned and the windows rattled. She drank the whiskey in a single gulp. "I suppose this will go on all night?"

She meant the wind, but also the tense air of discomfort between two strangers.

A wry grin turned Bracken's lips. "The villagers tell stories of those driven mad by the sound of it."

In the firelight he appeared as nothing more than a normal mortal man. A very handsome mortal man, but no more than a man. So different from the black-winged warrior with brimstone eyes who had captured her so easily two nights before.

Selene wrapped her hands around her empty glass. "Do you think I am mad?"

The smile slipped from his lips. "If I did, I would not have agreed to bring you here."

She burrowed deeper into the cushions. "You didn't agree to bring me here. You were commanded to do so by the queen and the Primordial Council, for the sole purpose of making sure I haven't turned into some sort of murderous monster."

The dark line of his brow rose. "You overheard."

She shrugged and set the glass onto a circular side table. "I was in the next room, and you are all rather loud conversationalists."

Shadows painted the hollows beneath his cheekbones and the taut flex of his jaw. "You're not mad."

His solemn declaration soothed her fears more than she cared to admit. "How can you be sure?"

"It's just a feeling."

"I had a feeling today," she responded softly.

"About what?" he inquired.

She pulled the blanket tighter around her shoulders. "About that ravine. The place where you found me."

A fierce stiffening rippled through Bracken's shoulders, and his neck and face, as well.

Selene prodded softly, "The bridge, and that broad stone plateau. What happened there?"

Curse the shadows—shadows that used to hide nothing from her Amaranthine vision. They obscured his expression. But just as telling was the way he sat taller, more imperiously in his thronelike chair, leveling his shoulders against the seat back. "There are no stories or legends to be told. It's just a dangerous place."

"But—"

"Don't go there again, Countess."

Selene bristled, unaccustomed to being told what she could and could not do. Though Avenage was her host and observer, he was not her master.

"I think I'd like to retire," she whispered.

"Very well." He stood, looking both tense and relieved. "I bid you good night."

Silence hovered between them as he, she supposed, waited for her to stand. At last, he glanced to her ankle on the cushion.

"Oh, yes," he muttered. "I see."

He did not hesitate in his duty. With strong arms he lifted her off the sofa. Selene bit her lip at the sudden shot of pain through her ankle.

"I'm sorry." He shifted her in his arms, gently canting her toward him.

By necessity, she looped her arms around his neck. Her corseted breasts crushed against the solid plane of his chest. The feel of him . . . the scent of him . . . sent her thoughts into an unfamiliar blur.

"Don't be," she murmured, staring at his ear, which was encircled by a mahogany swath of his hair. He had small ears. But not too small. Delicious ears. Perfect for kissing.

He conveyed her from the room and down a narrow hallway lit by flickering caged lanterns on either side. She was no delicate flower. She stood taller than most mortal men, and yet she—who had never wanted or needed a protector—felt safe and softly feminine in his arms. The muscles of his neck and shoulders flexed under her palms as he proceeded up the stone stairs without a single curse, groan or glimmer of perspiration at bearing her weight. All too quickly he'd twisted the handle of her door and pushed inside. Neither his touch nor his glance lingered as he deposited her on the bed.

"I'll start a fire."

"Thank you."

He knelt at the hearth. It seemed only a moment later that flames leapt above the brass firedogs and he repeated his good-night. With a curt tip of his head, he moved toward the door.

Realizing her predicament, she called out after him. "Avenage."

"Yes?" He turned, one dark eyebrow lifting higher than the other.

"I'm afraid I require further assistance." She touched the buttons at her throat.

His gaze swept over her bodice and skirts. Perhaps the dimness of the light played tricks on her mind, but a flush appeared to rise to his swarthy cheeks.

She offered a woeful smile. "I might as well be wearing a suit of armor. If I can't bear weight on both feet while I try to remove it all, I'll surely topple over."

He swallowed visibly. "All right."

Selene almost laughed aloud. Avenage was so handsome . . . so powerful and desirable. He seemed the sort of man who would have vast experience with women. And yet he stared at her and her garments as if they were on fire. In that moment, he became even more attractive in her eyes, although she felt rather certain the infatuation was one-sided. Regardless, she did need help getting out of her blasted garments.

"There's no need for either of us to feel awkward," she assured. "We're peers, both Shadow Guards. You wouldn't hesitate to offer the same assistance to one of your fellow Ravens, would you?"

"Of course not," he answered, his response registering somewhere between a growl and a hiss.

"So why should it be unsettling for you to assist me?"

"It isn't unsettling," he retorted tightly. He stared at the space just above her head.

"Then help me."

"By tomorrow I'll have hired a woman from the village to assist you."

"But tonight, Avenage—"

"Yes, of course." His lips compressed into a thin line.

Selene shifted, giving him her back, careful not to jar her leg. "If you can undo the buttons to start with . . . I believe that once everything is unfastened, I can manage on my own."

His boots shifted quietly on the carpet. She tilted her head and waited.

A low, rough sound issued from his throat.

"What is it?" she inquired.

"Your hair."

The rich timbre of his voice reverberated through the room. Through *her*. She reached behind her neck and twisted the length of her hair so that the weighty mass draped over one shoulder and down between her breasts.

He plucked at the first few buttons. To Selene's surprise, she heard him chuckle. The sound inspired a shocking wave of pleasure that rolled from the top of her head, down through her toes. An effect of her quickly downed whiskey, no doubt.

"They're so damn small," he said.

He worked his way from her neck, down her spine, to her lower back. Bit by bit, the heavy wool sagged open and cool air touched the bare skin of her neck and shoulders. She felt the gentle tug of her overskirt being untied.

"And this?" he murmured, touching her corset fastenings lightly.

"If you please." Selene closed her eyes and bit into her lower lip.

He moved even closer. She heard his trousers brush against the counterpane and felt the sensation of his heat against her back. Tiny pricks of awareness rose upon her skin. She resisted the urge to rub them away. Instead, her breath hovered in her throat, captured there by an anticipation so strong that she feared she might actually scream at the first brush of his fingertips against her skin. His fingers dragged, ever so softly, across the center of her back.

"Are you in pain?" he asked.

"Why would you ask?" she whispered.

"You gasped."

"Don't be silly," she retorted. "I'm not a gasping sort of woman."

"Are you?"

"Am I what?"

"In *pain*."

"I . . . well . . ."

His hands slid into her gaping bodice to firmly press against her corseted torso. Even through the silk and boning of her corset, she felt the imprint of his hands like a searing brand.

Selene squeezed her eyes shut and braced her palms against the mattress. "Perhaps a little pain."

It was true. Being this close to him, having his hands on her was pure, wicked torture. No . . . pleasure.

Pleasure-torture.

He said, "Perhaps in the fall you broke a rib, and because of the tight structure of your undergarments you simply did not realize—"

Cursed, passion-inspiring hands. They skimmed over her rib cage, just beneath her breasts.

She exhaled sharply.

"That, my lady, was a *gasp*."

"It's not my rib."

"Then what is it?" he demanded gruffly.

She gripped his splayed, long-fingered hands with both of hers, halting their movement, and stared down at the swirling pattern on the counterpane.

"If I must explain that to you, my dear Lord Avenage, then you have kept to your Raven's perch inside the Tower of London for far too long."

KIM LENOX

NIGHT FALLS DARKLY

A Novel of the Shadow Guard

Ever since an accident took away her memory, Miss
Elena Whitney can't recall the secrets of her own past.
All she knows is that with her mysterious benefactor
Archer, Lord Black, returning to London at the behest of
Queen Victoria, she should seize the chance to get
some answers.

A member of the immortal Shadow Guard, Archer has
been summoned to London to eliminate the soul of an
evil demon—Jack the Ripper. Archer feels not only
bound to protect the women of the night, but also his
beautiful young ward, Elena, whom he spared from death
two years before. But with a wave of panic spreading
across London, Archer fears that Elena is his weakness—
a distraction he can't afford, especially since she's likely
to become the Ripper's next target...

"Lush, dangerous, and darkly sensuous...The
Immortals have arrived!"
—*New York Times* bestselling author Kerrelyn Sparks

Available wherever books are sold or at
penguin.com

COLLEEN GLEASON

The Rest Falls Away
THE GARDELLA VAMPIRE CHRONICLES

In every generation, a Gardella is called to accept the
family legacy of vampire slaying, and this time, Victoria
Gardella Grantworth de Lacy is chosen, on the eve of her
debut, to carry the stake. But as she moves between the
crush of ballrooms and dangerous, moonlit streets,
Victoria's heart is torn between London's most eligible
bachelor, the Marquess of Rockley, and her enigmatic
ally, Sebastian Vioget. And when she comes face to face
with the most powerful vampire in history, Victoria must
ultimately make the choice between duty and love.

"Sophisticated, sexy, surprising!"
—#1 *New York Times* bestselling author
J.R. Ward

Also Available in the series
Rises the Night
The Bleeding Dusk
When Twilight Burns
As Shadows Fade

**Available wherever books are sold or at
penguin.com**